Children of the Dawnland

As Twig fell asleep, an eerie glitter started behind her closed eyes, and the dream swept over her like an icy flood. . . .

A deep groaning rumble erupts, followed by a loud boom! Several smaller booms shake the ground beneath my feet, and I stagger as a strange, orange gleam swells. The blue light vanishes.

The rumble grows to a roar.

When I look up, the sky explodes, and torrents of fire consume the night. As the rumbling, crackling flames roll across the heavens, the Star People vanish, and the entire world glows brilliant orange. A flaming ball of light rolls right over the top of me; then the earthquake strikes like the fists of the gods. I'm slammed against the ground. The Ice Giants roar and scream as they split wide open. Somewhere in the distance, I hear ice cliffs crashing into water . . . and people running, running hard. Three heartbeats later, a wave of heat hits me. It's as though I've been thrown into the midst of a raging forest fire.

I scream.

CHILDREN
— OF THE —
DAWNLAND

Kathleen O'Neal Gear
AND W. Michael Gear

A TOM DOHERTY ASSOCIATES BOOK · NEW YORK

CHILDREN OF THE DAWNLAND

Maps and illustrations by Ellisa Mitchell

A Starscape Book
Published by Tom Doherty Associates, LLC
175 Fifth Avenue
New York, NY 10010

www.tor-forge.com

ISBN 978-0-7653-5986-5

First Edition: July 2009
First Mass Market Edition: June 2010

Printed in April 2009 in the United States of America by Offset Paper Manufacturers, Dallas, Pennsylvania

0 9 8 7 6 5 4 3 2 1

To Tedi, Jessie, Ben, and Shannon,

our faithful friends,

and the purest hearts we've ever known.

Ice Giants

ICE GIANT LAKE

Lands of the People of the Dawnland

Lands of the Thornback People

The People of the
Dawnland's
Villages

Oakbeam Village
Sunhawk Village
Starhorse Village
Clearwater Village
Buffalobeard Village
Screech Owl's Cave
Hoarfrost Canyon
and Cobia's Cave

Cobia's Cave

Hoarfrost Canyon

Oakbeam Village

N

Sunhawk Village

Starhorse Village

Clearwater Village

Screech Owl's Cave

Buffalobeard Village

INTRODUCTION

At the peak of the last Ice Age, 20,000 years ago, ice covered most of Canada and extended south into the United States as far as Iowa and central Illinois. The largest glacier, the Laurentide Ice Sheet, was almost three miles thick over Hudson Bay. The immense weight of the glacier depressed the earth's crust more than 3,250 feet below its current elevation. Then a global warming period began. These "interstadials," or periods of ice retreat and rising ocean temperatures, generally occur for the same reasons that global cooling occurs—shifts in the earth's orbit and axis. The earth's orbit is not round, but elliptical, so when the earth moves closest to the sun in its orbit, the planet warms up. In addition, the earth does not sit straight up in space, but tilts at an angle; this is called the earth's "axis." When the tilt of the axis reaches its minimum— that is, when the northern hemisphere is tilted more toward the sun—summers are longer, glaciers melt, air and ocean temperatures rise. Every system, however, experiences moments of "abrupt climate change" that don't obey these rules, and this is what happened 12,900 years ago. *Children of the Dawnland* is set at this time, in what is today the northeastern United States and Ontario, Canada.

The great glaciers that had covered most of North America had been melting for about 7,000 years, creating a massive meltwater lake around the edges of the ice. Lake Agassiz, which is named after nineteenth-century Swiss geologist Louis Agassiz, covered more than 80,000 square miles and was the largest body of freshwater in the world. What is now Winnipeg, Canada, was under approximately 650 feet of water. As the glaciers continued to melt, the size, shape, and depth of the lake changed, sometimes rapidly.

At around 12,900 years ago the lake suddenly dropped by over 300 feet, and 85 percent of Lake Agassiz rushed through the Great Lakes, out into the Champlain Sea (today it's called the St. Lawrence River), where it flooded into the North Atlantic, shut off the ocean current that transports heat from the equator to the high latitudes (called the thermohaline current), and raised sea levels around the world. This event brought on a global cooling episode known as the Younger Dryas that lasted for 1,400 years.

We will discuss what caused Lake Agassiz to drain at the end of this book, but for now let's just say that the massive flood that resulted, combined with the Younger Dryas, provided a one-two punch for Clovis Culture. There are no Clovis sites younger than 12,900 years ago.

It must have been a terrifying time, especially for Paleo-Indian children. It must also have been a time of great heroes. . . .

CHILDREN

— OF THE —

DAWNLAND

A DEEP, AGONIZING GROAN trembled the air, and Old Mother tern tipped her wings to dive closer to the Ice Giants. Below her, glaciers stretched for as far as she could see. In places, the ice had broken and cracked, forming great dark canyons where she could see no bottom. In other places, massive blocks of blue ice resembling jagged mountain ranges thrust up so high they raked the bellies of the Cloud People.

Another groan erupted, followed by softer whimpers, and she tilted her white wings and headed south.

Old Mother's flock regularly flew great distances. She had seen much of the world in her forty summers, and knew something was changing. The air and oceans were growing warmer. Flowers were blooming earlier in the spring, and the short-faced bears were waking up from their winter slumbers earlier. Even more disturbing, in just her lifetime the size of the meltwater lake to the south of the glaciers—where her flock nested—had almost doubled. Once, she had tried to find the far western shore of the lake. She'd flown for twenty days straight, and never found it. The lake seemed to go on forever. Every summer, the water rose and forced her people to build their nests farther and farther south.

Unfortunately, that had not stopped the humans from hunting them.

That was her mission today. She was scouting for human hunters.

She flapped her wings harder and flew out over the vast blue lake. Icebergs the size of small mountains floated in the water, bobbing and twisting, and far to the south, she saw the smoke from the human campfires. It rose into the cold air and created a gray smear over the treeless tundra. Old Mother tilted her tail and angled down toward the village.

The humans made strange nests. She had watched them erect the wooden pole frames and cover them with mammoth or buffalo hides, and wondered how such nests could ever be safe for their children. When a fox attacked a tern nest, the fledglings could leap up and run in less than a heartbeat. Human children, on the other hand, could be cornered in their hide nests and slaughtered. She had seen that happen, for all was not well in the world of humans. They seemed to be constantly at war with one another, and they—

Old Mother's eyes widened. Far below her, she saw a line of children walking toward the lakeshore, in the direction of her flock's nesting area.

Her heart raced. She soared down for a closer look. Each child carried a hide bag. In terror, she let out a high-pitched squeal to warn the rest of the flock, and dove straight for the last child in line—a boy with a dog trotting at his side.

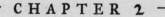

CHAPTER 2

GREYHAWK LET OUT a shriek, and Twig spun around in the trail to look. The afternoon was freezing cold. Every time Twig exhaled, a crystalline halo encircled her heart-shaped face and frosted her long black hair.

"Where's Greyhawk?" she asked.

Rattler, Twig's friend, stopped to wait with her. "I don't know. I don't see him at all."

Rattler was Twig's age, twelve, but much prettier than Twig. She had a beautiful oval face, with slanting eyes and a broad, catlike nose. Silky black hair hung to her waist.

The other ten children in the egg-gathering group filed down the trail with their heavy buffalo coats shining, leaving Twig and Rattler far behind. The hide bags they carried over their shoulders swung at their sides. Their leader, an old woman named Snapper, was hobbling out front with her thin white hair whipping in the wind. As she did every spring, Snapper led the children to Ice Giant Lake to collect bird eggs. The rocky shore was covered with tern nests and seemed to be a fluttering, squealing sea of white. When they returned home at dusk, the entire village would boil, bake, and scramble eggs for supper.

"Twig, I think we should go on," Rattler said. "Snapper will be very angry if we fall too far behind."

"I know, but I have to wait for Greyhawk. The Thornback raiders have been prowling the trails, stealing children to take home as slaves. Grandfather told me last night to keep watch for them."

"All right, silly girl. I'll see you sssoon," Rattler hissed, sounding very much like a snake, and sprinted away as fast as she could.

Twig adjusted the bag on her shoulder and looked for Greyhawk again. Where could he be? They'd been walking since long before dawn, and had traveled much farther to find the terns' nesting ground than last spring at this time. Grandfather said that the world was changing, and by next spring the lake would flood their village, and they would be forced to move again.

But moving wasn't unusual. Her people moved their

village constantly to match the movements of the animals. In the autumn, they moved into the southern forests to harvest walnuts, persimmons, and acorns. Then, just before winter set in, they moved far south to hunt buffalo and white-tailed deer. Finally, when the spring thaw arrived, they moved back to the shore of Ice Giant Lake to fish, and to wait for the terns to return to their nesting grounds.

Rattler shouted, and Twig spun around in time to see Grizzly, the village bully, trip Rattler and send her tumbling headfirst to the ground. Rattler leaped to her feet, and she and Grizzly got into a shouting match. Elder Snapper was hurrying to break them up.

Twig turned back and called, "Greyhawk?"

Yipper, Greyhawk's dog, barked. Greyhawk had gotten Yipper as a puppy when he'd seen three summers. Since that day, they'd never been apart.

Twig waited for another fifty heartbeats; then she ran back to find them. She stopped when she saw moccasin tracks veer off the trail and head toward a big pile of tumbled black boulders.

"Greyhawk?"

Yipper barked again. "Greyhawk, where are you? Answer me!"

From inside the boulders, she heard him call, "I'm not going, Twig."

"Oh, Greyhawk, you're going to get in trouble!"

A cascade of gravel rolled out as he and Yipper climbed higher into the boulders.

Twig followed their tracks, and found Greyhawk crouching among the highest boulders, watching the other children heading for the nesting grounds. Yipper, who was half wolf and pure black, wagged his tail when he saw Twig. He had yellow eyes that seemed to glow even in broad daylight. Greyhawk, on the other hand, scowled at her. A bloody gash marked his cheek.

"What happened to you?" she asked, and pointed to the gash.

"A tern dove right out of the sky and smacked me in the head!"

She squinted at him. "Well, come on. We have to go."

Greyhawk nervously wet his lips. He had a moonish baby face, with large brown eyes and a small nose. "Elder Snapper will never miss us. We'll just wait here until everyone comes back with their bags full of eggs; then we'll sneak into line and go home."

"Of course she'll miss us," Twig said sternly. "Do you want to get punished when you get home?"

Greyhawk slumped down on a rock. The long fringes on his hide sleeves were shaking. "You go on without me, Twig. I don't want you to get punished, too."

Greyhawk was two summers younger than she, ten, and one of the smallest boys in the village, which meant he got teased a lot. And the hat he wore today hadn't made things any easier for him.

Twig propped her hands on her hips. "I wish you hadn't worn that hat. That's why everyone has been teasing you. You look stupid."

"Don't you remember what the terns did to me last spring? They hate me." He adjusted the hat. Made from woven strips of rabbit fur, it looked like he was wearing a dead cottontail on his head.

"They're just birds, Greyhawk."

"No, they're not. They're evil Spirits straight out of the darkest underworld. Just wait, you'll see. They'll peck my brain to pieces."

Terns ferociously guarded their nests. A person did have to be careful, but it didn't take long to fill a bag with eggs, so it was over fairly quickly, and mostly fun.

"Greyhawk, if you don't go, Snapper will tell your father, Reef, that you spent all day hiding in the rocks. Is that what you want?"

Greyhawk's mother had died when he'd seen barely three summers, and his brothers and sisters had died in an epidemic, so he tried very hard to make his father proud of him. That was one of the reasons they'd become best friends. Twig's father had died, too, before she was born. At the time, they were the only two children in the village with just one parent. She and Greyhawk had both been sad and lonely until they'd started talking to each other.

"I'm not going, Twig."

She sat down on the rock beside him and looked out at the nesting grounds in the distance. Old Snapper kept turning around and looking back up the trail. Was she counting heads? It wouldn't be long until she realized they were gone. Twig tried to think of something to say that would take Greyhawk's mind off the terns, something even scarier.

In a low voice, she said, "If you think terns are scary, I . . . I had the dream again, Greyhawk."

He jerked around to stare breathlessly at her. "About the flaming ball of light?"

"Yes."

Twig had dreams that came true. Her people called them Spirit dreams, because Spirits from the Land of the Dead brought the dreams.

"I think Mother's afraid I'm a Spirit dreamer."

"Why would she be afraid? She's the village Spirit dreamer."

"Yes, but truly great Spirit dreamers are terrifying. They can see the future, and call down fire from the heavens to burn up their enemies. Nobody likes them."

"You mean like"—Greyhawk cautiously looked around and whispered—"Cobia."

"Don't say her name out loud!" Twig shouted.

Cobia was supposedly a white-haired hag who lived deep in the heart of the Ice Giants. She had left Buffalobeard village twenty summers ago. No one had seen her since, though people frequently tried to find her cave to ask if she would dream the future for them. Their own village chief, Chief Gill, had just dispatched a search party to seek her out for that very reason.

"Twig! Greyhawk! Where are you?" Snapper shouted hoarsely.

Twig leaped up to peer through the boulders. The old

woman stomped up the path with her fists filled with rocks.

Twig said, "Oh, we're in trouble, Greyhawk. You can come with me, or stay here hiding in the rocks. But you know what will happen if you don't come. The other boys will torment you even more than they usually do."

Twig sprinted away. When she looked back over her shoulder, she saw Greyhawk clench his teeth. After several moments, he stood up.

"Wait, Twig, I'm coming."

Greyhawk trotted down to meet her.

When Snapper saw them, she started flinging rocks at them and yelling, "Get down here! Where have you been?"

A rock whizzed past Twig's head, and she called, "We're coming!"

They broke into a run, racing down the hill. All the while, Snapper tried to hit them with rocks. Fortunately, they were both fast and managed to dodge before they were knocked unconscious.

Just before they reached the egg-gathering party, Twig heard a loud squeal and saw a white bird plummet out of the sky; it struck Greyhawk's hat hard enough to make him stumble, and ripped out a tuft of rabbit fur before it flew away.

Snapper yelled, "Greyhawk! What did you do to the tern?"

"It wasn't my fault!" Greyhawk sputtered at the unfairness. "They h-hate me. I've told you a hundred times."

"How would they know you from any other child out here today?"

"Maybe they can smell me, I don't know." He hurried on down the trail and wormed his way into the midst of the other children.

Grizzly snickered and pointed at Greyhawk's hat. "You let a bird beat you up? You are such a baby."

Grizzly's nose had been broken when he was a child, and it still pointed to the left. He had small dark eyes and a mouth like a fish's, but his shoulders spread as wide as a man's—and he had seen only eleven summers. He whispered something to his young brother, Little Cougar. They both laughed, and Greyhawk hid behind Rattler.

"Stop it!" Snapper growled. "Get in line." She picked up a big rock to hit anyone who disobeyed.

All of the children scurried into line, but Grizzly kept glancing over his shoulder at Greyhawk and giggling.

"Be quiet," Old Snapper called. "We don't want to get the birds too excited."

Thin white hair blew around Snapper's wrinkled face as she resolutely walked out into the nesting area where hundreds of nests, packed closely together, dotted the treeless tundra. The children followed.

OLD MOTHER saw them coming. She let out a series of loud sharp squeals, and thousands of terns rose up and hung in the air like a noisy white cloud, waiting for her command to attack.

When she shrieked her war cry, tucked her wings, and dove, the entire flock plummeted down behind her.

As Twig bent down to gather the eggs from the first nest, she heard two quick *fwaps!* followed by a small shriek from Greyhawk. She swung around in time to see him fall to the ground with his arms over his head. Two dying birds, still kicking, rested at his side.

Black Locust, a homely little girl who had seen nine summers, stared at the birds, awestruck. "Look at that. They hit you hard enough to break their necks."

Greyhawk struggled to his feet. "That's because they're trying to kill me."

Grizzly called out to the other children, "Don't stand next to Greyhawk or the terns will rip off your ears." He pointed upward.

Everyone looked, and Twig's mouth dropped open. There had to be one hundred terns circling right over Greyhawk's head.

Greyhawk shrieked and started running around in circles, which upset Yipper. He started leaping and snarling at Greyhawk's heels.

Snapper shouted, "Greyhawk! Stop that!"

"He's such a worm." Grizzly picked up a handful of tern poop and threw it at Greyhawk. It splatted on his rabbithide hat.

All of the children except Twig roared with laughter.

Grizzly picked up another handful to throw, and Snapper yelled, "That's enough!" She swatted Grizzly in the head with her hide bag. "Start gathering eggs. If we aren't quick, you will all be late for tonight's Storytelling."

As the children dashed out into the nesting area, grabbing eggs and filling their bags, the cries of the terns rose to a deafening roar. The birds squealed like rabid bats, dove, and tore at the children's hands and clothing.

Greyhawk ran.

Twig called, "Greyhawk, wait!"

"No! I don't care if I do shame my father," Greyhawk shouted and kept running. Yipper charged out in front of him, leading the way home.

"Yes, you do!" Twig ran harder, caught up with him, and grabbed his arm to stop him. "Don't you want to be a great warrior, like your father? If you leave now, you'll be staring at your feet for the rest of your life."

Greyhawk faced her with his jaw clenched tight. Like all children between the ages of eight and twelve, boys and girls, he was studying to be a warrior. On any other day, except today when he needed both hands to grab eggs, he would have had his weapons with him.

"Are you coming or not?" she asked.

Finally, he threw up his arms. "All right, but if the terns pluck my brain out, I expect you to scoop up every piece and carry it home to my father."

"Whatever they don't choke down."

He gave her a disheartened look as he strode past her and dashed out into the nesting area. Yipper worked himself into a frenzy barking and snapping at the attacking birds.

"Hurry!" Twig yelled. "Once our bags are full we can leave!"

She whacked at terns with one hand while she grabbed eggs with the other, then sprinted for the next nest. Greyhawk stayed close beside her. His hat took most of the hits, but occasionally a tern flew right into his face and bashed him hard. His nose was bleeding.

After another hundred heartbeats, a high-pitched scream rang out, and Grizzly ran past them batting at his head. Two terns had grabbed locks of his hair and were ferociously trying to rip it out by the roots. Grizzly shouted, "Get them off me! Help! Somebody help me!"

Snapper stalked over and whacked him in the head with her bag again, which knocked the terns loose and sent them squealing into the sky. "Stop playing with the terns and get back to gathering eggs," she ordered.

Grizzly looked at her as though she were dim-witted, but ran to obey.

In a short time, most of the children's bags were full, and one by one, they began to race out of the nesting area and back up the trail.

Once they were all assembled, Snapper yelled, "Now, stay together! We have to walk fast, or you will be late for Elder Bandtail's Storytelling."

By the time they reached Buffalobeard Village, Father Sun had already slipped into the underworld, and a misty purple haze was rising from Ice Giant Lake.

CHAPTER 3 ————

AT THE EDGE of the village, the children split up and sprinted for their own lodges. Twig called, "I'll see you at Storytelling, Greyhawk."

He lifted a hand and trotted away with Yipper at his side.

Twig removed the egg-filled bag from her shoulder and looked around. Thirty-two people lived in the village. One family, often including grandparents, lived in each of the fourteen lodges that were arranged in a rough oval around the big central fire pit. Few people were out at this time of night. Most were inside eating supper, though she saw four old people sitting by the central fire, chewing the last scraps of meat from the bones of a roasted caribou. The remainder of the carcass, still suspended from a pole over the fire, was sizzling, filling the village with the wonderful fragrance of roasted meat.

Twig walked past two lodges before she reached her own. She and Mother lived alone. Mother was the village Spirit dreamer and needed privacy to perform the rituals that kept their village safe.

Firelight streamed around the edges of the door curtain as Twig called, "Mother, I'm home," and ducked inside.

Mother knelt before the fire, adding branches to the blaze. She had a narrow face, and a slightly hooked nose. Her hair was black and waist-length. The deer-hide cape she wore was painted with the images of running black bears. "Twig, I was getting worried. What took you so long?"

Twig's eyes drifted over the interior of the rounded lodge. Built upon a woven willow-pole frame and covered with thick buffalo hides, the lodge was three body-lengths across and just tall enough for an adult to stand up in. Through the smoke hole in the roof—a gap in the hides that allowed the smoke to escape—she saw the Star People glittering. In the rear, thick piles of rolled hides marked their beds.

The buffalo hides on the floor cushioned her steps as Twig walked over and handed her bag to Mother. "We had to walk much farther this time. I swear Ice Giant Lake has risen more than my height since last spring."

"Yes, the Ice Giants are melting very fast these days. That's why the gullies and creeks are all wider and deeper. They're being washed out by the runoff." Mother gestured to the fire. "Your supper is in the bowls on the hearthstone. I've been keeping it warm for you. If you don't eat quickly, Bandtail will punish you before you even have a chance to sit down at the Storytelling."

"I know. Elder Snapper made us run almost all the way because she was afraid we'd be late."

Twig knelt and reached for the two wooden bowls, one turned upside down on top of the other. When she removed the top bowl, the scent of fried rabbit rose. She grabbed a piece of the rich meat and bit into it hungrily.

Mother walked to the tea bag hanging from the tripod at the edge of the fire. "Do you want some hot tea?"

"Yes, Mother, thank you."

Mother pulled two sticks out the woodpile and very carefully used them to lift a hot rock from the fire pit, which she dropped into the hide bag. Steam exploded as the tea came to a boil. Mother waited for a few heartbeats, until the boil slowed down; then she dipped a wooden cup into the bag to fill it, and handed it to Twig. "Here, this should warm you up."

Twig took the cup and sipped it. The tea was almost too hot to drink. Made from spruce needles and bumble-bee honey, it had a sweet, tangy flavor. "It's delicious, Mother."

Mother dipped a cup of tea for herself and sat down beside Twig. "Did you see any sign of Thornback raiders?"

Around a mouthful of food, Twig said, "No. Not even a single track."

"That's a relief." Mother sipped her tea and seemed to be thinking about something. Her eyes were focused on something far away.

"Why? Is something wrong?"

"No, no," Mother said quickly. "It's just that a runner came in today. He was from Sunhawk Village, and he said his hunting party had stumbled over the bodies of Deputy Walleye and his search party."

"The warriors we sent to find Cobia?"

"Yes. Our chief wanted Cobia to dream the future for us, but our search party was ambushed near Cobia's cave. The runner talked with War Chief Puffer, and Puffer came to talk with me right after the runner left. Puffer wondered if I had dreamed anything about the Thornback raiders."

"Did you?"

Mother tucked a lock of black hair behind her ear. "No."

For a time they sat in silence. Twig watched Mother from the corner of her eye while she ate. Mother looked frightened. What else had Puffer said? There had to be more to the story, something so bad that Mother didn't want to tell Twig about it.

Finally, Mother said, "What about you? Did you remember anything else from the dream that woke you last night?"

Without thinking, Twig squeezed her eyes closed, and the dream came back. . . .

The wave of heat hits me, and it's as though my skin is peeling from my face!

"Help!" I cry out. "Someone help me!"

"I'm right here. Come to me, Dreamer."

The ground is heaving and shuddering. I try to see who spoke, but I don't see anyone. "Where are you?"

"Come. Fly to me. Your people need your help."

The gentle voice echoes from the snow, and on the crest of the high ice ridge, I see a young woman sitting. She wears a white mammoth hide over her shoulders, and black hair whips around her beautiful face. Behind her, strange, half-transparent things dance. They don't seem to have any arms or legs.

I shout, "But I've only seen twelve summers! What can I do?"

The woman smiles. "You can save them, Twig. If you're brave enough. Just remember that to step onto the path, you must leave it. Only the lost come to stand before the entrance to Cobia's cave, and only the defenseless step over its threshold. You—"

"Twig?" Mother said sharply. "I asked about your dream. Answer me."

The memory died. Twig shuddered before she could stop it. "N-no, Mother. I don't remember anything else. Really. I just remember seeing the green ball of light and being scared. That's all."

Mother stared at her unblinking. "You didn't tell anyone about the dream, did you?"

Twig took another big bite of rabbit and chewed it for several heartbeats before she lied, "No. You told me not to. But I still don't understand why I can't—"

"Yes, you do. The story would travel through the village like lightning. Within days the elders would call a council meeting to question you to determine if you are a Spirit dreamer. Do you want to be made an outcast?"

"But you're a Spirit dreamer, and you're not an outcast. Spirit dreamers are only made outcasts if they become too strange to live among other human beings. I won't change—"

"How do you know that? You have powerful dreaming blood. You could become as crazy as Screech Owl, or—or worse, Cobia. That's why your grandfather was sent to kidnap Cobia. She was a power child, and everyone knew it. Everyone wanted her to dream the future for them. Do you want someone to come and kidnap you?"

Twig swallowed hard.

Mother lowered her voice and hissed, "Ever since you were born, I've seen Cobia's shadow hanging over you, as though you are her daughter, not mine. The two of you are linked, Twig. I don't know how or why, but it frightens me."

The fear in Mother's voice terrified Twig. She ate the last bite of meat from the rabbit leg and set the bone down in her bowl. "Did Cobia ever dream the future for our people?"

Mother sat back and seemed to be thinking. "Cobia

had seen four summers when our Spirit dreamer, Chief Minnow, first asked her to dream for him. From that moment until the day she left, people never left her alone. She dreamed constantly, for anyone who asked, and her dreams always came true."

Mother looked away and stared at the lodge flap, as though she expected Cobia to walk right through it at any instant. "I don't know how she stood it. She must have been exhausted."

Twig hesitated for a long time before she worked up the courage to say, "Mother? Maybe I should go ask Screech Owl about my dream. He's very powerful. He may know—"

"Absolutely not!" Mother shouted. "He's lost his human soul, Twig. There's no telling what kind of animal soul is living in his body. It could be a rabid wolf that will chew you up! I don't want you going anywhere near Screech Owl."

Mother didn't like Screech Owl. He was an odd old hermit who lived in a cave down at the Snake Rocks. Every time Twig went to see him, he was very kind to her. Strange, but kind. Twig picked up her tea and concentrated on drinking it.

In a softer voice, Mother said, "Besides, I need you here in the village. The Buffalo Way ceremony is coming up. There is a lot to be done, and you have to help me."

"Yes, Mother."

Mother waited until Twig finished her tea and set her cup down; then she said, "Well, you had better get to the

Storytelling. You don't want to be late. Elder Bandtail can be peevish."

Relieved to be going, Twig ran across the lodge and ducked out into the night. Children had already started to gather around the big plaza fire. She could see their faces shining in the light.

CHAPTER 4

GREYHAWK SAT YAWNING between Twig and Grizzly, listening to Elder Bandtail's old voice drone on. He was totally bored, not to mention covered with bloody gashes where the terns had ripped hunks out of his face and hands.

Greyhawk tried to focus on anything but the story Bandtail was telling. The old woman had withered cheeks, a hunched back, and a large, bulbous nose the size of his fist. Her gray hair hung around her face like greasy twists of weasel fur, making her look like a hag from the darkest underworld.

The other twelve children around the fire looked as

bored as he did. Little Cougar stared off at the glistening Ice Giants. Yellow Gull retied her moccasins for the third time, and Muskrat was watching the Star People glitter. The night smelled of wood smoke, and the roasted caribou and boiled tern eggs villagers had had for supper.

"I'm going to fall asleep," Twig whispered to Greyhawk.

"I wouldn't if I were you. She'll bash you in the head with her walking stick. I know. I still have the dent from three moons ago, when she—"

"Are you talking?" Bandtail's eyes narrowed. "No talking while I'm telling stories!" She pointed her walking stick at him.

Greyhawk shut up. He swore she could hear the softest whisper from a day's walk away.

Once a moon, each of the clan elders gathered together with all the children who had seen less than thirteen summers and told them the Old Stories. When the children became adults, at thirteen or fourteen, they would be expected to recite the sacred stories flawlessly. His least favorite elder was Bandtail, from Twig's clan, the Blue Bear Clan.

Greyhawk decided he would join Muskrat and stare up at the Star People. They were very bright tonight, so bright he could almost reach out and—

Bandtail pounded her walking stick on the ground, and Greyhawk jumped at the same time that Yipper, who had been sound asleep at Greyhawk's feet, barked and scrambled to his feet with his hair standing straight up. A low growl rumbled in Yipper's throat as he scanned the village, searching for whatever monster had awakened him.

"It's okay, boy," Greyhawk said, and petted Yipper's back. "Everything's all right."

Yipper wagged his tail, stared up at Greyhawk with love in his yellow eyes, then flopped on his side and went to sleep again.

Bandtail leaned forward and stabbed her stick at Greyhawk. "What happened then?"

Greyhawk, who had not heard a word she'd said, blurted, "After what?"

Twig leaned over and whispered the answer to him, but her voice was so low all Greyhawk heard was the word *tortoise*.

Bandtail's wrinkled mouth puckered up like a dried plum. While still glaring at him, she called, "Who knows what happened next?"

Buzzard, a five-summers-old boy, shouted, "Tortoise brought up mud!"

"That's right," Bandtail praised. "Tortoise brought up mud from the depths of the oceans, and Earthmaker fashioned the mud into the land, trees, animals, and humans. Then what happened?"

In a high-pitched little girl voice, Black Locust called, "Earthmaker breathed Spirit into the world, just like we breathe Spirit into our atlatls and spears, and all living things chose their own colors. The trees turned green, and the animals—"

"Good." Bandtail rocked back on her hips and glared

around the circle, as though selecting her next victim. She glared at Greyhawk again for good measure. "After Earthmaker had finished his creation, he realized with a shock that he'd forgotten to leave room for rivers and creeks. But he'd made everything so perfect that he hated to start ripping gashes. He didn't know what to do. He waited so long that the trees started drooping and the animals were dying of thirst. Muskrat came to him with his tongue hanging out and told Earthmaker he'd better do something fast." She aimed her stick at Buzzard. "Buzzard, what did Earthmaker do?"

"Earthmaker made rivers!" Buzzard slurred around the finger in his mouth, only to be shouted down by the other children yelling, "No, he didn't! Stupid! Not yet."

"You, Rattler," Bandtail said. "What did Earthmaker say to Muskrat?"

Greyhawk looked at her and sighed. Rattler was so beautiful. Every boy in the village prayed for a single glance from her. Unfortunately, she made a habit of sneering at anyone who paid her the slightest attention— including Greyhawk.

Rattler sat up straighter. "He said he didn't know where to put the rivers."

"That's right. Earthmaker said, 'Yes, yes, you're right, Muskrat, but where shall I put the rivers and creeks? Do you have any ideas?' Together, Earthmaker and Muskrat went to the rim of the sky to peer down upon the world. From their height, the only things they could see clearly were the huge serpents that Earthmaker had created first.

They slithered all over the land, creating squiggles. But when a dark shadow skimmed over the face of the world—it was Red-Tailed Hawk looking for dinner—the serpents instantly froze. Only their forked tongues darted to scent the air for danger."

"Then Earthmaker made rivers!" Buzzard shouted, trying again.

"Yes," Bandtail agreed. "Muskrat pointed at the snakes and said, 'There! Look at those magnificent patterns! Put the rivers where the snakes are. Isn't that beautiful? Not even you could have found better places than Red-Tailed Hawk.' So Earthmaker turned all the giant serpents into rivers."

Bandtail cracked her walking stick on one of the hearthstones to wake everyone up. "Next moon, Elder Blood Duck will tell you the story of the hero twins, the Blessed Wolf Dreamer and his evil brother, Raven Hunter, who fought and killed all the monsters in the Beginning Time."

Buzzard let out a happy shriek and threw his arms around Bandtail's neck. "No, please, tell us another story tonight, Grandmother," he begged.

Greyhawk softly groaned, "Oh, not another one."

Grizzly snickered, and Twig hissed, "Shh!"

As though Bandtail had heard, one of her eyes started to twitch. She called out in a loud hoarse voice, "Children, Greyhawk the Wise is going to tell you a story of long ago. A true story of Cobia and the evil creatures that come at her bidding. Go on, Greyhawk, since you seem to know so much."

"Which story?" he asked.

"The story about how she called to me when I had seen only fourteen summers."

Greyhawk looked around the circle at the other children. They seemed to be waiting. Twig was biting her lip. "I don't know that story. How could I know what Cobia said to you when you were fourteen summers old?"

Bandtail waved her stick in front of his face. "Then perhaps if you don't know anything, you should listen better."

Children laughed, and Greyhawk wanted to crawl under the log and hide. "Yes, Elder," he said in shame.

Bandtail leaned forward and stared each child in the eyes before she continued, "I heard Cobia crying. It was in the middle of the night, and I was worried about her. She'd just come from the Duskland, far, far to the west. She was only two, and helpless. I rose from my hides and walked across the village toward the Spirit dreamer's lodge. Cobia was crying harder and harder. I had a little girl of my own at the time, named Hopleaf. She was pretty, with big brown eyes, and I kept imagining how Hopleaf would feel if she'd been kidnapped and dragged away to a strange land, with no family or friends."

Buzzard had tears in his eyes. "Was she afraid of the dark?"

"I don't know, but it was very dark that night. Yes, indeed. I couldn't see my hand in front of my face, but I kept marching, pushing on through the blackness to get to her. The lodge flap was swinging when I arrived, as though someone had just entered. A thin line of light seeped around the edges, lighting the ground at my feet."

Buzzard began to wring his hands in his lap. "Was she dead?"

Bandtail hissed, "She was laughing. It was a sweet sound, and I thought maybe the Spirit dreamer's wife had picked Cobia up and started playing with her. I pulled back the lodge flap to see . . . and I gasped."

Terrified, Buzzard asked, "What did you see?"

"I don't know what they were. Spirit Helpers of some kind. Huge things, with no arms or legs. They danced around her bed, their enormous beaks clacking like thunder while they spun and leaped in time to music I couldn't hear."

Everyone, including Greyhawk, sat as if frozen, staring at Bandtail. Twig looked especially terrified.

Bandtail's mouth hung open for so long that a bead of spit formed at one corner and dribbled down her chin.

Rattler asked, "What did you do?"

Bandtail croaked, "I screamed in fear, and a green demon with a twisted face flew at me. He drove me across the entire village, clutching at my hair and dress while I screamed my throat raw. When I finally scrambled into my lodge, my baby girl, Hopleaf, was dead."

Greyhawk glanced at Twig, but Twig didn't seem to notice. He said, "What happened to Hopleaf?"

"She'd been witched, stupid boy. Witched by Cobia, because I'd seen the evil Spirits she'd called to keep her company."

Greyhawk said, "Cobia is a baby killer?"

"Not just babies—everyone. She's too powerful. As she grew up, the Spirit dreaming twisted her soul into knots. She'll kill a person just for walking near her cave. That's probably what happened to Deputy Walleye and his search party. Remember that, in case any of you ever get curious about her and decide to go find her cave—like Little Badger and Sunmoth did last year."

Absolute silence fell.

Both children had died horribly. It had taken War Chief Puffer five days to find their wolf-chewed bodies. They'd been half buried in ice, their frozen eyes wide open, staring at the distant Ice Giants as though terrified.

Bandtail leaned on her willow stick and grunted to her feet. "Now, all of you get to your hides and sleep well tonight."

The children scattered, racing for their lodges. Greyhawk, Twig, and Rattler headed in the same direction.

As they ran, Rattler said, "My father says that Walleye's party was ambushed by Thornback raiders, not Cobia."

"Maybe," Greyhawk answered, "but I heard no one really saw men. Whatever killed Walleye and his warriors floated through the trees like black ghosts."

Twig shuddered.

From across the plaza, Grizzly called, "I'm going to beat you up tomorrow, Greyhawk!" Then he turned to run off for his lodge.

When they were alone, Twig grabbed Greyhawk's arm and stopped him.

He said, "What's wrong?"

Twig looked around to make sure no one could hear them; then she whispered, "Greyhawk, I have to go see Screech Owl to talk to him about my dream. Mother told me not to, but after what Elder Bandtail said about Cobia . . . I—I have to. There's a woman in my dream. I think it may be Cobia. I'm going to go tomorrow. Do you want to come with me?"

"Screech Owl!" he half shouted. "Are you crazy? He's not human."

Twig gave him a pleading look. "I'd go alone, like I always do, but with the raiders out there, I'm afraid to. Please, come with me."

The tone of her voice made him feel instantly guilty. It would be very dangerous for her to go alone. In addition to the evil raiders, short-faced bears and saber-toothed cats prowled the trails. Greyhawk definitely did not want to go with her. Just the thought of looking into old Screech Owl's inhuman eyes made his belly curdle.

"I—I'll decide tomorrow, Twig."

Greyhawk ran off toward his own lodge, leaving Twig standing by herself in the darkness.

Just before he ducked into his lodge, it occurred to him that if he did go with her, it would get him away from Grizzly's promised beating. And, well, he didn't actually have to go into Screech Owl's cave. He could just stand outside and wait for her.

Maybe he would go with Twig.

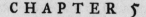

CHAPTER 5

THE NEXT MORNING, as they ran for the Snake Rocks, Greyhawk yelled, "Twig, this is a terrible idea! Let's go home!"

Twig dodged a patch of ice that hid in the shadows of the boulders and continued running down the hill. Dead grass snatched at her doeskin dress as she leaped a deep gully filled with rushing water. On the other side, she turned to watch Greyhawk to make sure he could jump the gully.

Yipper leaped it in one bound and turned to bark at Greyhawk, as though to tell him it was easy. Greyhawk stopped and grimaced at the gully. He wore a buckskin shirt that hung down to his knees and had many fringes on the sleeves. "I thought you said Screech Owl's cave was close! How much farther is it?"

"It's right there." She pointed to the black boulders piled in the valley bottom like a lumpy snake. At the far end, gigantic oaks grew. "Screech Owl's cave is behind those trees."

Greyhawk cupped a hand to his mouth and shouted, "Twig, we shouldn't go see him! My father says he's an old witch."

"I have to talk to him, Greyhawk. He's the only one who understands my dreams. And he knows Cobia better than anyone. He raised her."

"Are you sure it was Cobia in your dream?"

"No. That's why I have to talk to Screech Owl. I have to know for sure."

Greyhawk frowned down at the gully again; then he leaned over to sniff it. Yipper's ears went up, and he sniffed the gully, too. Greyhawk and Yipper liked to smell things—some of them pretty putrid. Once last summer he had taken Twig to a recently abandoned wolf's den and gotten down on his hands and knees to sniff the ground alongside Yipper, telling her he could distinguish the pups' sleeping places from the adults' just by the smell of the wolves' urine.

Twig couldn't see any use to such knowledge. She could tell the difference by the look of the tracks. Who wanted to smell wolf urine?

"Come on, Greyhawk!" she said. "You've made it this far."

Yipper barked at Greyhawk and wagged his tail, as though wondering what was taking his master so long.

Greyhawk yelled, "I'm coming!"

He nerved himself and took a flying leap across the gully, but stumbled on the other side and fell to his knees in a puddle. Water splashed up around him. As he dragged himself to his feet, Greyhawk made a low sound of disgust.

Twig said, "Did you hurt yourself?"

"Of course not." He shook water from his hands and straightened his buckskin shirt. "I swear that gully is twice as wide as it was a moon ago."

"It is twice as wide. Mother says the Ice Giants have been melting faster, flooding the creeks and gullies, washing them out."

Greyhawk flung out an arm to point west and said, "I'm telling you, we should do this another day. Thunderbird is coming."

Twig turned and saw blue-black Cloud People walking across the earth on spindly legs of rain. Thunderbirds lived in the bellies of Cloud People. They guided the storms and brought rain and snow to heal Mother Earth, but sometimes they could be violent.

"You've dodged lightning bolts before," Twig said. "Besides, we'll be at Screech Owl's cave soon, and there's a big rock ledge just above the cave. It's always dry beneath it."

"But . . . Twig," Greyhawk said nervously. "I talked to Father last night. He said the village elders banished Screech

Owl from living with humans because he had the soul of a wolf."

"He has a kestrel soul now. He says his soul has had many shapes. You'll like him. He tells great stories."

Greyhawk didn't move. He was biting his lip and glancing back toward Buffalobeard Village. Yipper followed his gaze, as though expecting to see something dangerous bounding toward them.

"What's wrong?" Twig called.

Greyhawk made a face. "I'm not going."

"Greyhawk! He's not as crazy as people say. Screech Owl is . . . different, but he's not bad. Come on, you'll see." She waved him forward.

"But what if Screech Owl does something to us, like casts a spell on us?"

She groaned. "A spell? What kind of spell?"

"I don't know! Maybe he'd witch us to make us lose our human souls so he can put kestrel souls in our bodies."

Twig spread her arms and whirled on her toes, imitating a soaring bird. She felt absolutely free. "I've always wanted to fly, Greyhawk. Haven't you?"

"No!"

Twig put her hands on her hips. "Then go home! I'll go by myself. I should have known you were too young to bring along. But I'm telling you the truth, Screech Owl is no witch, and he's not crazy either. He's just a little—"

Thunderbird chose that instant to crackle lightning

bolts over their heads, and she saw Greyhawk leap off the ground and collapse into a trembling heap. Yipper frantically licked his face to comfort him.

"See?" Twig grinned. The first drops of rain started to fall, cool and wonderful on her face. "Even Thunderbird agrees with me. You're a coward, Greyhawk!"

She turned and raced for Screech Owl's cave.

Rain began falling harder, soaking her dress and the long black braid that bounced against her back.

Thunderbird roared again.

"Wait!" Greyhawk yelled as he scrambled to his feet. "Wait for me, Twig!"

"Well, hurry!"

As she dashed for Screech Owl's cave, the hair on her arms started to prickle. Spirit power did that; it rode the wind like tiny teeth until it could find a human and chew its way inside to coil around the soul.

From a short distance away, she called, "Screech Owl? It's Twig. Are you here?"

No one answered.

Twig ducked beneath the low branches and into the dry spot created by the big rock ledge above the cave. Rain beat the ground, growing in strength.

Greyhawk stumbled through the branches behind her. With wide eyes, he hissed, "Is—Is Screech Owl here?"

"I don't think so," she said, disappointed.

Yipper was sniffing the tattered hide door curtain that covered the cave. After ten heartbeats he lifted his leg. . . .

"Yipper, no!" Greyhawk shouted, and dragged Yipper

away before he could mark the curtain as his personal territory.

Yipper looked totally confused, probably because he wasn't the first dog to do such a thing.

Greyhawk said, "Twig, crawl inside his cave. If Screech Owl isn't here, we can run home right away." He longingly looked at their back trail. Water had started to puddle in the low spots.

Twig got down on her hands and knees, shoved aside the leather curtain that covered the cave, and crawled halfway inside. It was dark, but she could see the smoldering fire pit in the middle of the floor, and the tripod, made from three long sticks tied together at the top, that stood beside the pit. A hide bag hung from the tripod; it was probably filled with water or tea. The cave was large, fifty hands across. Her people measured distances by the length of a person's hand, from the base of the palm to the tip of the longest finger. Power symbols covered the gray walls: red spirals, black crescent moons, purple starbursts, and many dancing buffalo, some playing bone flutes. The old man's woven rabbit-fur blankets lay in the back of the cave.

"What's that strange smell?" Greyhawk's nose wiggled as he scented the air. "It smells like poison."

"Screech Owl probably made another potion for his eyes. He tries new ones all the time. Nothing seems to help. He just can't see very well these days. At least not close up. I think he's getting old."

"How old is he?"

"I don't know. He's lived maybe sixty summers."

Screech Owl's cave always smelled odd. The fragrances of wood smoke and Spirit potions hung in the air. All along the walls, brightly colored baskets of dried blossoms, fish scales, snake heads, Spirit plants like coughgrass root, as well other things that Twig couldn't remember made bulges in the shadows . . . but Screech Owl was gone.

Twig sighed and slumped down outside the cave. "What am I going to do now? I really need to talk to Screech Owl."

Greyhawk eased down beside her and propped his elbows on his drawn-up knees. "As soon as the rain lets up, we should go home."

Twig watched the rain move down across Ice Giant Lake in the distance. Flashes of lightning struck at the tallest icebergs as Thunderbird took the storm north.

Greyhawk said, "Why can't you just tell your mother about your dream? She's a Spirit dreamer. And the keeper of the Wolf Bundle. She's supposed to understand Spirit things."

The Wolf Bundle was old. It had been handed down from Spirit elder to Spirit elder. Made of leather, like an old pouch, it was covered with paintings of spirals, buffalo, and wolves. A big yellow spider stared out from the middle of the bundle. Inside the bundle lived the Stone Wolf, a tiny black obsidian carving of a wolf. Legends said that the ancient hero, Wolf Dreamer, had carved the Stone Wolf right after the creation of the world. It had enormous Spirit power . . . though Mother said she could never seem to feel it.

"Can't she just ask the Stone Wolf?" Greyhawk said.

"She has more important things to do." Twig left it at that.

Her mother didn't have Screech Owl's knowledge or power, but Twig couldn't explain that to Greyhawk. He would think she meant something bad about her mother, and she didn't, not really. Her mother had actually studied with Screech Owl for a while, so she did know important things about Spirit dreams.

Greyhawk looked at her from the corner of his eye. "Twig, what's the old man like? If everyone in our village thinks he's crazy, he must be."

"No, he's not. Really. He's a good man. And he's smart. I helped him fix a rabbit's broken leg last spring. We tied sticks around it to keep it straight. Then Screech Owl built a cage and gathered grass and flowers for the rabbit to eat."

"He fixed its leg instead of eating it? He doesn't sound very smart to me," Greyhawk grumped, and suspiciously sniffed the air again. "We should go. He's not here, and if your mother finds out that we—"

Loud shrieks erupted when two kestrels swooped out of the sky and dove straight for them.

Greyhawk grabbed Twig's arm in a death grip. The birds pulled up just before the cave and floated on the air currents, chirping to each other as they eyed Twig and Greyhawk.

Yipper growled and leaped into the sky to try to catch one, but the birds easily got away.

"Who are they?" Greyhawk whispered hoarsely. "Part of Screech Owl's family?"

"If they are, I've never met them before."

Sand trickled over the ledge, and they heard steps, like something heavy moving through the rocks above them. Twig and Greyhawk craned their necks to look.

"Can you see it? What is it?" Greyhawk hissed in panic. "A dire wolf? A short-faced bear?"

Dire wolves were much bigger than regular wolves, and short-faced bears were the most terrifying predators in their world. They had heads twice the size of grizzly bears.

Twig got to her feet. "I don't see anything!"

Just then a shaft of sunlight pierced the clouds, and in the boulders high above them, someone shouted, *"There it is! Kill it!"*

CHAPTER 6

GREYHAWK LET OUT a hoarse scream, and he and Twig crashed into each other as they tried to dash away in opposite directions. Yipper started growling and running circles around them. But before they had gone ten steps, Screech Owl's tall, skinny body dropped from the ledge. He staggered sideways with his gray hair spiking out wildly. He had a long beaky face with deep wrinkles. His wolf-hide shirt and cape were little more than rags.

"Look at it!" Screech Owl shouted, and began grabbing up rocks and smashing them into the ground. "Hurry! Get some rocks. We have to kill it. It pounced on me first thing this morning! Tried to eat my soul!"

Greyhawk clutched Twig's shoulders and hid himself behind her. She could feel his heavy breathing warm on her neck. They stared in utter terror at the tiny mouse that darted from rock to rock.

"Screech Owl!" Twig blurted. "That's a mouse. What are you doing?"

The old man stopped throwing rocks in mid-swing and bent forward to squint at it. "It's a mouse? Are you sure? I thought it was a baby mink."

"No! Look at it."

Screech Owl squinted harder; then he slammed his rock down and sighed. "Twig, I wish you'd come earlier. I wasted all morning chasing that mouse through the rocks."

He strode forward in a whirl of ragged wolf hides and lifted her off her feet to hug her. "In fact, I wish you'd come moons ago. I've done some very strange things this winter. I think I'm changing form again. I may be turning into a mink. Look how sharp my teeth are getting." He opened his mouth very wide to show her.

Twig pried herself loose from his grip when she heard Greyhawk make a strangling noise. "Screech Owl, we'll talk about it later, all right? This is my friend, Greyhawk."

She extended her hand to Greyhawk, who had flattened himself against one of the boulders and was breathing as though he had just finished a tough race.

Screech Owl stared. "Why, yes, of course. Reef's son, from the Smoky Shrew Clan. I remember the night you were born. What a nasty hailstorm that was. It actually cracked people's skulls." He shook his head and clucked noisily. "Yes, I recall that well. Of course, I wasn't much help with the rescue. I had the soul of a vulture at the time, and I was always hungry, so I—"

"Screech Owl!" Twig cut him short when she saw Greyhawk's eyes bug out. "Why don't we have some tea? I need to talk to you. I had a strange dream."

"Oh, forgive me," Screech Owl said. "You've come such a long way." He knelt and pulled aside the leather curtain to the cave. "Please, go inside and sit down."

Twig winked encouragingly at Greyhawk before she ducked inside. Yipper followed her and began roaming around sniffing things. The ceiling was just high enough for her to walk upright across the dirt floor and sit down on a soft pile of fox hides in the rear.

Outside, she heard Screech Owl say, "Come on, Greyhawk, you little rodent. I've got baskets full of your dead kin in there for you to look at. Hurry it up! Do I have to cast a spell on you to get you into my cave?"

Greyhawk darted through the doorway and scrambled over to sit by Twig, whispering, "I told you! You didn't believe me. We'll be lucky to leave here with our human souls!"

Screech Owl smiled as he hooked the curtain back over the peg hammered into the wall, then entered. Cool wind gusted into the cave. "My, it's good to have someone come to see me again. It's been such a long winter. And how are you, Twig? Did you have another Spirit dream?"

"Yes." She watched Screech Owl move about. Because

of his height, he had to stand in a hunched position while he gathered kindling to add to the fire. "In the dream, I'm . . ."

She stopped when a single tern—a sharp-eyed little bird with white wings—fluttered down to stand in the doorway and gaze suspiciously in at them.

Greyhawk pointed, and hissed, "Who's that? Who's *that*?"

Screech Owl turned, saw the bird, and chirped to it, which made Yipper prick his ears. When the tern chirped back, Screech Owl said, "Why, thank you, Old Mother. No, I didn't know that."

"What did she say?" Greyhawk asked.

"Hmm? Oh, she said a very bad storm is coming. It will be here by tonight. So make sure you pile lots of hides over you before you go to sleep."

The tern hopped into the cave, glared briefly at Greyhawk, then flew away.

Screech Owl knelt in front of the fire pit and blew on the smoldering embers until the kindling caught and flames leapt up. Orange light flickered over his elderly face. He tossed two round rocks into the middle of the fire, then sat down and gazed wide-eyed at something on the ceiling.

Twig and Greyhawk looked up, but saw only soot-coated rocks and the crack in the ceiling through which the smoke escaped. They shrugged to each other.

"Twig," Screech Owl said, "tell me more about your dream while we wait for the rocks to heat up."

She tried to lean forward to answer, but Greyhawk was

holding her sleeve too tightly. He seemed to be examining the painting on Screech Owl's wolf-hide shirt, where a black tortoise spread its red legs across the old man's chest. From the end of each red leg, a green spiral spun out.

Twig said, "The dream begins with the sky exploding, but at the very end, I'm standing next to a woman on a sandy beach. The shore is covered with thousands of shells, and out in the water enormous monsters float, blowing fountains from their backs. It's a beautiful place."

"Ah," Screech Owl said with a nod. "That's the Duskland. Far, far, to the west, along the great ocean."

Twig's heart almost stopped. In hushed awe, she whispered, "You've been there?"

Only the greatest holy people journeyed to the Duskland. It was a powerful vision quest. They went in search of the tunnel where Father Sun disappeared into the underworld at night. Legend said that if a person could find that cave, they could live forever—just as Father Sun did.

"Oh, yes," Screech Owl said, "many summers ago, when I had the soul of a dolphin. The Duskland sits on the shore of a vast sea that stretches to the edges of the world. And out in the middle of the sea is a bright glowing spot that marks the tunnel that leads to the underworld."

"Who do you think the woman in my dream is?" Twig asked.

Screech Owl didn't seem to hear her. He reached into a blue-and-red woven basket, pulled out a handful of leaves, and dropped them into the water bag.

"What's that strange smell?" Greyhawk sat up straighter to sniff the tangy fragrance that filled the cave.

"My own tea mixture," Screech Owl answered. "It's made from spruce needles, grass seeds, and dried snail guts."

"Snail guts? Why would you put that in tea? What does it do to a person?"

"Do?" Screech Owl blinked. "Why, it clears the head and takes the soul up—"

Screech Owl stopped abruptly to watch a feather that floated around the ceiling. To make matters worse, the kestrels outside let out low chirps and took wing, shrieking as they soared away.

Greyhawk rose to his knees, ready to bolt. "It takes your soul up where?"

"Up where?" Screech Owl repeated as if he had never heard the words before. He snatched at the feather, missed, and asked, "Where what?"

"You said the snail gut tea takes the soul up somewhere. I want to know where!" A tremor had invaded Greyhawk's voice.

Screech Owl broke into a grin. "You're an inquisitive little rodent, aren't you? Did you know that a person's entire future can be read in the wrinkles of dried mammoth dung? I've spent forty summers making collections for nearly everyone in Buffalobeard Village. Here, let me see if I can find yours. If I recall correctly, it's . . ." He grabbed a big hide sack, dragged it across the floor, and proceeded to pull out chunks of dried mammoth dung.

Twig sighed. "Screech Owl, we were talking about my dream. About the far western Duskland? I wanted to know about the woman. Do you know who she is?"

He studied her as though he had no idea what she meant. "Who who is?"

"The woman. In my dream."

"What woman? . . . Oh, wait! I remember." He threw the sack down, heedless of the fact that two chunks of dung bounced out onto the floor and cracked into a thousand pieces. Greyhawk looked appalled, as if half of his life had just turned to dust. "That's right, we were talking about the great western ocean. Let's see . . ." A distance filled his gaze, as if he looked back across time. His voice gentled. "It all started with Cobia. Yes, Cobia and her people, the People of the Duskland."

Twig remembered the story Elder Bandtail had told, and a shiver ran up her spine.

Screech Owl made a delicate gesture, the way he would push aside a cobweb. "Yes, it started forty summers ago. The mammoths were all gone. No one had even seen one in many summers. Our people were starving. Then the great Spirit dreamer, Chief Minnow, told us that a powerful little girl was calling all the mammoths to the west, to the Duskland. He said we had to go there and kidnap the girl, then force her to call the mammoths only for us."

"And did Cobia call the mammoths?" Greyhawk asked.

"A few mammoths returned after Cobia came to live in Buffalobeard Village, but not many." In a softer voice, Screech Owl added, "Your grandfather, Halfmoon, led that battle-walk, Twig. That journey took two summers."

Greyhawk whispered, "Did Elder Halfmoon kill all of Cobia's people?"

"No. Just the people who tried to stop him from taking her."

"Elder Halfmoon is a very great warrior," Greyhawk said solemnly. "His burns and scars prove his courage."

"Yes," Screech Owl whispered, "Minnow got more than he bargained for in Cobia. By the time she'd turned ten, she had great power. Cobia could dream the future and kill with a shout."

"She can kill with a shout? Did you ever see her do that?" Twig asked.

Screech Owl jerked his chin up, startled by the question. "Oh, yes. She killed her first victim at the age of thirteen summers. Then, when she was nineteen, I saw her kill an old man."

Greyhawk hunched forward and whispered, "Cobia is a baby killer, too, isn't she?"

Screech Owl leaned toward Greyhawk until their noses almost touched, and whispered back, "What would make you think that?"

Greyhawk frowned. "Well, you just said—"

"Come here!" Screech Owl grabbed hold of Greyhawk's head and started rapping on the top of it with his knuckles, as though sounding it out.

"What are you doing!" Greyhawk shouted and squirmed, trying to get away.

Screech Owl released him and said, "Well, that's too bad," and duckwalked back to the fire pit. He used a buffalo-horn spoon to scoop up one of the hot rocks and dropped it into the tea bag. Steam gushed up around his face in a glittering veil as the water came to a boil.

Greyhawk rubbed his head. "What do you mean too bad? Too bad what?"

Screech Owl flicked a hand. "Oh, it's just that humans are born with cracks in the top of their heads through which they can talk to Earthmaker, the creator. In most people, the cracks close up when they're very young and reopen only at death to let the soul depart to the Land of the Dead. But!" He shook his finger emphatically. "A person can learn to keep them open if he tries. I thought maybe you'd been getting messages from the Spirits about Cobia. Turns out you were just guessing." He paused thoughtfully. "But you know, I do brain operations. I could fix that for you."

Greyhawk choked and started coughing.

Screech Owl grabbed for a wooden cup, dipped it into the tea pot to fill it, and handed it to Greyhawk. "Here, drink this."

Greyhawk shrieked, "No!" and continued coughing.

Screech Owl offered the cup to Twig, who took it. She'd had the tea before and knew how good it tasted. Nothing had ever happened to her soul because of it.

Screech Owl said, "Tell me more about this dream, Twig. Did you see people?"

"Yes, running. But it's the woman I want to know about. She was young, maybe twenty, and had a beautiful face."

"Did you talk to her?"

"Yes, but I didn't understand anything she said. It was all gibberish. Things like, 'To step onto the path you must leave it.' I don't know what that means, do you?"

Screech Owl dipped himself a cup of tea and took a long sip. "No, not a word." He grinned at Greyhawk.

Greyhawk scowled back. He was over his coughing fit, but kept clearing his throat.

Screech Owl said, "What else happened?"

"There was a loud boom," Twig said, "and an earthquake."

"An earthquake?" Screech Owl tilted his head to the left. "Where did it come from?"

"From the Star People, I think. I see a ball of light roll over the top of me. It's huge. It flies south in a roar, like a thousand lions are running inside the light."

Screech Owl set his cup on the floor with a sharp crack. "The light flies south?"

She nodded.

Screech Owl shot to his feet and turned first one way and then another, muttering, "So it comes from the north. Blessed Spirits, I hope that doesn't mean . . ."

"Mean what?" Twig asked.

His stooped position and the curious tilt to his head

made him look like a demented stork. "Don't worry, it doesn't necessarily mean they're coming for us, but if they are, we'd better be ready."

Greyhawk put his mouth against Twig's ear to whisper, "He's as crazy as a rabid skunk! I'm getting out of here. Are you coming?"

"Please, just give me a little longer," she whispered back.

Greyhawk slumped to the floor again, but kept his slitted eyes on Screech Owl, who was walking around the cave, talking to himself and touching the colorful Spirit symbols on the walls. After a few moments, he stopped. When he turned back to gaze at Twig, a prickle climbed her spine.

"What is it, Screech Owl? What are you thinking?"

"Hmm?" he asked, studying her with unnerving concentration. "Thinking? Oh, I wasn't thinking at all . . . except, well, last moon Old Mother brought me news that a new Star Person had been born in the night sky far to the north. The Star People are very clannish—they don't like new people—but Old Mother said this new person is very bright."

"Do you think this new Star Person has something to do with my dream?"

Screech Owl's bushy gray brows lowered. "I pray not. Once, long ago, the Star People made war upon humans. Huge rocks rained down from the night sky. Many were killed."

"But why would the Star People send me a Spirit dream?"

"Maybe they sent you the dream so that you could tell Greyhawk. He's studying to be a warrior, isn't he?"

"Who? Me?" Greyhawk asked in panic. "I'm just a boy! I can't do anything. Can I?"

Screech Owl threw another branch onto the fire. "Well, I certainly can't answer that until I find the chunk of mammoth dung that tells the story of your life. Where could I have put it?"

He started grabbing for new bags and dragging them across the floor to search them. Yipper danced around each bag, as though suspecting it held something edible.

Greyhawk hissed in Twig's face, "I'm leaving before he can find it!"

Greyhawk rushed for the door and was out into the sunlight before Twig even started to stand up. Outside, she heard the squeal of a tern; then Greyhawk yelped, and his moccasins pounded the ground as he charged away. Yipper dashed outside growling, and ran after Greyhawk.

Twig heaved a deep sigh and finished her tea in three long gulps. After she'd set the cup on the floor, she said, "Screech Owl, I guess I should be going. We have to be home before sundown. Thank you for the tea and for talking to me about my dream."

"Twig, do you want me to talk with your grandfather about your dream? All of the elders should know about this. They—"

"No. No, Screech Owl. Thank you, but Mother doesn't want anyone to know I'm having Spirit dreams."

Screech Owl frowned and looked away. "I'm not surprised. Power always terrified her."

"Why?"

"Oh, I'm probably to blame. I think I may have pushed her too hard. Cobia had just left the village, and we needed another great dreamer. A Spirit dreamer who truly sees the future can save the lives of everyone in the village. I thought your mother could be that dreamer."

"But you're a great Spirit dreamer. Couldn't you do it?"

"Well," he said with a smile, "people didn't like me very much. I knew sooner or later I was going to be made an outcast."

His face slackened, and an odd tinge of fear entered his voice. "Twig, about your dream . . . if the Star People do make war on humans, everyone could be killed. We *need* to tell the elders."

"But what if my dream is wrong? I'm only twelve. I don't know anything about dreaming."

In the wavering firelight, his brown face seemed older, more wrinkled, but the twinkle returned to his eyes. "Do you want me to teach you how to be a Spirit dreamer? I might be able to convince your mother—"

"No. I—I'm not sure I want to be a Spirit dreamer."

He smiled and nodded. Softly, he said, "I understand. It is a hard life. But you should at least talk to the Stone Wolf about your dream. Or maybe Cobia, if you can convince your grandfather to take you to see her. He's probably the only one brave enough to do it. And if Cobia is the woman in your dream, she may actually let you find her."

Twig's hand quaked before she let it fall to her side. "But Mother doesn't like me to get near the Stone Wolf. And Elder Bandtail has forbidden us to go near Cobia's cave. Two children who were curious about her died last year trying to find it. What makes you think—"

"Power has taken to the wind again. The Stone Wolf and Cobia will know that. There's no saying who or what Power is trying to corner. Maybe you, my only friend." He rapped the top of her head, listened speculatively to the hollow sound, then smiled and said, "Oh, good."

Twig laughed. "Thank you again. I'll try to come back soon."

"Very soon, I hope. I've missed our talks."

"Me, too." She walked to the door, but turned back just before she ducked outside. "Screech Owl? We're having the Buffalo Way ceremony tomorrow night. Why don't you come? I'm sure no one would mind."

He tilted his head uncertainly. "The last time I went to a ceremony people threw rocks at me to drive me away."

"But they won't this time. I'll ask Mother to speak with Chief Gill about letting you come."

"Well, I'll think about it. Now, you'd better go. Grey-hawk's probably halfway home already."

She ducked out the cave entrance into the sunlight, and shielded her eyes to see if she could spot Greyhawk. A tern dove and soared over the trail in the distance, and she thought she heard vague yells and barks coming from below the bird.

Twig began running with all her might, trying to catch up with Greyhawk.

CHAPTER 7

WIND WOMAN HOWLED and tore at Twig's
lodge as though she wanted to rip it to pieces.
Just as Old Mother tern had warned, snow
had begun falling just after dark, and already the drifts
outside were more than six hands deep, and ice filled their
water bags.

"Where were you today, Twig?" Mother asked. She
sat across the fire stitching yellow porcupine quills onto a
new buckskin dress. Her long black hair draped over the
front of her cape, almost covering the images of the running black bears. "I looked all over the village for you.
You promised to help me get ready for the Buffalo Way

ceremony. I had to do all the cooking and washing by myself."

Twig pulled her cape more tightly around her shoulders. When she and Greyhawk had returned at sunset, Twig had seen Mother on the lakeshore pounding their clothing with rocks to loosen the dirt, then sinking them in the water to rinse them. She'd felt guilty, but . . .

"I—I went rabbit hunting. Didn't spear any, though."

Mother's mouth quirked, as though she didn't believe Twig's story, but she just sewed another quill onto the dress. She was creating beautiful chevrons around the neck.

"Twig?" Mother's voice changed. "Did you go see Screech Owl today? Greyhawk's mother said he came home shivering and hid under a pile of hides until she ordered him out for dinner. Do you know anything about that?"

"About him hiding? No."

Mother's brows lowered. "Did you go see Screech Owl?"

"Well . . . Mother," Twig said. She thought about making something up, but figured Mother would find out the truth eventually, and when she did, the punishment would be worse. "Screech Owl gets lonely. He needs people to come see him every now and then. And he needs to come to the Buffalo Way ceremony tomorrow night. It would be good for him. Do you think you could ask Chief Gill if Screech Owl can come?"

Mother lowered her sewing to her lap. In a low shaking voice, she said. "You make me so angry. I can't believe you disobeyed me. How many times have I told you that he's dangerous? You never know what Screech Owl will do. One moment he has the soul of a raven, and the next he's a dung beetle. No one wants him here."

"But why not? He wouldn't hurt anyone."

Mother's hands clenched the dress for an instant before they relaxed again. "I want you to stay away from him."

"But I like him, Mother. Didn't you ever like him, even when you studied with him?"

"Yes, I did, but that was a long time ago, before . . . well, before a lot of things happened."

"Before my father died?"

Mother hesitated for so long that it made Twig fidget. "Mother, why don't you ever tell me about my father?"

"There isn't much to tell. We were married for only one summer, and he was gone most of that time."

"To go on battle-walks." She beamed at Mother in pride. People in Buffalobeard Village told stories on long winter nights about what a great warrior her father, Shouts-at-Night, had been.

"Yes, he was a very great warrior."

Twig hesitated before she asked, "Is that when you studied with Screech Owl? When my father was gone raiding?"

"Yes."

"Why did you stop studying with him? He has great power. I'll bet he could have taught you a lot more."

Mother's eyes drifted to the Stone Wolf. She'd left her

medicine bundle open near her bedding hides, as though she'd forgotten to tie it closed after her nightly prayers. The Stone Wolf stood on top of the bag. Black, tiny, it glimmered like a speck of molten midnight.

Mother said, "I'm sure he could have. He just scared me too often."

Twig kept looking at the Stone Wolf.

She could feel the Stone Wolf's power from all the way across the lodge, like the sticky feel of a cricket's legs on her arms.

Silently, she mouthed the words, *Do you know anything about that dream I had two days ago?*

The sensation of power grew, and Twig heard a faint rumble, like the distant roar of a flash flood before it wipes the face of the land clean. Fear gripped her. She started shivering.

"Is something wrong?" Mother stared at her.

"No, it's just that I . . . it's the Stone Wolf. It was looking at me."

"Well, don't worry. It's quiet tonight."

Twig frowned, and glanced at the Stone Wolf. It had started to shimmer, as though firelight lived and breathed in its glassy heart. "Mother, didn't you feel that wave of power?"

"I didn't feel anything." Mother's eyes narrowed. "Why? Did you?"

Wind gusted, and snowflakes fell through the smoke hole. As they drifted down to vanish over the fire, Twig worked up her courage. Finally, she asked, "Mother, would it be all right if I . . . I—I know you've told me never to go near the Stone Wolf, but could I just talk to it? Maybe hold it for a little while?"

Mother set her sewing down and walked across the lodge to her medicine bundle. She stuffed the Wolf inside and tied it firmly closed. For a long time, she just stared at her bundle. Finally, she turned back. "Did Screech Owl tell you to ask me that?"

The way Mother said it meant she already knew the answer. "Yes, Mother. He thought maybe the Stone Wolf could help me—"

"You are never to go see Screech Owl again. Do you understand? If you're not careful he'll send you on a Spirit journey to the Land of the Dead and forget to tell you how to get back."

Twig's heart thumped her ribs. "D-did he do that to you?"

"Yes, of course. He had the soul of a rat snake at the time, and was so busy trying to stuff a whole mouse down his throat that he forgot I didn't know how to get back. It's a miracle I survived. Tell me you understand and you won't go there again."

Twig looked down into the fire and watched the flames flickering. Quietly, she answered, "Yes, Mother. I understand."

"And?"

"And I . . . I won't . . ." It hurt to say the words. "I won't go see him again."

CHAPTER 8

As TWIG FELL asleep, an eerie glitter started behind her closed eyes, and the dream swept over her like an icy flood. . . .

I AM HUDDLING in a cavern filled with blue light. Towering ice spires rise around me, and from somewhere far away, I hear inhuman chanting. . . .

Fear clutches at my heart. I start to run, screaming, "Is anyone here? Hello!"

I race up the icy trail, and when I reach the top, I slip and fall, landing hard. The sharp ice rips my shirt and tears a long gash in my right arm. Hot blood soaks my sleeve.

Everywhere I look, glittering, frozen apparitions dance in the curious blue glow. They have no arms or legs.

"Where am I?" I cry in fear.

"You are in the future, young dreamer."

I sit up, expecting to see the strange woman. But she is not here. Instead, a bizarre creature perches on an ice ledge above me. It has a human body, but wings and a bird's beak, and its skin shimmers, as though it's snakeskin.

I'm terrified, shaking, but I force myself to stand up.

"Please, h-help me?" I stutter. "Who are you?"

It gives me a sad smile. "I am Eagle-Man, your Spirit Helper. Do you hear it, Dreamer? Listen."

"W-what?"

At first, all I hear is the roaring wind.

Then . . .

Faint screams creep up from every sparkle in the snow, and fear clutches at my heart. All around me, colors swirl and form pictures. I see Screech Owl's terrified face and hear Mother shrieking. . . .

"What's happening?" I cry.

Eagle-Man just smiles.

A deep groaning rumble erupts, followed by a loud boom! Several smaller booms shake the ground beneath my feet, and I stagger as a strange, orange gleam swells. The blue light vanishes.

The rumble grows to a roar.

When I look up, the sky explodes, and torrents of fire con-

sume the night. As the rumbling, crackling flames roll across the heavens, the Star People vanish, and the entire world glows brilliant orange. A green flaming ball of light rolls right over the top of me; then the earthquake strikes like the fists of the gods. I'm slammed against the ground. The Ice Giants roar and scream as they split wide open. Somewhere in the distance, I hear ice cliffs crashing into water . . . and people running, running hard. Three heartbeats later, a wave of heat hits me. It's as though I've been thrown into the midst of a raging forest fire. My skin is peeling from my face!

I scream.

"TWIG! TWIG, WAKE up!"

She felt Mother's hand on her shoulder, shaking her, and bolted up in her buffalo hides. Cold sweat drenched Twig's body. Outside, an owl hooted as it glided through the darkness.

"Mother?" she cried in fear.

"You scared me half to death. Are you all right?"

"Mother, I—I had a bad dream. You were screaming!"

"Well, it was just a dream." Mother hugged Twig. "Everything is all right. Look at me. I'm right here and I'm perfectly safe. We are both safe."

Twig hugged her hard. "I'm sorry I woke you."

Mother smoothed her damp hair from her face. "It's all right. Do you want to sleep with me?"

"Yes."

Twig crawled beneath Mother's hides and watched

Mother throw another branch on the fire. Sparks shot out and floated up toward the smoke hole in the roof. When Mother got beneath the hides, Twig snuggled against her.

Mother said, "Tomorrow is going to be a long, busy day. Let's get as much sleep as we can."

Twig inhaled a deep breath, trying to calm herself enough that she could go back to sleep. As the fire ate into the branch, the eagle-feather prayer fans and dried Spirit plants that hung from the roof poles spun and fluttered.

Twig sighed and rolled to her side . . . and her arm hurt.

She sat up in bed again. There was a rip in her sleep shirt. Through the hole, she could see the long gash that tore her right arm. And blood. Dark and clotted. The drops looked like black tears.

CHAPTER 9

IT WAS ONLY mid-morning, but so warm that most of last night's snow had already melted to puddles that made shining spots across the tundra.

As Twig and Greyhawk trotted through the plaza, they passed two clan schools. All of the children from the Crabkiller Clan had gathered to learn to flake stone tools. Twig glanced at Grizzly and Little Cougar as she ran by. They sat with a piece of leather over their left hands and a deer antler tine in their right hands. To sharpen the piece of chert that lay on the leather, they pressed the antler tine to the edge and applied pressure. When a flake of stone popped off, they blew on the stone to clean it, and continued pressure-flaking the edge. If they'd done a good job, at the end they would have a beautiful sharp spear point. If they'd done a bad job, they'd have an ugly stone knife. Twig knew. She'd made lots of ugly stone knives when she'd studied flint knapping.

A little farther down the path, they passed the Waterweed Clan school. Elder Cove was showing the children how to use a stone scraper to clean animal hides, to get them ready to tan. An enormous brown buffalo hide lay draped over a pole, drying in the bright sun. Five girls and three boys were working to scrape it clean. Gray buffalo brains filled a big wooden bowl a short distance away. When the hide was clean, the children would lay it on the ground and rub the brains into the hide to tan it. It was backbreaking work. Twig was glad this was her clan's day for children to carry water—which Twig had done all morning.

"What did you tell your mother?" Greyhawk asked as they took the trail that led down the hill to the eastern side of the village. Yipper leaped and bounded out in front of them.

"I told her the truth," Twig replied. "I said we were going to see Grandfather."

"Did you tell her that you were going to ask him to take you to see Cobia?"

"Shh!" she hissed. "Keep your voice down!"

Greyhawk rolled his eyes. "That means you didn't tell her."

"Well, she wouldn't have understood. I told her we

wanted to hear Grandfather's story about how he captured Cobia."

"But we've heard that story a thousand times."

"Yes, but it makes Mother happy that I like Grandfather's stories. And I always learn new things when he tells the story again."

"Yes, me too."

Part of Greyhawk's warrior training involved memorizing the stories of the greatest warriors who had lived among their people—like Grandfather Halfmoon. Depending upon which clan you belonged to, the stories might be different. Twig had finished her training last summer.

From now on, the Blue Bear Clan would expect different things of her. She would be expected to begin the path to womanhood, to marry, and have children to increase the clan's numbers. Twig most wanted to become a healer. Mother had been teaching her about Spirit plants, and she was good at making poultices and brewing healing teas.

Greyhawk said, "Did you know that after your grandfather stole Cobia, he was chased by a hundred warriors and had to fight them off by himself? It was a miracle he lived."

Twig looked over at Greyhawk. Black hair flapped around his face as they ran. He carried his spear—as long as he was tall—in his left hand and had his atlatl tied to his belt. An atlatl was a throwing stick about as long as the thrower's forearm. When a warrior inserted the hollow end of his spear into the hook on the atlatl and cast, his spear flew much farther.

Twig said, "I've never heard that part of the story."

"Of course not," he said with his chin up. "They only teach it to boys from the Smoky Shrew Clan. It's part of our secret training. Your grandfather came in to tell us how he did it. He almost died before he slithered into an ice tunnel on his belly and lost them. He had to stay there for four days, and Cobia shrieked the entire time."

Twig frowned. "If it's a secret, why did you tell me?"

"You're my best friend. If I can't tell you, who can I tell? You won't tell anyone else, will you?"

"Of course not," she said indignantly.

They swerved in front of the big rocky ridge—really a massive boulder pile filled with sand and dirt—that encircled the eastern half of the village. When they got to the far end of the ridge, Twig saw Grandfather sitting in front of his lodge, talking with the village war chief, Puffer. Puffer was tall and muscular for a woman. She'd seen twenty-eight summers and had short black hair, cut in mourning for a friend she'd lost one moon ago in a battle with the evil Thornback People. She was of Greyhawk's Smoky Shrew clan, and her bravery was legendary. In her hand, Puffer carried her atlatl. Red, black, and white designs encircled the shaft.

"Let's stand here and wait until they're finished talking," Twig said.

Greyhawk nodded. "They could be making life-or-death plans for our village."

When they stopped, Yipper turned to look at them, wondering what they were doing; then he trotted back and sat on his haunches beside Greyhawk. His black fur shone today, as though coated with flakes of gold.

Sitting beside Puffer, Grandfather Halfmoon looked very old and frail. He had seen fifty-eight summers. Deep scars cut grooves across his forehead and cheeks, and his eyes had started to turn white, as though the winter snow collected in them and never melted. His graying black hair hung over his shoulder in a long braid.

Grandfather was placing rocks on the ground, saying, "This is where Starhorse Village was, and Sunhawk Village is over here. Farther up the trail, you'll come to Oakbeam Village. The trail you want"—he drew a line in the dirt with his finger—"runs past Oakbeam Village and down into a narrow ice canyon that the local villagers call Hoarfrost Canyon."

Puffer nodded. "The entry to her cave is at the end of the canyon, isn't it?"

"Yes, but I doubt you will see her. She'll see you before you arrive, and be long gone. She knows that honeycomb of ice tunnels better than the lines on her own palm."

Puffer exhaled hard. "Probably, Elder, but we need Cobia's help to defeat the Thornback raiders. If we can just get her to dream the future for us, we will know where and when they plan to attack us. Then we can prepare to fight them." She bowed her head for a long moment. "Walleye's search party failed. Someone has to try again."

Grandfather looked at Puffer with shiny white eyes.

"Be careful. The trails will be muddy. And Cobia will not be happy to see you. You know that, don't you? When she left here twenty summers ago, she said she'd kill anyone from Buffalobeard Village who tried to find her."

"Yes, Elder, I know." Puffer stood up. "If she chooses to kill me, at least I won't have to worry about what the Thornback raiders are up to."

Grandfather stood and embraced Puffer, saying, "I pray the Spirits watch over you. And don't worry: While you are away, we will start building a rock wall around the village. It won't be much, but at least our warriors will have something to hide behind to launch their spears."

"Thank you, Elder. We'll try to be home tonight before the Buffalo Way ceremony starts. Then, tomorrow, I'll assign every warrior the task of helping to build the wall."

They patted each other on the back.

When Puffer turned and walked away, Grandfather's blind eyes followed her. He shook his head, as though deeply troubled.

Puffer walked to meet her deputy, Black Star, who stood with the rest of the war party at the lakeshore trailhead. Black Star was Grizzly's father, and a muscular man with massive shoulders. Puffer spoke to the party briefly; then she led the way up the trail at a trot. None of them looked happy.

"Now we can go see him," Twig said, and trotted for her grandfather, calling, "Hello, Grandfather!"

Yipper charged forward with his tail wagging.

Halfmoon turned, and squinted hard, as though trying to see her. "Twig? Is that you?"

"Yes, Grandfather. It's Twig and Greyhawk."

Grandfather knelt and opened his arms. Twig ran into them, and he hugged her. "How are you today, my beautiful granddaughter?"

"Fine. How are you? Are your eyes better?"

Grandfather smiled sadly. "No, they get more and more blurry every day—though I see a little better after Father Sun goes down." He turned to Greyhawk. "And how are you, young warrior? Are you practicing with your atlatl and spears?"

"Yes, Elder Halfmoon. I practice every morning and night. I'm getting better, but I can't slice the ear off a wolf at a hundred paces like you can."

"That was in the old days. Today, I can't even see a wolf at a hundred paces." Grandfather sat down on the mat before his fire again. "Come, children. Sit down. I have some roasted fish left from breakfast if you're hungry. It's there, in that bowl." He pointed to the wooden bowl that rested on the hearthstone, keeping warm.

They both sat down cross-legged beside the fire, and Greyhawk reached into the bowl for a chunk of white fish meat. He smelled it first, took a bite, and gave Yipper a bite, which the dog choked down in one swallow.

Twig licked her lips nervously, trying to muster the bravery to ask Grandfather to take her to see Cobia.

"What's wrong, Twig?" Grandfather asked. "You're being very quiet."

Instead of getting to the point, she said, "Mother told me I could never go to see Screech Owl again, but I have to, Grandfather. He needs me. I don't understand why she doesn't like him."

A gust of wind blew Grandfather's graying black hair around his wrinkled face as he said, "She did like him. Once. A long time ago. I don't know what went wrong between them, but it happened before you were born. Is she afraid he'll turn you into a slug?"

Twig laughed. "Maybe."

Around a mouthful of fish, Greyhawk said, "What did Screech Owl do to get banished from the village? It must have been really bad."

Grandfather picked up a stick and prodded the fire, which caused sparks to crackle and spin upward in the morning air. When his sleeves pulled back, Twig saw the burn scars that covered his hands and lower arms. "Not bad, not exactly. He was always doing curious things, like sniffing people's tracks as they walked by, or leaving wet spots in front of their doors."

Twig cocked her head. In the distance, over Grandfather's shoulder, the Ice Giants groaned and a rumble shook the earth. Grandfather listened for a long time, and looked worried.

Twig said, "Did Screech Owl have the soul of a dog then?"

"A wolf, or so he said. Then there was the time he dug a hole under Chief Gill's lodge and filled it with dead mice. After five or six days, the smell drove the chief's entire family out of the lodge."

Between bites of fish, Greyhawk said, "Did Screech Owl cover them up and forget they were there?"

"All I know is the chief had had enough. He told Screech Owl to get out of the village and never come back."

Twig reached into the bowl to grab the last piece of fish before Greyhawk could eat it. Yipper snapped for it, but Twig stuffed it in her mouth and chewed. It tasted warm and delicious. "I have to go see him, Grandfather. He gets lonely by himself, and I'm his only friend."

Grandfather's white eyes moved, as though trying to see Twig. "Does he have a human soul yet?"

"No, a kestrel's; but I don't think he's buried any dead mice in a long time." She wiped the fish grease from her hands onto the sand and took a deep breath. This may be the best chance she would have. "Grandfather?"

"Yes?"

"Screech Owl told me to ask you a question."

Grandfather shifted as though expecting the worst. "What question?"

Twig glanced at Greyhawk, who looked back with his mouth quirked, as though he thought she was insane for wanting to go see Cobia, the baby killer.

"Screech Owl said I should ask you to take me to see Cobia, because you were the only one—"

"*Cobia!*" Grandfather half shouted. "I'm not taking

you to see Cobia! That's a death sentence. She hates me and my entire family. Do you want to die?"

Twig nervously licked her lips. "But . . . Screech Owl—he said I needed to talk to her about my dream, and you were probably the only one brave enough to take me."

Grandfather tossed his stick into the fire and glared at it as it burned up. Finally, in a softer voice, he said, "You had another Spirit dream?"

"Yes, Grandfather."

"What was it about?"

"I saw a flaming ball of light flying south through the night. It filled the entire sky. Screech Owl said that the Star People might be planning to make war on us. It scared him."

Grandfather reached over and stroked her hair. "I'm sorry I raised my voice. I didn't know you'd had another Spirit dream. Your mother didn't tell me."

Twig swallowed hard. "She . . . she doesn't want anyone to know."

"Why not?"

"I don't know."

Grandfather's mouth tightened, as though it hurt him to hear that. "Twig, you must be kind to your mother. Spirit dreaming comes easy to you. After all the praying and fasting your mother has done, it's hard for her to understand why Spirits are always walking in your dreams, and not hers. I think she's a little jealous of you."

Twig whispered, "But Grandfather, I don't ask them to walk in my dreams."

Grandfather put a hand on her shoulder and squeezed it tenderly. "I know you don't. But I suspect that's why your mother doesn't want you to see Screech Owl. She's afraid you will become more powerful than she is, and the village will make you an outcast, just like Screech Owl."

"But Grandfather, I—"

"I'm glad you told me about this, Twig. I need to warn the elders. Right now they are far more concerned with the Thornback raiders, but later they may want to question you."

Twig nodded. "Screech Owl said they should know."

"He's right. Is there anything else you need to tell me?"

"No. Well . . . maybe that I invited Screech Owl to come to the Buffalo Way ceremony tonight. I asked Mother if she would talk to Chief Gill about it, but she wouldn't. Now I'm afraid Screech Owl will come and people will throw things at him to make him go away."

The wrinkles around Grandfather's eyes got deeper. "I'll talk to Chief Gill. I think he'll allow it. He doesn't mind seeing Screech Owl, so long as it's on rare occasions."

"Thank you, Grandfather." She leaped to her feet to hug him around the neck.

When she sat down again, she saw Greyhawk studying the lines drawn into the dirt. He pointed at one and said, "Elder Halfmoon, are the Thornback People going to raid us?"

Grandfather reached out and felt for Greyhawk's hand where it hovered over the line, then pulled Greyhawk's fingers down to a rock. "Do you know the name of this village, young warrior?"

"That's Starhorse Village," Greyhawk said. "I went there with my father two summers ago, to trade beaver-hides for shell beads."

Grandfather released his hand. "Well, you won't be going there again. It no longer exists. The Thornback raiders destroyed it ten days ago."

Greyhawk's eyes went wide. He frowned at the rocks and the lines between them, as though following out the trails in his head, before he pulled two more rocks from the fire ring. As he placed them on the ground in a line with Starhorse Village, he said, "Did I do that right, Elder?"

Greyhawk took Grandfather's hand and moved it down to touch the rocks.

Grandfather felt them, then felt the other rocks and said, "You did that perfectly. Do you understand what it means?"

With his eyes still on the rocks, Greyhawk said, "They're coming up the lake trail, destroying every village in their way? It looks like Clearwater Village is next, or maybe Oakbeam Village."

"It appears so."

Greyhawk's hand dropped to the spear on the ground at his side, as though he feared he might need it. "Why are they killing people?"

Grandfather paused and frowned. "They have a new

Spirit dreamer. His name is Nightcrow. He's powerful and evil. I think he wants to destroy every other village in the world."

"Then shouldn't we pack up the village and move, just in case?" Greyhawk asked.

"I've already discussed that with our council of elders. There are too many people who do not agree with me. They're frightened."

Twig said, "But we need to move, Grandfather. Why are they frightened?"

Grandfather exhaled hard. "It's springtime. The rivers and creeks are all flooded. Most of the trails are underwater. Not only that, bears have just started coming out of their dens. They're starving, eager to hunt for food. If we move, there are those who believe many of our children and elders will die."

Twig could feel the fear in the air.

She reached out and put her hand on Grandfather's wrist. "Grandfather, maybe I can help. If I can just go see Cobia, she can help me understand my dreams, and then maybe I can *dream* the safest way for us to go."

"Forget about Cobia. I'm not even sure she's still alive. And the journey is extremely dangerous. There are raiders on the trails, and Grandfather Brown Bear's people live all around her cave. We'd be torn apart and eaten before we got halfway there. Besides, Screech Owl taught Cobia to be a Spirit dreamer. He can teach you just as well as he did her."

"But, Grandfather . . ." Twig almost couldn't speak.

"I—I'm afraid to be a Spirit dreamer. Mother doesn't want me to be, and she told me I could never go see Screech Owl again."

Grandfather grabbed her hand and got to his feet. "Lead me to your mother. I'll talk to her right now. She'll let you study with Screech Owl, I promise."

Their people, the People of the Dawnland, traced descent through the men. That meant that Grandfather was the leader of their family and had the last word. Whatever he told Mother to do, she had to, or the Blue Bear Clan elders would punish her severely.

As Twig led Grandfather back toward her lodge, she gave Greyhawk a terrified glance. She *needed* to understand her dreams, but she was afraid that Mother was right. If she became too powerful, her own people would be frightened of her, and might cast her out of Buffalobeard Village. Where would she go? Whom would she live with? Would she be alone for the rest of her life, as Screech Owl and Cobia were?

Twig suddenly felt lost and frightened, like her insides were melting.

CHAPTER 10

SITTING ALONE OUT on the treeless tundra, Chief Nightcrow heard steps pounding up the trail and opened his eyes. His Spirit vision died like mist on a hot day. War Chief Hook and a young warrior named Player trotted up the trail.

Nightcrow rose to his feet. The wind was cold on his face. He shivered. To the south, the forests had just started leafing out. A green haze whiskered the distances.

Images from his vision taunted him. He saw men screaming in fear, trying to protect their families; then he saw himself cleaning and preparing the bodies of the bravest of his warriors for the blessings of the afterlife.

The cowards, of course, would receive no such rites. On the contrary, he would send their souls spinning away into eternal darkness.

Nightcrow's eyes narrowed. He was a man of spells and magical words, more feared than any other Spirit dreamer in the history of the Thornback People. He could kill with a look, or the lightest touch. When he'd been a boy, and his powers had first started to come, his own parents had tried to kill him. They had failed. Then the assassins sent by the chief had failed. Finally, an entire war party had vanished trying to track him through the snow.

Since then no one had dared try to harm him. He had seen thirty-three summers pass, married three wives, sired eleven children, and seen six grandchildren born in the past two summers. Life had been good. But the world was about to change.

The end was coming soon. In his visions, Nightcrow had seen the sky explode and the land burn. The dead scattered the charred ruins of villages like slaughtered animals, and hunger stalked the land. War broke out as people fought for the scraps from each other's supper fires.

Nightcrow had already ordered Hook to start attacking their enemies first. His reasons were simple: If there were no other villages, there would be no fighting over scraps. His people would have everything.

Nightcrow inhaled a breath as Hook—a tall, muscular giant, with broken, yellow teeth—stopped before him and bowed. Many scars cut across Hook's face. He wore a knee-length black shirt, as did all Thornback warriors.

"Chief, forgive me for disturbing your visions, but important news has reached us."

"What news?"

"Buffalobeard Village has sent out another war party. We think they are trying to find Cobia."

A small thread of fear warmed Nightcrow's veins. There was only one person in the world who frightened him. Cobia. "Cobia will not help them. She hates them. They stole her from her people and lied to her about it for nineteen summers. She wants the People of the Dawnland dead as much as I do."

Young Player stepped forward. He was thin, with a long black braid dangling over his shoulder. His skin shone with sweat from his run across the tundra. "She may want the People of the Dawnland dead, my chief, but I have heard that there is one old man, the man who raised her, that she would die for. His name is Screech Owl. If he asked Cobia for help, she might agree."

"Do you think so?"

"I think we must consider it, because if she agrees . . ."

"If she agrees . . . what?"

Player closed his mouth. He seemed to realize his mistake. The young warrior had just suggested that Cobia was more powerful than Nightcrow, that she might be able to defeat him and destroy the Thornback People.

Nightcrow's gaze slid to Hook, seeing if his war chief understood the insult. Hook showed no emotion at all.

He was a wise man. That's why he had ascended to the position of war chief.

Nightcrow walked to stand very close to Player. The warrior stiffened, and Nightcrow could smell his fear sweat. "You didn't mean to suggest that Cobia was the most powerful Spirit dreamer alive, did you?"

Player nervously licked his lips. "No, my ch-chief, of course not. I would never—"

"Good." He turned back to Hook. "What did you find at Starhorse Village?"

Hook frowned for an instant, then reached into his belt pouch and drew out a beautifully carved deer-bone stiletto. Nightcrow grabbed it, and power prickled across his palm. "This was their most powerful sacred object?"

"Yes, that's what the survivors told us just before we killed them."

Nightcrow studied the magical stiletto. Images of buffalo, mammoths, and birds covered the bone surface. It was a truly beautiful thing. Their Spirit dreamer must have cherished it.

Player leaned forward to stare at it, and Nightcrow plunged it into the young man's throat. As blood shot from Player's wounded artery, he fell onto Nightcrow with open arms. Nightcrow grunted and shoved him away. Player's body thumped hard on the ground. Nightcrow watched him writhe for one hundred heartbeats, until the life went out of his eyes; then he turned back to face Hook.

"Was there anything else you wanted to tell me, War Chief?"

Hook clenched his fists at his sides and shook his head. "No."

"Good. Find the Buffalobeard war party. Kill them. Then come back."

"Yes, my chief." Hook bowed, then trotted back down the trail toward the village.

Player's blood soaked the carvings in the bone stiletto, making them appear to be alive. The prickling sensation of Spirit power grew.

Nightcrow exhaled a deep breath and closed his eyes. The wind on his cheek felt especially pleasant, the fragrance of the tundra wildflowers especially sweet.

He kicked Player's dead body, sat down, and returned to his vision quest.

TWIG PANTED AS she scrambled up the massive pile of boulders on the eastern edge of Buffalobeard Village. Greyhawk, Grizzly, and Muskrat climbed above her. The dirt cascading from beneath their moccasins kept rolling down over her head. Twig spat gravel from her mouth and climbed faster.

After Grandfather Halfmoon had spoken with Mother, Mother had been very quiet for a while; then in a cold voice she'd ordered Twig to start carrying rocks for the defensive wall being built around the western side of village. Twig had carried rocks all afternoon, until her arms and back ached so badly she could barely straighten up. It was only when Mother had to begin the preparations for the Buffalo Way ceremony that she'd released Twig to go and play. And Twig had the feeling that carrying rocks was only a small part of the punishment to come for telling Grandfather about her dreams.

In the village below, people laughed and walked around the central plaza. While quarters of buffalo roasted, suspended from heavy poles over the main bonfire, there were many smaller fires where racks covered with strips of goose meat and fish stood. The racks had been arranged over low fires. Then wet wood was added, causing a lot of smoke to rise and smoke the sweet meats to a golden brown.

"Hurry up, Twig!" Greyhawk called from the top of the rocks. His chin-length black hair glistened with sweat. He waved impatiently, and Yipper barked at her. "We're going over!"

Grizzly propped his fists on his hips and sneered over the edge at Twig. "Come on, girl!" Grizzly yelled, and turned to the other boys to say, "Let's leave her. She's been hauling rocks all day. She's too tired to keep up."

"I'm coming!" Twig cried as she watched the boys charge over the rocks and out of sight. At the top of her lungs, she added, "I'm the oldest. I should be the leader!"

No one answered.

She slid her knee onto the next ledge and dug her fingers into the crevices to pull herself up, but the rocks gave way, and she slipped and fell, landing hard on a lower ledge. Blood trickled warmly from a scraped knee. She bit her lip to drive back the hurt and tackled the rock face again, climbing until she could crawl over the top ledge.

The boys were huddled together, shoulder to shoulder, behind a rock thirty paces away. They butted each other playfully as they fought for the best position.

Twig got up and trotted toward them, but her steps faltered when she realized where they were. They must be looking down on the dressing area of the masked dancers. The dancers would conjure the Spirits of the buffalo in tonight's ceremony. If they did everything right, with reverence, the buffalo would smile upon them, and bring their herds north where Twig's people could hunt them and use their meat to feed their families.

She bent low and sneaked up on cougar-silent feet to see what occupied them so thoroughly. On the grassy flat below the rocks, two women stood painting each other's faces with bright red spirals.

Twig called, "You turkey brains! Do you want to ruin the ceremony? You know nobody's supposed to see the dancers until they come into the plaza tonight. You're bringing bad luck. Do you want the buffalo to go away forever, like the mammoths have?"

Shamed, Greyhawk slid backward on his hands and knees, but Grizzly grabbed him by the shirt and hauled him back up.

Greyhawk let out a yowl while he chopped at the bigger boy's meaty hands. "Quit that, Grizzly! Let me go!"

When Grizzly laughed, Yipper went into a barking,

snarling frenzy and leaped for Grizzly's hand where it held Greyhawk.

Grizzly shrieked, let go of Greyhawk in the nick of time, and ran backward to get away. Yipper positioned himself between the boys and stood with his teeth bared, growling at Grizzly. The hair on his back stood straight up in a black bristly line.

"What are you doing listening to a girl?" Grizzly shouted, and looked at his hand to make sure he still had all of his fingers. "What does she know?"

Twig narrowed her eyes. "A lot more than you do, ugly boy, at least about our sacred ceremonies. My mother is the village Spirit dreamer and the keeper of the Wolf Bundle."

"So what?" Grizzly shouted. "She doesn't have any power."

"Yes, she does!" Twig yelled back.

Grizzly threw his huge shoulders back and stalked toward Twig like Grandfather Brown Bear walking on his hind legs.

She let out a yell and ran.

Grizzly was right behind her, chasing her down like Wolf does Mouse. When she jumped a bush to reach the trail that led back to the village, her hurt knee gave way, and she fell against a pile of boulders, a little dizzy.

Grizzly bawled in triumph as he dove for her, but Twig somehow scooted out of his way, rolled to her feet, and stood with her jaw thrust out and her fists up. "Stop it, Grizzly, or I'll break your nose again!"

Greyhawk and young Muskrat raced up as Grizzly kicked Twig in her sore knee. When she screamed, he grabbed her hand and growled, "Now I've got you!"

He swung his clenched fist at her cheek. Twig ducked and rammed her head into his stomach, then sank her teeth into his hand before flinging herself backward to break his grip.

Grizzly roared in pain, stared at his bloody hand, and shouted to his friends, "Come on! Let's get her!"

Greyhawk glanced at Twig, then at Grizzly, trying to decide whose side to take. Muskrat, who had seen only eight summers, didn't have much courage yet, so he jumped from foot to foot as though totally confused. His long black braid dangled in a fuzzy mass over his left shoulder.

Twig braced herself for the battle. "Greyhawk! Help me. You're my best friend!"

"I know it!" he said, but he made no move to run to her side.

"Your best friend is a girl!" Grizzly taunted. "You've got the brain of a tree stump! Come on, Muskrat, help me get her!"

Muskrat gritted his teeth so hard in indecision that his head shook. Finally, he ran to Grizzly's side.

Twig almost wet herself. She glared at Greyhawk, trying to look fierce but knowing that her expression quickly changed to pleading. "Greyhawk? Your grandfather was my great uncle's third cousin!"

It meant that Twig and Greyhawk were only very distantly related, but she was still praying that kinship might work.

Greyhawk blinked, apparently trying to remember if that was right; then he grudgingly nodded and trotted to stand beside her. Throwing out his chest, he declared, "Leave my cousin alone!"

Twig grinned at Grizzly, but he didn't seem to appreciate her accomplishment. He hunkered down, spread his arms like Falcon ready to soar into the sky, and roared, "All right. We're coming!"

Grizzly and Muskrat lunged for them. Greyhawk kicked out, catching Grizzly in the knee, but Grizzly only stumbled. When he regained his balance, he whirled around and slammed a fist into Greyhawk's back that sent him sprawling across the ground like a dead spider.

Twig planted her feet, preparing for Muskrat's attack. He ran straight at her, yelling with his mouth wide open, so she took her fist and jammed it down his throat. His teeth made a crunching sound at the same time that her hand split in agony.

"Ach!" Muskrat screamed and backed off to wipe his bloody mouth on his sleeve. "You broke one of my front teeth!"

"You deserved it!" Twig stared at her bloody knuckles, shook them to fight the pain, and spun to face Grizzly, who had managed to drive Greyhawk ten paces up the slope and was coming back for her.

"Don't do it, Grizzly!" she threatened. In a stroke of genius, she pointed at the sky. "Eagle-Man is my Spirit

Helper. If you hurt me, I'll call out to him and he'll come and carry you all the way up to the Cloud People before he drops you on Buffalobeard Village! There will be nothing left of you but a pile of bony mush with a tongue sticking out!"

Grizzly laughed—a low, disbelieving laugh—and kept coming. "You're only twelve. You're too young to have a Spirit Helper."

"I am not too young. Cobia had Spirit Helpers when she had seen two summers!" Twig called, and refused to give ground. She grabbed up a rock and stood with her knees trembling, thinking it was probably a good day to die.

As his shadow fell over her, a large rock plunged out of the blue and smacked Grizzly in the ear.

He screamed, "Ow!" and staggered backward.

A tall figure wearing a kestrel mask rose with ghostly stealth from behind one of the rocks up the slope. Grey and white feathers sleeked down over the thing's face and formed a ruff around its neck. Twig's eyes went wide. She knew it wasn't Eagle-Man, but she doubted Grizzly did.

Grizzly backed up and shouted, "Get away from me, Spirit!"

The figure crept down the hill, and his huge wooden beak slowly creaked open, showing glimpses of a puckered mouth beneath. Then a high-pitched shriek flooded out, sounding so real that Grizzly stood petrified.

In a flash, the figure swooped down the slope, holding

out the woven edges of its rabbit-fur cape like wings, screaming something nobody could understand.

Grizzly clutched at his heart with one hand and his wounded ear with the other before dashing down the path toward the village with Muskrat wailing behind him.

Greyhawk slipped his spear into the hooked end of his atlatl and lifted it as he ran back to defend Twig against the masked Spirit creature. "Stay back!" he shouted, ready to cast.

Twig couldn't believe it. Greyhawk had never done anything like this before. He must be learning a lot in his clan warriors' school.

The Spirit creature propped age-spotted hands on bony hips and said, "Twig. Greyhawk. You should stay away from Grizzly. He has a twisted soul. Did you know his grandmother used to suck fish eyes for fun? She kept a batch rolling around in her cheeks all day long. I never did like her." He reached up and tugged off the mask, revealing Screech Owl's white-painted face. Black streaks ran below his eyes, just like they did Kestrel's. A single gray spot covered the middle of his forehead.

"Screech Owl!" Twig shouted in glee and ran to grab him around the waist. "When did you get here? I thought you would wait until nightfall, when people couldn't see you so well."

Screech Owl grinned. "No, no. This way if people chase me out of the village, I can still make it back to my cave before midnight."

"No one is going to chase you. It took Grandfather

most of the afternoon to convince Chief Gill that it was all right for you to come, but he finally agreed. You're safe here."

The lines at the corners of his eyes crinkled. "It was kind of Halfmoon to ask him. And kind of you, Twig, to ask him for me."

She patted his arm affectionately. "I wanted you here."

Screech Owl put a hand on top of her head, paused for several moments, and asked, "Who is Eagle-Man?"

A shiver climbed Twig's spine. "He told me he's my Spirit Helper."

"He came to you in a dream?"

"Yes. Last night."

Screech Owl's bushy white brows drew together. "What did he look like?"

"He was very strange. He had a bird's wings and beak, but a human body with snakeskin."

Screech Owl's gaze searched the horizon, as though thinking about that. Finally, he looked down at her. A somber expression lined his elderly face. "You have a very powerful Spirit Helper, Twig. Remember that. The most powerful Helpers combine many worlds in themselves: human, reptile, bird. The more worlds they combine, the more powerful they are. You are very fortunate."

Twig nodded. "I'll remember."

The crimson face of Father Sun hung a hand's breadth from the horizon. In the stillness, she could hear voices climbing the slope—soft voices, as if the approach of the ceremony turned the world as frail as a blossom, so that it had to be treated gently.

Twig said, "We should be going. The ceremony starts at nightfall. We don't want to be late. Mother is already mad at me."

"Why?"

"I told Grandfather about my dreams. As punishment Mother made me carry rocks all afternoon."

Screech Owl frowned, but he didn't say anything. They took the trail down to Buffalobeard Village.

"Twig, did you ask your grandfather to take you to see Cobia?"

She gazed up into that long, beaky face with its unruly frame of gray hair. "He won't take me. He says it's too dangerous. There are raiders on the trails, and Grandfather Brown Bear's people live all around Cobia's cave. Besides, he said you could teach me just as much as she could."

Screech Owl tilted his head as though he did not agree and said, "Are you sure you want to study with me? The last time we talked, you said you didn't—"

"I—I know, but I guess I have to. Grandfather said so."

He patted her shoulder gently. "Well, I'm a poor substitute for Cobia, but I will do my best. Which means we should immediately start teaching you how to see through the eyes of Snake and Bird. The sooner the better."

She glanced up at him from the corner of her eye. "Will I have to give up my human soul, like you have?"

"Yes, for a while."

Her heart started to pound against her ribs. "Screech Owl?"

"Yes, Twig."

"What if I'm scared?"

He smiled. Father Sun cast reddish light over his face, and his wrinkles stood out like dark cobwebs. "You should be scared. Spirit quests are very dangerous. I wish . . . well, I wish you could come and live with me for a while. That way I could teach you all the little things about changing souls."

Twig tried to imagine what it would be like to live with Screech Owl instead of Mother. She didn't know if she liked the idea. She had always lived with Mother, and close enough to Greyhawk to hit him with a rock if she wanted to. But she loved Screech Owl just the same. Maybe she could. She would talk to Grandfather about it.

"Will the Spirits let me choose the kind of bird and snake souls I get? Maybe I could get Water Snake's soul or Falcon's soul?"

"You can try. But often when you're looking for a new soul, one comes to you that you didn't expect."

"You mean like the mink that's trying to take over yours?"

Screech Owl looked around uneasily. "I wish you hadn't mentioned that, Twig. He could be out there right now, ready to pounce on me."

"I don't blame you for being scared. I've seen minks

attack animals ten times their size, pull them down, and chew their throats out. They're very fast and ferocious."

"Yes." He gulped a swallow. "I know."

They reached the foot of the trail and walked toward the plaza, where dozens of people stood talking.

"Screech Owl? What if I never learn to see through the eyes of Bird or Snake, No matter how hard I try?"

"I wouldn't worry about that," he said mildly. "Eagle-Man will help you. Besides, it's usually when you give up searching for Spirit power that it leaps upon you like Grandfather Wolf with his teeth bared."

Twig frowned at the sunlight slanting across the village. She decided not to ask him the next question, but it repeated in her soul anyway:

And he chews you up? Does Power chew you up? Is that how it kills your human soul?

CHAPTER 12

WHEN THEY WALKED into the village, people started pointing at Screech Owl and whispering behind their hands, but he didn't seem to notice; he just smiled at everyone.

Twig took Screech Owl by the hand and led him to Grandfather's place around the central fire where the buffalo roasted. It was a special place, close to Chief Gill's family. Mother wasn't there yet, but Grandfather was. He sat with an old mammoth-hide cloak around his shoulders, staring blindly out at the western trail. Mammoths were so rare these days that having such a hide was a mark of great honor.

Twig sat down cross-legged beside Grandfather and said, "Look, Grandfather! Screech Owl came!"

Grandfather turned, and his long graying black braid pulled over his shoulder. "Screech Owl? Is that you?"

Screech Owl crouched before Grandfather and said, "Yes, Elder Halfmoon, thank you for your kindness. It's been a long while since I was invited to a village ceremony."

Grandfather smiled. "Well, I always liked you. You know that."

"Even after I chewed up your moccasins that day?"

"Well, not as much after that. Those were my favorite moccasins. But, yes, even after that."

Grandfather gazed, again, up the western trail, and Twig wondered if he was afraid that the Thornback raiders were about to attack them. Then she remembered War Chief Puffer saying that she would try to be back before the Buffalo Way ceremony started. She searched the village, and didn't see Puffer. Was Grandfather worried about her?

Screech Owl sat down beside Twig, and she felt better, safer, sitting between two of the people she loved most in the world. "See?" she said to Screech Owl. "I told you everything would be all right."

"So far. But keep your eyes open for thrown rocks. You can never be too sure."

A sudden hush fell over the village. All heads turned toward Twig's lodge. She got up on her knees—wincing at the sore one—and saw Mother duck from beneath their lodge flap and walk across the plaza toward the fire. She looked beautiful. Her long cape was painted with red, white, and black pictures of running buffalo and yellow suns. Her hair had been freshly washed, and she'd coiled her black braids around her ears and pinned them with polished fish-bone combs. She carried a hollow buffalo horn in each hand.

No one spoke as she made her way through the crowd to stand before the fire where the buffalo roasted.

Mother stopped and lifted her hands toward the heavens. The village went totally quiet.

In a ringing voice, Mother called, "When legends die, dreams end, and there is no more greatness. Remember that every buffalo is a legend. They are not like oak leaves that fade and fall to the ground to be blown away by the slightest breeze. Instead, they are like the Star People who shine forever. Let us thank Buffalo Above for the gift of her children's lives."

Mother carefully placed Buffalo's horn sheaths before the fire, pointed west, and everyone in the village rose to their feet.

When Mother started the sacred song, Twig closed her eyes and sang. The words came from the depths of her soul, eddied around the village, and seemed to hang like a veil.

She sang:

> Look upward, Brother Buffalo, to the Road of Light
> that streaks the night sky.

We pray that Buffalo Above will come and take your soul running to the Land of the Dead, where you will never be hungry again, where it is always warm, and you'll never have to shiver in deep snow.

We thank you, Brother, for giving your life to us, so that the One Great Life of all might continue unbroken.

Come, Buffalo Above. Come and take the soul of our Brother running on the Road of Light.

When Twig opened her eyes, she saw Screech Owl smiling down at her. His gray hair looked like handfuls of frosty twigs. The ragged wolf-hide shirt that he wore beneath his cape had been worn so thin she could see his knobby ribs sticking out through the hide.

"You sang well," he praised.

"So did you. I didn't know you had such a deep beautiful voice."

One by one, people sat down on the hides spread over the ground. Twig, Grandfather, and Screech Owl kept standing until the Buffalo Dancers appeared out of the darkness and shuffled to their positions around the fire to begin the dance.

Twig studied the dancers. Their painted faces gleamed in the firelight, as did the decorated buffalo headdresses they wore. The thick brown fur of their capes had been turned inside for warmth, and the outside was painted with magnificent hunting scenes.

Twig started to say something to Grandfather, but Grandfather made a small sound of surprise, rose to his feet, and hurried to where Chief Gill sat with his family. By the time Grandfather got there, Chief Gill was standing. They headed out into the darkness. Twig couldn't see anyone out there . . . but she hoped Puffer had returned.

"Screech Owl? I've never seen Grandfather this worried before."

"I noticed that War Chief Puffer was not at her position guarding the trails as we came into the village. Is she gone on another battle-walk?"

"Chief Gill sent her to find Cobia and ask if she will dream the future for us, and help us defeat the Thornback People. Grandfather is afraid they're going to raid us. That's why we've been building the rock wall around the village."

Screech Owl looked out at the half-finished rock wall. "Then it's no wonder your Grandfather is worried."

"Do you think Cobia can help us defeat the Thornback raiders?"

"She may be the only person who can . . . if she chooses to. Her soul walks constantly in the Land of the Dead. Powerful Spirits are always close to her. Once, when she was just thirteen summers, she got into a fight with a village boy, and I saw her kill him with a word. Cobia pointed at him and shouted a strange word, and the boy fell down stone dead."

Twig pulled up her knees and hugged them to her chest. That scared her. "What was the word?"

"I don't know. It wasn't our language, or any language I had ever heard before. It frightened me."

It scared Twig, too. Is that what Chief Gill wanted Cobia to do to the Thornback raiders? Kill them with a word?

"Then there was the death of Minnow. That's when she left."

"What happened?"

"Oh, it was a long time ago, twenty summers. Cobia had just learned the truth about her past. She—"

"What truth?"

Screech Owl bowed his head for a long moment before he said, "I'll tell you, if you promise not to hold it against your grandfather. He was just obeying the orders of his chief."

"I promise." But her heart started to pound. She wasn't sure she wanted to hear anything bad about Grandfather.

"When Halfmoon first arrived with Cobia, she'd seen less than two summers. She grew up knowing she'd come from the Duskland, but she didn't know her mother had been murdered, or that she had been pulled from her dead mother's arms and kidnapped. She learned that from a visiting trader when she'd seen nineteen summers."

"Is that when she left?"

"Yes, but not before she took her revenge on the man responsible, Old Minnow."

Twig's mouth had gone dry as dust. When she spoke, her voice was gravelly. "What did she do?"

"She walked up to him, opened her hand, and blew across it, and he fell dead. Then Cobia turned around and left. No one has seen her since, though people have hunted for her many times."

"To get her to dream the future?" Twig shivered.

"Yes." Screech Owl put his arm around her and hugged her. "Let's talk about your dreams instead. Are you well? Have you had that dream again?"

"About the ball of light that roars over the top of me? Yes."

"Did you tell your grandfather?"

She nodded. "He said he would talk to the council about it. I think we should move our village, Screech Owl."

"Move where?"

"Far to the west. That's all I know."

Screech Owl ran a hand through his gray hair while he stared absently at the dancers. The flames leaped and crackled behind them, turning them into dark moving shapes. When they shook their buffalo hoof rattles, the very air seemed to shudder.

People started joining the Buffalo Dancers, singing with all their hearts.

Screech Owl said, "I fear you are right, Twig. Buffalobeard Village should move. I'll try to talk with Chief Gill about it. I hope he listens."

CHAPTER 13

THE MUSIC OF a bone flute woke Twig where she dozed, shivering, beneath her cape. She'd danced for as long as she could; then she'd eaten a big helping of delicious buffalo meat and gone to join the other children who sat on the south side of the village. Most were curled beneath their hides, sleeping. Moon Maiden had just peeked over the eastern horizon, but her light was faint on this cold night. Twig pulled her cape up over her icy nose so she could breathe down the front and warm her chest.

Old Man Blood Duck, with his maimed leg, stood at the edge of the dance circle and sang as he swayed. He had the scratchiest voice in the village, but it didn't matter. The only thing that mattered tonight was that Earthmaker saw the goodness in their hearts. If they kept their souls pure and treated each other and the buffalo well, as Earthmaker had taught, then great herds of buffalo would come. The raiding would stop. And they would never be hungry again.

Greyhawk mumbled something in his sleep and elbowed Twig before he rolled to his side.

"Are you awake?" she asked.

"No."

She looked back at the dancers. They blurred together in her tired vision, seeming to sink into the darkness and cold. Only their voices and the shell bells on their moccasins told her they hadn't been sucked up by the Water Spirits that haunted the ceremonies. All of the colors that humans used for painting their bodies came from the bones of the Water Spirits, and on nights like this one, when so many colors flashed, the Spirits were drawn to the souls of their dead ancestors. They came to watch from the shadows, sometimes to dance, and sometimes to steal a bad child and take him to their home beneath Ice Giant Lake.

A gust of wind swooped over the rocky ridge and soared down to blast Twig and other children. Several groaned and slid deeper under their hides.

Greyhawk said, "I'm cold. When is the dance going to be over?"

Ice had formed on the edge of the hide next to his nose.

"I'm cold, too. But you know we can't go in until the dance is finished. Buffalo Above might get angry and take her children away."

"I know." He propped himself up on one elbow. "Twig, what did you and Screech Owl talk about this afternoon?"

She hesitated, not sure she wanted to tell him yet. "Nothing. Just about the ceremony."

"I don't like him. He's too strange."

She shifted to study Screech Owl. He stood a head taller than anyone else in the village, so it was easy to spot him in the dance circle. He looked skinny, the way he twisted in the dance. He had been dancing next to her mother all night, which Twig found very odd, since Mother didn't like Screech Owl. "I might go live with Screech Owl for a while, Greyhawk."

"What for? You might never come back! At least, not as a human."

"I guess there are things, dangerous things, he can teach me only if I live with him."

"You mean he's going to teach you how to be a Spirit dreamer?"

She drew her cape more tightly around her shoulders. "Yes."

Greyhawk obviously didn't know what to say. He blinked and looked away, as though scared. Finally, he said, "Do you want to go live with him, Twig?"

"I don't know."

"Won't you be scared to live with someone who isn't human?"

"Of course not." She shook her head valiantly. "I live around sloths and giant beavers and other animals right now. They don't scare me. Do they scare you?"

"Well, no, not when they're in their own bodies," Greyhawk replied. "Why can't he come and teach you here?" He paused and scowled. "No, that would never work. Somebody would whack him in the head for chewing up their moccasins, and you'd feel bad."

"Yes. I would."

Greyhawk combed hair out of his eyes. "Twig, I'm afraid that you'll become a very powerful Spirit dreamer and you'll be cast out of the village, like Screech Owl. Is your grandfather going to make you?"

"I think he wants me to."

Greyhawk's eyes narrowed, as though in pain, and he stared out at the dancers for a long time. "Well, if you have to go live with Screech Owl, I—I'll try to come and visit you. If Father doesn't forbid—"

They both jumped when Old Man Blood Duck let out a shrill cry of joy and tried to dance on his bad leg.

"Here they come!" Greyhawk said excitedly. He sat up, eager for this final moment of the ceremony.

All around the edges of the plaza, old people and children opened their eyes to look.

A rumble like an earthquake trembled on the cold air. From out in the darkness, a chant echoed, deep and powerful, calling to the Spirits of the plants and animals. Then the last dancers trotted into the plaza. Big men, they were dressed like buffalo and charged around the fire, making the deep-throated calls of playing, happy buffalo. The first dancers fell into line behind them, and together they danced out of the plaza into the darkness.

Finally, Mother came back to the fire and began sprinkling grass seeds on the ground and on people, so that each person could carry the buffalo's prayers for lush spring grasses to Earthmaker in his dreams. Perhaps, if they all dreamed well, Earthmaker would hear them.

Twig laughed when a huge kestrel leaned over her. Wind fluttered its feathers. Through its open beak, she could see Screech Owl's grin. "Come on," he said. "Your mother invited me to have nutcakes and tea, and I'm starved."

"Mother *invited* you?" she blurted as she struggled to stand up.

"Yes. She hasn't been herself tonight," he answered. "It's been very nice. I'm a little worried that she wants something."

Greyhawk cast one glance at Screech Owl. "I'll see you tomorrow, Twig!" he said, and ran.

"Sleep well, Greyhawk!" she answered.

Twig held Screech Owl's hand as they made their way across the plaza. People swerved wide around them, still not sure that Screech Owl ought to be allowed in human company, even though he had danced with all his kestrel soul.

When they turned the bend in the path, she could see that firelight already gleamed around the edges of the door-hanging to their lodge. But Twig smelled something else. She sniffed noisily. "That's Mother's special raspberry tea, Screech Owl."

He sniffed too. "Yes, it smells good."

Twig gave him a quick look, wondering why her mother would make it for Screech Owl when she wouldn't make it for Twig except on important occasions. She slipped out from under his arm and trotted for home. As she ducked inside, her head brushed the eagle feathers that dangled from the ceiling.

"You looked beautiful tonight, Mother," she said, and ran across the lodge to crawl into her warm buffalo hides.

Mother smiled. She had changed out of her ceremonial clothing and wore a white doeskin dress with black-and-red starbursts painted on the hem and across her chest.

"So did you, Twig. I was proud of you. I—"

Screech Owl called softly from outside, "It's me, Riddle. Are you ready for me yet?"

"Come in, Screech Owl. We're ready. The tea isn't, but we are."

Screech Owl ducked under the lodge flap. He had taken off his mask and was holding it reverently. His gray hair spiked out around his long face. He winked at Twig before crouching by the fire, where the tea bag hung from its tripod. Mother had already added hot rocks to boil it, and the lodge smelled like a raspberry patch.

Screech Owl smiled awkwardly at Riddle, and she smiled back before rising to fetch the plate of nutcakes.

"Are you hungry, Twig?" her mother asked.

"No, just tired."

"Then why don't you try to sleep? Screech Owl and I are going to talk for a while."

Twig snuggled deeper into her hides, but she kept her eyes slitted to watch what happened.

Mother knelt beside Screech Owl and offered him a nutcake.

"Thank you, Riddle. It's been a long time since I've had one of your cakes." Screech Owl took a bite and said, "They're as good as I remember."

Neither one of them said anything for a long time, and Twig felt the tension rising between them.

Finally Mother said, "Screech Owl, I wanted to talk to you about something that's happening. I don't understand it."

His eyes widened. "What?"

"It has to do with the Thornback raiders. Do you know that Chief Gill sent Puffer and a war party to try and find Cobia?"

"Yes, Twig told me. Why?"

Mother sank down to the floor. "Just as the dance began, one man returned: young Searobin. I saw him come in, but of course I couldn't go to him. I had to lead the dance. In the middle of the dance, Father came to tell me that Puffer and the others are dead."

"Oh," Screech Owl said so softly that Twig almost didn't hear. Grief twisted his face. "Was it Cobia? Did she kill them?"

"I don't know. Father was in a hurry. He barely spoke

to me. He and the chief were on their way to Searobin's lodge to spend the night hearing the details of what went wrong. That's why I wanted to talk with you."

"Ah, I see. Are you feeling guilty because you didn't dream about it before they left and warn them? You shouldn't. Dreamers do the best they can, but they aren't infallible. They—"

In a tight voice, Mother said, "Why would Cobia kill them?"

Screech Owl sat so still that his dark eyes caught the firelight and held it like polished mica mirrors. "I'm not sure she did. She might have, but Puffer's war party might also have run into the Thornback raiders. In any case, it means Buffalobeard Village has lost many of its best warriors."

Mother extended her hands. "What are we going to do, Screech Owl? Tomorrow we're meeting to discuss whether we should pack up and move the village. Do you think we should?"

He sighed. "This is a dangerous time. The ice is melting; rivers have swollen to twice their normal sizes. Grandfather Brown Bear is hunting every trail. If we move, many of us could die."

"Yes, I know. Have you . . . have you dreamed anything?"

He gave her a sad smile. "If you asked me here because you hoped I'd dreamed the future, I haven't. I'm sorry. I didn't know about any of this. But"—he took another bite of nutcake and chewed it thoughtfully before he said—"Twig might have. Has she told you about her dreams?"

Mother shot a glance at Twig, and she pretended to be fast asleep. When Mother looked away, Twig opened her eyes again.

Screech Owl tilted his head. "She hasn't told me any of the details," he lied, "but I know she's having Spirit dreams. I can feel it."

Screech Owl's eyes flared for a moment before he added, "Riddle, there's something else I'd like to talk to you about."

"What is it?"

Screech Owl's lips pressed into a tight line. "If Twig wishes to, I'd like her to live with me while I'm teaching her. So I can make sure she's safe." He glanced up hesitantly. "Will you allow it?"

"Well, I—I don't know. I'll have to think about it."

Screech Owl glanced at Twig, then stepped to the lodge flap and pulled it aside. "Please, come outside with me so we can talk about this more."

"Don't push me, Screech Owl. I told you I have to think about it."

"Usually that means your answer is no."

"If you don't stop pushing me, the answer will be no!"

His gaze rested on Twig again. She lay absolutely still, watching the worry in his elderly eyes, as if he saw something so terrible in her future that he almost couldn't bear it.

"Riddle," he whispered, "don't I even have the right to teach her how to be happy?"

"She's my daughter, Screech Owl. You have no rights regarding her." Mother folded her arms and turned away. "Please go."

"You know she'll be miserable if she can't control the dreams. Soon they'll begin stalking her." At the hard look on her mother's face, Screech Owl said, "Please, I beg you. Just give me the chance to teach her for a few days."

"I knew I shouldn't have invited you here," Mother snarled. "Leave."

Screech Owl closed his eyes wearily for a moment before he ducked beneath the flap and disappeared into the night.

Tears filled Twig's eyes. She didn't understand it. She loved Mother and Screech Owl, but they were always fighting and arguing. It broke her heart.

Twig waited until Mother turned to pick up the plate of cakes before she slipped completely under her buffalo robe to cry.

AT FIRST, ALL I hear is the roaring wind.

Then . . . the dream begins.

I'm freezing. Freezing to death, and terrified. The woman is standing beside me, smiling.

Faint screams creep up from every sparkle in the snow, and fear clutches at my heart. All around me, colors swirl and form pictures, becoming flaming spears that flash through the air.

"What's happening?" I cry.

The woman just keeps smiling.

Far below, I see a village. It looks tiny from this high. When the flaming spears land on top of the lodges, they burst into flame, and a brilliant fiery wall rises. I see women and children lunge from their blazing homes and run away into the haze of smoke that billows into the starry sky.

"What am I seeing? Where is this?"

"You don't recognize it?"

"No, I—"

"You will. Soon. You must remember that you will not find Cobia's cave without Greyhawk. You must be braver than you have ever thought possible. Learn every lesson Screech Owl teaches you."

She leaps into the frosty, twinkling hearts of the Star People . . . and the screams and cries of war fill the air. I turn, and the Ice Giants are black, black as coal, and sparkling.

"Wait. Wait!" I shout. "Don't leave me! How do I get home?"

A deep groaning rumble erupts, followed by a loud boom! Several smaller booms shake the ground beneath my feet, and I stagger as a strange orange gleam fills the night.

The rumble grows to a roar.

The earthquake strikes like a giant fist slamming the earth.

And a boy's voice calls my name. . . .

CHAPTER 15

S TARLIGHT GLISTENED ON the roof poles over
Riddle's head. She lay warm in her hides, listening
to Twig, who was dreaming.

"No," Twig said softly, and Riddle could tell she was
crying. "Help me. Please, help me."

Riddle rolled to her side to study her daughter. Only
the top of Twig's head showed over the edge of the buffalo hide. Her long black hair snaked across the sleeping
mat. Twig whimpered and turned over onto her stomach. Her hands clenched and opened, as if she were trying to reach for someone.

Riddle threw off her hides and went to kneel by Twig.

"Twig?" she called softly. "Twig, wake up. It's all right. Twig?"

"Mother?" Twig whispered, her voice sleepy.

"Yes, I'm right here. You're safe."

"Oh, Mother, I had the dream again! This time I saw a village on fire. And the Ice Giants turned black!" Tears ran down her cheeks.

Riddle stroked Twig's hair gently. "What else did you see?"

Twig took a breath as if to speak, then shook her head. "There was a—a boy's voice . . . and a blue spiderweb. I—it . . . never mind. I'm sorry I woke you."

Riddle's heart sank. Twig didn't want to tell her, and she knew why. Riddle feared powerful Spirit dreams. She often shouted at Twig when she claimed to have had one. Mostly because Riddle had never learned how to control them, so on the few occasions when they came to her, they controlled her with such terrifying power that she thought she was dying.

Twig squeezed her eyes closed, a clear signal that she didn't want to talk anymore. "Thank you, Mother, but you can go back to sleep now. I'm all right, really."

Riddle let out a tense sigh. "Twig? Do you want to go live with Screech Owl?"

Twig opened her eyes. For several heartbeats she didn't answer. Finally, she whispered, "Do you want me to?"

"No, not really, but he could teach you a great deal, and maybe . . . well, I've tried hard to kill the power that lives inside you, Twig. But if you really are destined to be a great dreamer, you could save our people. I just, well, I pray the dreaming is not as hard on you as it is on me."

"Why is it so hard?"

"Oh, Twig, everyone in the village relies on the Spirit dreamer to see the future, and when she's tired, or sick, or just disheartened, and she can't dream, they all blame her for the bad things that happen. It's not an easy life . . . and I hoped yours would be."

"Was it hard when you were growing up?"

"Yes, I just wanted to be a normal little girl. But my grandfather made me study with Screech Owl."

Twig swallowed hard. "Is that why you don't like Screech Owl?"

Mother nodded. "His lessons are very difficult. Sometimes, they hurt, as you are about to find out."

They stared at each other for a long time before Mother said, "Tomorrow we'll pack your things, and I'll take you to Screech Owl. I don't know how long you'll be able to stay. We may be moving soon. But I'll give you as much time with him as I can."

Twig hugged her hard. "I'm afraid, Mother, but I will try to learn to dream better."

"Good. Terrible things are happening. If you learn enough, and try hard enough, maybe you will dream a way for us to escape."

Since I can't, someone has to.

Across the lodge, from the Wolf Bundle, Riddle thought she heard the Stone Wolf call out to her . . . as if in approval.

CHAPTER 16

"OH, GREAT MAMMOTH, there he is," Mother said in an unhappy voice. "Do you see him?"

Twig shielded her eyes from the bright morning sunlight. They had been walking since long before dawn to get to Screech Owl's cave. Twig looked at the huge oaks out front, then searched the black boulders . . . and finally saw him.

Screech Owl was balancing on his belly on a pointed rock that stuck out high above his cave. He had his arms and legs thrust out into thin air, as though he was imitating the ravens soaring above him. The birds cawed, and Screech Owl cawed back. The big raven, obviously the leader of the flock, swooped down and hovered in front of Screech Owl's face. He tipped his wings illustratively. Screech Owl moved his arms in the same way, but couldn't quite get it right. He kept thrashing around.

Twig said, "What's he doing? Flying?"

Disgusted, Mother said, "He probably thinks so. Come on. Let's get this over with."

As they got closer, Twig heard Screech Owl say, "I'm sorry. I just can't get it right. Maybe in my next life, Earthmaker will let me have wings so I can fly better; then—"

"You are such an old fool," Mother called up to him.

Startled, Screech Owl lost his balance and fell off the rock. Twig didn't see where he landed, but a cloud of dust rose, and she heard him shout, "Riddle! Twig! What are you doing here?"

Mother lifted a brow. Her long hair, as blue-black as magpie feathers, fluttered about her shoulders. "Walk down here like a human, and we'll discuss it."

"Of course! I'm coming."

Screech Owl climbed through the boulders and onto the ledge that stuck out over his cave, where he jumped off. He landed hard and stumbled sideways before he caught himself. "My, it's good to see you both! Come in. Have some tea."

He hurried to pull the door curtain aside so they could enter the cave. "Please, go in and sit down. I'll have the tea boiling in no time and—"

"Screech Owl," Mother interrupted him. She made no move to go into his cave. "You've been right all along.

I'm sorry I tried to prevent Twig from becoming a Spirit dreamer. I was just trying to protect her. You know—"

"Yes." He gave her a kind smile. "I do know. The life of a Spirit dreamer is very hard, and you love Twig very much."

Mother folded her arms tightly across her heart. "You have five days. I wish I could give you more time to teach Twig, but I'm not sure we have more."

"What do you mean?"

"The village council will be meeting this afternoon. Father is going to tell the elders that we must pack up and move the village far to the south, away from the ball of light Twig has been dreaming about and the Thornback raiders."

Screech Owl just stared at Mother with hurt in his eyes, as though he was worried about her. "Then I'll do the best I can in five days." He extended a hand toward his cave. "Now, please, come in and have a cup of tea. You've walked a great distance this morning."

"No, I can't. I must get back to prepare for the meeting."

Mother slipped the hide pack from her back and dropped it beside Twig, and then she knelt to hug her. "Learn as much as you can," she whispered. "Perhaps you'll be able to learn the things that I couldn't."

Twig hugged her back. "I'll try, Mother," she said bravely. "And don't worry. Screech Owl will take care of me."

"I know he will." Mother rose slowly to her feet and

turned to Screech Owl to ask, "Should I come and get her in five days, or will you—"

"No, let me bring her home."

Twig said, "I can go home by myself. I've done it a hundred times."

"Yes, but things change once you sprout a Spirit dreamer's wings," Screech Owl said. "Your soul will be concentrating on other things. I don't want you to get lost. I'll take you."

Twig blinked, curious and not understanding, but accepting his decision just the same.

Mother touched Twig's hair lovingly before she began backing away. "I'll see you soon."

"I love you, Mother."

Twig watched her until she vanished behind the boulders up the trail; then she looked up at Screech Owl. "Well, I guess I'm here."

"Yes, and I'm so glad. How did you manage it?"

"I had the dream about the strange woman last night. I woke Mother. After that she decided I could come and live with you."

Screech Owl seemed to be studying the nervous twist to her mouth. "And what about you? Did you think it would be all right to come and live with me?"

She flapped her arms helplessly. "I have to find out what my dreams mean, Screech Owl. You know I do. I want you to teach me how to dream better."

"Good. Then let's get started."

"What? Right now?"

"We only have five days, Twig, and a long way to go." Screech Owl pulled back the door curtain to his cave and said, "Let's go inside and grab the things we'll need."

She wrung her hands. "What do I have to do?"

"First," he said, "you learn to fly so that you can go and talk with your Spirit Helper, Eagle-Man."

Twig glanced uncomfortably up at the rock where Screech Owl had been balancing on his belly. "I have to fly?"

"Yes, didn't you see me flying when you arrived?"

Twig narrowed her eyes. "Screech Owl, that didn't look like flying."

"No? What did it look like?"

"Well, I don't know exactly. You were thrashing around like a turtle whose head was being chewed off by a wolf."

"Ah!" he exclaimed in delight. "That's exactly it! Learning to fly is like having your head chewed off. Come on. As soon as your human head gets devoured, you'll grow bird eyes and be able to see the tunnel that ties Mother Earth to Father Sky. Then you'll find Eagle-Man's nest."

As she ducked beneath the door curtain and into his cave, the scent of old dry mammoth dung rose. "I don't like the idea of getting chewed up, Screech Owl."

His expression turned dark and serious. For several heartbeats, he just stared at her. "No one does, Twig. But every great dreamer, at some point, must step into the mouth of the Spirit that wants to chew her up."

CHAPTER 17

SUNLIGHT PIERCED THE smoke hole and flickered over War Chief Hook's lodge, casting his shadow like a dark monster over the elk-hide walls. The Thornback People made lodges similar to those of the People of the Dawnland, but much larger. His lodge stretched six paces across, and was twice his height. A fire burned in the middle of the floor, sending smoke up to be sucked out through the smoke hole in the roof. Human scalps and finger-bone necklaces decorated the willow pole frame.

Hook paced while he watched his wife, Dry Cloud, dip a piece of hide into the water bag and place it on their young son's fevered forehead.

"How is Slate?" Hook asked.

"I think . . . I'm afraid he may be . . ." She couldn't finish the sentence.

Hook loved his ten-summers-old son, but Slate had always been weaker than his four brothers, sick more often, too easily hurt in play. The boy would never be a warrior, or a hunter of any account. But he always told himself that not every man could be skilled with weapons. Hook just prayed that when the time came for Slate to marry, he could find a woman who would have him. If he lived that long.

Dry Cloud stroked Slate's black hair. "Can you hear me, Son?"

Slate's eyelids fluttered, but he didn't open them. He just moaned and twisted on the buffalo hide where he lay.

Hook reached down and touched the purple knot that swelled just below his son's navel. It was hot and hard, like a fiery rock buried beneath the skin. The pain had been growing worse for days.

"He will get well, won't he?" Dry Cloud asked. She had an oval face, with a straight nose and large dark eyes. Her deer-hide cape was painted with zigzag slashes of yellow lightning.

"He's been sicker than this before. Do you remember the time he fell from the cliff and landed flat on his back? I thought he would be permanently paralyzed, but two moons later, he was walking again."

Tears filled Dry Cloud's eyes. She nodded. "I remember, but this is different. I've seen knots like this before, when men lift rocks too heavy for them—it tears something inside."

"I've seen such things, too. The men often get well."

She put a hand to her trembling lips, but nodded.

Both of them looked up when the lodge curtain was tugged aside and brilliant sunlight washed across the floor. Chief Nightcrow stepped inside. Dry Cloud sucked in a sharp breath and leaped to her feet.

"I—I didn't send for you, my chief," Dry Cloud said. "Did you, Hook?"

"No."

Nightcrow stared at them. His eyes were wolflike and wary, and there was no mercy in them. He had greased his long black hair with bear fat and tied it back with a braided grass cord. The style made his long pointed nose look as sharp as a spear point. The polished shell beads that hung from his ears and circled his wrists flashed as he moved. "Your uncle Snow Bear came to tell me your son was dying."

Hook stood frozen, watching as the chief crossed the lodge and knelt beside their son. Slate mumbled something.

"How long has he been sick?" Nightcrow did not look at them. He was frowning down at Slate.

"Seven days," Dry Cloud said, and glanced uneasily at Hook.

"And you did not think to call me? This boy has an evil Spirit in his belly that will kill him if we do not act quickly."

"My chief, we are at war," Hook said. "You have more important things to worry about than my family. We have had three healers here, but none have been able to cure our son. I didn't wish to—"

"Do you see the color of this knot?" Nightcrow asked, and turned to fix Hook with a glare. "It cannot be burned off, or cut out, or cured by a Spirit plant. *It is alive.*" He put his hand on Slate's belly again and closed his eyes, as though concentrating. "I can feel it breathing. It has a heartbeat. If we do not kill it, it will eat your son's insides and leave him a hollow husk."

As though to show them, he squeezed the knot, and Slate cried out and sat bolt upright in bed, staring at Nightcrow with wide, shocked eyes.

Dry Cloud rushed to her son's side and stroked his sweat-drenched hair. "The chief is trying to help you, Slate."

Nightcrow said, "Even now, the evil Spirit in his belly fights me. What would you have me do? Leave? Let it consume him? Or shall I perform the dark ritual necessary to save his life?"

Dry Cloud said, "Please, heal him."

Nightcrow didn't seem to hear her. He kept his gaze on Hook, waiting for him to ask for help. Hook never asked for help. It was something he was not good at.

Hook met Nightcrow's gaze, and a chill ran through him. The coppery odor of rotted blood always surrounded the chief, though no sign of it stained his clothing. "What do you need to cure him?"

"This is a dangerous ritual. I may die saving your son. Be prepared for that. If I do, you will need to act swiftly to elect a new chief."

"Please don't talk that way," Dry Cloud said. "We—"

"I will need two things: Bring me an orphaned slave, one of the young children whose parents we killed in our last raid, and I'll need the yellow deer-hide bag in my lodge. Go and get both immediately."

Dry Cloud left at a run. Another flash of sunlight blazed in when she ducked beneath the lodge curtain.

Nightcrow sat down cross-legged beside Slate and began to rock back and forth and chant in the strange alien tongue that Hook did not understand. The longer he rocked, the more his eyes rolled back in his head, leaving only the whites visible. Hook recoiled from the sight.

Several hundred heartbeats later, Dry Cloud threw back the lodge curtain and entered dragging a young slave boy, maybe eleven summers, and Nightcrow's yellow bag. "I brought them, my chief."

The slave boy looked around the lodge and swallowed hard. Less than a moon ago, Hook had clubbed the boy's father to death and ripped him from his weeping mother's arms to carry him home as a slave. When the boy's gaze landed on Hook, hatred filled his eyes.

Nightcrow continued to chant as he reached out and dragged the slave boy closer. The boy struggled, but halfheartedly. He had been beaten often since his capture. He obviously didn't wish another one. "Hold still."

In a vicious thrust, Nightcrow shoved his fingers deep

into Slate's belly and twisted the knot. Slate screamed, and in a flash, Nightcrow ripped a bloody creature from the wound. It flipped around in his hand as though it were a writhing serpent.

"Blessed ancestors!" Dry Cloud cried. "Is that the evil Spirit?"

"Give it to me! I'll kill it!" Hook grabbed for it.

But Nightcrow jerked it from his hand. He pried open the slave boy's jaws and shoved the bloody creature past the boy's teeth and down his throat. When the boy tried to vomit it back up, Nightcrow held his mouth closed until the boy had swallowed it.

The slave stumbled backward, wiping at his bloody mouth, not sure what had just happened.

Nightcrow pulled a mammoth-hide bandage from his yellow bag and draped it across Slate's belly; then he rose on shaking legs. "Bandage your son's belly tightly. Do not remove the bandage for one moon. He should get well."

The chief stumbled toward the door like a man who'd been running for three days straight. Just before he left, he propped a hand on the lodge frame and said, "If you want to kill the evil Spirit, kill the slave boy. The Spirit will die with him."

An instant later, he ducked out into the morning and was gone.

The slave boy spun around to stare at Hook. "It was just a piece of meat! It tasted like venison. He was probably hiding it in his hand. It was a trick!"

Dry Cloud whispered, "Kill him."

Hook reached for his club, and the boy dodged out into the morning gleam and ran across the village with Hook right behind him.

When he caught the boy by the hair, he yelled, "Don't struggle and I will make it fast and painless."

"But it was a trick!"

Hook bashed the boy in the head, and the child slumped to the ground.

Hook tucked his club in his belt, stared into the boy's eyes to make sure he was dead, and started back for his lodge.

The icy gravel crunched so loudly beneath his moccasins that he almost didn't hear Nightcrow's voice call, *"Hook?"*

He turned and saw his chief crouching on the ground, holding his belly, as though too sick to find his way back to his own lodge.

Hook rushed to his side. "My chief? Do you need help? Shall I call for—"

"I do need help," Nightcrow said, and when he looked up, his eyes shone with sunlight. "There is a girl I want you to bring me."

"A girl? Another slave?"

"No. She is the keeper of the Stone Wolf . . . or she will be."

Hook cocked his head. He'd never heard of the Stone Wolf. "What is that, my chief?"

"It's a very powerful Spirit creature. I want it. And I

want the girl who owns it. She's learning to be a Spirit dreamer."

"Where is she?"

Nightcrow chuckled, but it was a dark, evil sound. "I don't know yet. My visions haven't shown me. But when they do, I want her brought to me immediately."

"Yes, my chief, of course."

Nightcrow rose on shaking legs. "Tomorrow, I want you to dispatch a war party to Clearwater Village. They have a sacred flute there; it's very powerful."

"I understand. I will dispatch the party at dawn."

Nightcrow sucked in a wheezing breath. "But do not send too many warriors. It will not be easy to capture the girl and the Stone Wolf. You will need every fighter we have left."

Hook bowed respectfully. "Yes, my chief."

Nightcrow stumbled toward his own lodge.

Hook walked back, and when he ducked beneath his lodge curtain, he found Dry Cloud touching Slate's belly, gently prodding it. Their son seemed to be resting easier. His face looked peaceful for the first time in days.

"How is he?" Hook asked.

Dry Cloud's mouth opened, but for a long time, she did not speak. Finally, she said, "I don't believe it. It's a miracle. The knot is gone. Completely gone."

CHAPTER 18

Twig smiled when she saw Greyhawk and Yipper running down the trail in the distance. She waved at them, and Greyhawk waved back. Behind him, dark brooding Cloud People filled the sky. She couldn't believe he had worked up the courage to run here by himself, especially with a bad storm on the way.

"Screech Owl! Look, it's Greyhawk and Yipper! They're coming to see us." She used her nocked atlatl to point at her friend.

"Yes," Screech Owl said without looking up. "Unfortunate. This is not a good time for visitors."

"Why not?"

"Don't you see the Cloud People? Thunderbird is bringing a storm here because he knows we are embarking upon a dangerous task."

Twig frowned at his back. "We are?"

"Oh, yes, very dangerous."

She studied him as he tiptoed across the gray rocks, his eyes glued to the ground. Black boulders lined the path, and contrasted sharply with the white hide shirt he wore. Though they had been hunting all morning, they hadn't found anything that Screech Owl would let her shoot, including a rabbit that had run right over the top of her moccasins. He seemed to be tracking some animal, but she didn't see any tracks.

Screech Owl suddenly froze with one foot in the air and whispered, "Twig, come look at this."

She lowered her atlatl and spear and trotted through the shadows cast by the boulders. "What is it? What did you find?"

Screech Owl slowly knelt and tapped a patch of bare rock covered with old spruce needles. "See them?"

Twig shook her head. "No. What?"

"The tracks," he said as though she were blind.

"I don't see any tracks, Screech Owl."

"You're not looking very hard. Look again."

Twig crouched and searched the rock carefully. The fragrant scent of spruce needles met her nose, but there weren't any tracks. "Screech Owl, this is bare rock. There aren't any tracks."

He made a face. "Twig, you're smarter than this. What do you see down there?"

"Rock."

"And what else?"

She glanced at the stone again. "A few spruce needles that were probably blown off by Wind Woman this morning."

"Yes!" He slapped her affectionately on the back. "Now keep your atlatl nocked and ready to cast. She's around here somewhere." He started off, taking one careful step at a time while his eyes diligently scanned the terrain.

Twig threw him a glance. *Blessed Thunderbird, we're not tracking a tree, are we?*

"Keep up, Twig."

She fell into line behind him. As she walked, she tipped her face to the cool wind. It had tousled her long hair all afternoon as they'd climbed.

The day smelled damply of water, and she could feel the new bite in the air. "Screech Owl, those Cloud People look like they're bringing snow. Maybe we should go back to your cave before—"

"Ha!" Screech Owl blurted. "More!"

Twig ran up to look. As she gazed over the top of his gray head, he tapped a finger beside another cluster of spruce needles.

"We're close, Twig, so be quiet. You'd better stay back and let me lead the way."

She nodded. "Sure. Go ahead."

He gave her a confident wink before tiptoeing forward like a long-billed sandpiper in a shallow pool of water.

"*Twig!*" Greyhawk called and waved. He ran up smiling and breathing hard. "Do you still have a human soul?"

Yipper leaped up and put his big paws in the middle of Twig's chest to lick her face. Twig laughed. "Yes, so far."

"Good. Father said if you were still human I could stay and talk to you. Otherwise, I had to come home right away."

"That's wonderful! Yipper, get down." She shoved him away, and he wagged his tail and loped off to sniff Screech Owl's moccasins. "I have so many things to tell you."

They hugged each other. Greyhawk's chin-length black hair had gotten sweaty and stuck to his tanned cheeks, which framed his brown eyes and small nose. He wore a soot-stained shirt that hung to his knees, and thick buffalo-hide moccasins.

"What are you doing?" Greyhawk turned to scowl at Screech Owl. "What's *he* doing?"

"I'm not sure yet. Come on."

They crept along behind Screech Owl, trying to see around his skinny body to where he was going. Every so often he would stop and point out more spruce needles, and Greyhawk would give her a quizzical look.

Twig just shrugged. She couldn't explain it to him, because she hoped she did not know what they were hunting. Yipper, however, was chasing a rabbit at full speed. He bounded across the slope, barking, until she lost sight of him.

"Twig," Screech Owl called. "You're falling behind."

"Sorry."

She and Greyhawk sneaked through a cluster of boulders where roots laddered the path. Screech Owl thrust out a hand to stop them from coming any closer. Then he knelt to stroke the roots reverently. When he turned, he stared at Twig so hard she was afraid to breathe.

"What is it?" Twig whispered. "What do you see?"

"I have to tell you something," Screech Owl whispered just loud enough for them to hear. "You know that spruces are sacred, but this tree is special. You have to hunt her correctly, with the proper ritual intent, or she'll kill you. Do you understand?"

Greyhawk's mouth pursed with disdain. "You're hunting a *tree*?"

Screech Owl leaned close to him and hissed, "Yes." Then he leaned toward Twig and breathed, "You had better be sure you understand. This is First Woman's tree. She grows in three worlds. Her roots are buried deep in the underworld next to First Woman's cave, but her trunk and branches stretch up through the earth and into the skyworld. Sometimes, Thunderbird lays his eggs in her top branches."

Twig listened in fascination. "And I'm supposed to kill her?"

Greyhawk said, "I don't think that's such a good idea."

"Don't worry; we just have to be careful and do it correctly."

Twig wet her lips. "But what if one of Thunderbird's eggs falls and breaks?"

"That would be very bad," Screech Owl said. "It might never rain again. Then the world would die, and you'd be to blame."

She nodded in fervent agreement. "I know. So, you know what, Screech Owl? I don't think I'm the one to do this." She thrust her atlatl and spear into his hands. "You do it." Twig took a step backward and swiftly clasped her hands behind her lest he think of returning the weapons.

Gently, Screech Owl said, "I can't. You're the one who wants to find Eagle-Man."

"Is he in that tree, too?"

"Oh, yes," Screech Owl responded darkly. "He's there."

"Well, but . . . I don't want to kill First Woman's tree."

Screech Owl gazed contemplatively at her small atlatl and spear. He rubbed his finger along the wood and canted his head to listen to its responding sound. His bushy gray eyebrows went up and down. "Well, at least your atlatl knows why."

Suspicious, Greyhawk said, "Twig's atlatl talks? Can I have it after First Woman kills her?"

"Everything in the world has a voice, Greyhawk—the trees, the stones, the clouds. People just stop listening to them when they start to grow up."

Twig said, "What did my atlatl tell you?"

Screech Owl pushed gray hair away from his wrinkled face and stared her hard in the eyes. "It said you must prove your courage to Eagle-Man before he'll allow you to come visit him in the Land of the Dead. You *do* want to talk to him, don't you, Twig?"

"Yes, but . . . well . . ."

"Twig?" he asked reprovingly.

"I do," she announced against her better judgment. "All right, Screech Owl. How do I hunt First Woman's tree?"

Under his breath, Greyhawk advised, "Maybe you'd better learn to chew bark like a beaver."

Screech Owl ignored Greyhawk and put his hand against Twig's back. "She's just behind that rock. When you go in, you have to cast your spear straight into her branches. Don't aim at her trunk, or Thunderbird will feel the tree shudder and send lightning shooting out the ends of the branches to get you."

"Because he'll think I'm trying to disturb his nest?"

"Yes, that's right." Screech Owl lifted Twig's nocked atlatl and handed it back. "Can you do it?"

She felt as though snakes were slithering around in her stomach, but she truly did want to speak to Eagle-Man. "I guess so," she admitted morosely, and took the weapons. "Just one spear will be enough?"

"It should be. But if she comes after you, you'd better spear her again."

Twig turned to Greyhawk. "You'd better nock your atlatl, just in case."

Greyhawk smirked, but pulled a spear from his quiver and nocked it into the hook of his atlatl. Almost laughing, he said, "Don't worry, Twig. If the tree comes after you, I'll kill her for sure."

Screech Owl sat on his haunches in front of Twig. "Now, go on, Twig."

Twig bravely stalked toward the rock. She eased around the boulder, and a shadow touched her face as the dark Cloud People covered the sky.

Twig edged farther, then stopped short. The cliff fell away in a sheer drop three times her height. But when she craned her neck to explore over the edge, she saw a tiny spruce tree clinging to a patch of soil no bigger than her foot. It was right over the edge, and no taller than her knees. She could have pulled it up by the roots if she'd wanted to.

Greyhawk came up behind her and looked over the edge. "*That* is First Woman's tree? It's not much to look at, is it?"

"No, but . . . I don't see any of Thunderbird's eggs in the top, do you?"

"Of course not. It's just a scrubby little tree."

Snowflakes started to fall. They glistened as they landed on the warm rocks and melted.

"Come on, Twig," Greyhawk said. "Spear the tree. I want to talk to you for a while before I have to run home."

Twig sighed, lifted her atlatl, and cast her spear into the branches. The tree wiggled, as though trying to dislodge her spear.

Greyhawk snickered, "I can't wait to tell Rattler that you speared a tree. She'll—"

A flash of lightning crackled through the air and blasted the boulders nearby. Greyhawk screamed as huge chunks of stone exploded all around them. They both dove for the ground and covered their heads. The roar of Thunderbird shook the ground so violently it felt like an earthquake.

"You must have hit the trunk!" Greyhawk shouted. "Run! He's coming after us!" He jumped up and took off like a scared rabbit, racing away down the rocky slope.

When Yipper heard Greyhawk's shout, he sprang up from beneath the cliff with a half-eaten rabbit between his teeth and charged after his master with shreds of fur flying around his black snout.

"I didn't hit the trunk!" Twig yelled. "I didn't!"

Screech Owl ran up and clutched her tightly against him. "Are you all right?"

"Yes, but I don't know what I did wrong."

It was snowing harder. Big fluffy flakes tumbled through the air and coated Twig's cape.

"Oh, Thunderbird is contrary. Sometimes he just does that to scare people. Did you kill the tree?"

"Well"—she had no idea how to tell—"I think so."

Screech Owl got down on his hands and knees and crawled to look over the edge at First Woman's tree. "Oh, yes. You did very well. Why don't you sit down while I cut off her top; then we'll go find where 'Greyhawk the Brave' is cowering."

Twig slumped down on the wet rock and wiped her drenched forehead. Hunting Spirits took a lot of strength. "Just the top? Why don't we take the whole tree?"

She could hear a soft zizzing as Screech Owl sawed with his stone knife.

"It takes only a very small portion to open a tunnel through which you can speak to Eagle-Man."

"A tunnel?"

"Yes. These branches are like hollow reeds. They connect this world to the skyworld."

"Do I have to crawl into the tunnel?" That possibility frightened her more than Thunderbird's wrath.

"Oh, yes, just like Snake. Tonight we're going to prepare you to die, and—"

"What?" She swung around to stare at him.

Screech Owl's knife halted in mid-motion. "Didn't I tell you?"

"No!" she protested. "You didn't tell me anything at all about having to die!"

He shook his head, said, "I'm getting so forgetful," and went back to sawing. When the very top of the tree came off in his hand, he placed prayer feathers near the trunk and sang his thanks to First Woman.

He extended the fragrant branches to Twig. "We have a lot of work to do. Let's go home. We have to build a death litter and prepare food for you to take on your journey to the skyworld. I guess we're actually lucky Grey-hawk is here. He can help." He studied the thick falling snow. "And it looks like he's going to be here for a long time."

"Screech Owl," she said in gut-wrenching terror, "I—I don't want to die!"

As he got to his feet, he lowered his voice and gravely said, "That's what happens when you step into the mouth of the Spirit that wants to chew you up. Didn't you understand that?"

Twig's heart slammed against her chest. "No, I . . . I mean, I didn't think dreamers *really* died."

"Well, they do. They must. Are you brave enough to walk into the Land of the Dead and face the ghosts of your ancestors?"

Twig looked down the trail and considered running away as fast as she could.

In a shaking voice, she asked, "This is what Mother feared, isn't it?"

"Yes," he said softly. "She could never cross the river that leads from life to death. She didn't have the courage. Do you? Your people need a great dreamer, Twig, but if you are not the one, tell me now. I don't want to waste my time on a coward."

Twig jerked as though she'd been slapped. She was not a coward! . . . Was she?

She glanced up at the sky. The snow was falling heavier, turning into a blizzard. By tonight, she suspected the drifts would be almost as tall as she was.

Deep in her memory she heard the hissing of the ball

of light that thundered through her dream. If she didn't learn to be a great dreamer, would it kill everyone she loved?

Twig exhaled a shuddering breath and said, "I'm not a coward, Screech Owl. Teach me."

CHAPTER 19

SNOW BLEW PAST the cave outside, and Wind Woman howled like a pack of hungry dire wolves. Twig shivered where she sat cross-legged on the floor near the fire. The flames crackled and spat, throwing Screech Owl's gangly shadow over the walls. He bustled around the cave, singing softly while he arranged Twig's hides on the death litter. Greyhawk crouched in the rear with a frightened, half-angry expression on his round face. When Screech Owl had told him he couldn't go home because of the storm, he'd tried to lunge past Screech Owl into the heavy snow, but Screech Owl had grabbed him by the shirt and dragged him back.

Greyhawk kept glancing outside, as though not fully re-signed to his fate. Yipper slept beside the fire with his paws twitching in dreams.

"We're almost ready," Screech Owl said as he tied two dried eagle heads, feathers and all, to the ends of the poles.

The litter resembled a ladder, except that it had long braided hair ropes, tied into nooses, stretched out across the floor in front of it.

Greyhawk kicked at one of the feathered heads. "Do you think it's smart to send Twig into the skyworld on scraps of her Spirit Helper's hide?"

"She'll be all right. My own grandfather, Silvertip, taught me how to do this." Screech Owl grabbed a yellow basket covered with red and black designs and filled it to the brim with rabbit jerky, lake rice, and a healthy sprinkle of spruce pollen. He set the basket at the foot of the death litter.

"Now, Twig, you have to remember that if Eagle-Man decides you're worthy, the journey will have stages. At first the road is easy, but the problems increase as you get closer to the Land of the Dead. There's a wide, rushing river that blocks the path. Only a very good dreamer can make it across."

"What happens if I can't?"

In a hoarse whisper, he said, "Something might eat you."

She stared into his unblinking eyes. They looked inhuman. "Like what?"

"Well, there are strange creatures up there. Snakes with wings. Buffalo that live under the water. I once had a toad with antlers try to gore me." He gazed absently at the ceiling, as though remembering. "Hmm. Well, so, when you get to the river, let your team pull the weight of the litter. Don't—"

"What team?"

Firelight reflected from his elderly face. "Your buffalo team. Spirit buffalo will pull the litter up into the sky-world. That is, if Eagle-Man agrees. He'll have to order them to pull the litter for you, or they won't. Buffalo almost never slip their own heads into the nooses just because a dreamer asks them to."

She twisted her hands in her lap. "Screech Owl, are you sure I'm ready for this?"

"If we don't try, we'll never know, will we?"

"No, but . . ."

Screech Owl's eyes went bright and alert, like a kestrel's when feeding on a fresh mouse. "Do you want to back out?"

Twig thought about it. "Did Mother back out?"

"No, not at this point. She tried to cross the river into the Land of the Dead. It was later that she gave up."

"That means it gets much harder, doesn't it?"

Screech Owl put a hand against her cheek and looked straight into her eyes. "Yes. It does."

Twig nodded. "All right. Tell me what I have to do."

"First, you must lie facedown on the litter."

She stretched out on the litter. The fox fur glistened in

the light as though covered with fireflies. She nuzzled its softness. "How's this?"

"That's good. Your chin is right over the spruce bough we cut from First Woman's tree. It's hidden under that top hide. Now turn your face so that your mouth rests against the fox hide."

Twig did.

He came and crouched by her side. "No matter what happens, I want you to remember that you are not the first child to set off on this Spirit journey, and you won't be the last. All young dreamers must do it. So, you are not alone."

"How many have died?" Greyhawk asked.

Screech Owl looked like he didn't want to answer that, but he said, "A few, but Twig is not going to be one of them."

"How do you know?"

"I know because she's going to follow my instructions perfectly, aren't you?" Screech Owl asked.

She nodded. "Yes."

"Good. Now, you just have to stay on your stomach with your mouth against the hide and call to Eagle-Man all night long. If he wants to, he'll answer you."

"And then he'll bring the Spirit buffalo to pull my litter?"

"That's right. Now," he said, patting her foot, "you'd better get started."

Twig pressed her mouth to the hides and called, "Eagle-Man? Eagle-Man, it's me. I need you to come. Eagle-Man, please come?"

She tilted her head and saw Screech Owl take Greyhawk by the shoulders and force him to sit down in the middle of a pile of folded wolf hides; then he began laying power objects in a circle around the bed.

Greyhawk said, "What are you doing?"

"Protecting you. No matter what, don't leave this circle tonight."

Greyhawk licked his lips nervously. "Why not?"

"Because any Spirit creatures that come into this cave will know *you* are not a dreamer, and they may kill you just for the fun of it."

"Fun? Killing me would be fun?" He gave Twig a horrified glance, and Yipper seemed to understand. He started whining and trotting around the cave with his tail tucked between his legs.

Twig kept her mouth pressed against the fox hide, but her hands started to tremble. Would the Spirit creatures know that she was a dreamer? How could they tell?

Screech Owl crossed to his own bedding hides, sat down, and carefully arranged a circle of painted rocks, eagle feather fans, skulls from predators like Marten, Badger, Coyote, Mink . . . He hastily thrust Mink's skull back into its basket. Instead, he picked up a huge bear paw and placed it in the circle. The long claws glimmered in the crimson glow of the fire.

Panic tingled Twig's chest. "Screech Owl, what are you afraid of?"

"Eagle-Man is your Spirit Helper, not mine. I don't know him as well as you do." He flicked a hand emphatically. "Keep calling him, Twig."

"Eagle-Man, Eagle-Man, Eagle-Man . . ."

Screech Owl stretched out, pulled a buffalo hide over the top of him, and closed his eyes. In almost no time, snores erupted from his mouth.

Greyhawk stayed awake a lot longer, but finally he, too, fell sound asleep.

Twig stared into Yipper's eyes. The dog had his head propped on his paws and was watching her as though curious as to why she wasn't asleep like everyone else.

A short time later, even Yipper abandoned her and went to sleep.

And Twig was alone.

No one could help her now. She had to do this by herself, and she knew it.

She sucked in a deep breath, and when she let it out her whole body shook in fear.

"I'm coming, Eagle-Man," she whispered into the fox hide. "I'm coming."

CHAPTER 20

WIND WOMAN WHIMPERED and batted at the leather curtain. Snow must have mounded into deep drifts on the rocks above the cave, because water dripped through the ceiling crack onto the glowing coals. A constant sizzling, like a snake's hiss, filled the cave.

"Eagle-Man, can you hear me? Eagle-Man? Eagle-Man?"

Her chant became a singsong. She called for what seemed an eternity, until her soul felt numb and her body had gone past aching. Her neck hurt so badly that she feared it might snap in two if she didn't soon roll onto her back.

She shifted to bring up her knees, feeling sneaky since Screech Owl had told her to lie flat on her stomach. But she kept her mouth pressed over the spruce bough. "Eagle-Man? Please bring the Spirit buffalo?"

The sacred symbols on the walls swayed and gleamed.

To the red spiral, she murmured, "I'm trying, Spiral. Can you help me?"

The spiral didn't answer, and she felt very close to falling asleep, but antlered monsters that lived under water lurked just beyond the horizon of her drooping eyelids. She dared not sleep.

"Eagle-Man? Why won't you come?"

She yawned. The tuft of branches beneath her chin made a lump under the sleekness of the worn hides. Twig blinked lazily at the threads of light reflecting on the wall.

"Eagle-Man . . ." Angrily, she growled, "Eagle-Man, Eagle-Man, *Eagle-Man!*"

Yipper jerked awake, stared at her as though worried, then flopped down beside Greyhawk again and closed his eyes.

More softly, Twig called, "Eagle-Man, please, I—"

A lonely buffalo called, a deep-throated rumble, trying to locate its herd in the gloom of midnight. From across the bluff, answering calls echoed. The first buffalo let out a delighted bleat, and the thundering of hooves rose in eerie cadence.

Twig's tired body floated on the sound, rocking like a leaf in a peaceful stream. She was almost asleep when she faintly heard the crunching of hooves in the snow outside. . . .

And a whisper of sound came from the branches beneath the hide.

Twig stiffened, too afraid to move. Timidly, she called, "Eagle-Man?"

"I heard you, young dreamer. I brought the buffalo."

An animal snuffled. She twisted around and saw two huge brown shaggy faces silhouetted in the cave opening. They had pushed the hanging aside with their noses. A fiery sheen glowed in their dark eyes. One of the buffalo took a step into the cave, a hoof lifted, waiting.

Twig got to her knees. Her throat had gone as dry as cottonwood leaves in the dusty radiance of autumn. Frightened, she croaked, "Can you tell them to pull the litter for me, Eagle-Man?"

"Yes, I'll give them the order, if you think you're ready."

Twig swallowed the lump in the back of her throat. "I have to learn to dream, Eagle-Man. My people need me."

"You are brave. Perhaps too brave. Hold on tightly. The flight into the skyworld is rocky, but the Spirits are waiting for you, Twig."

The buffalo walked across the floor, their hooves clacking on the stone, and dipped their noses through the nooses that Screech Owl had braided from his own hair.

She took a last look at Screech Owl's slack old face. His mouth hung open. Then she looked at Greyhawk. He'd covered his face with his hides, but she could see the outline of his sleeping body. Softly, she called, "I found

Eagle-Man, Screech Owl. Greyhawk, I'm going. I'll try to come back to you."

The buffalo lifted their heads and gazed at her. One flicked its tail as though waiting for instructions. Twig gripped the side poles of her death litter in tight fists. She was so scared she couldn't think straight. But she had to do this. If she didn't make it to the Land of the Dead, Mother and Grandfather and everyone she loved might die.

Her breathing turned shallow, and she found herself gasping for breath as she said, "I'm ready, buffalo."

The blackness rippled around her as they soared out of the cave and into the dark stormy sky.

CHAPTER 21

HIGH ABOVE ME, through the crystal green water, I see the overturned litter. The buffalo are dragging it away. . . .

I fight to swim, but my arms and legs feel like granite. They're so heavy.

As I sink deeper, the water ripples and shines. I'm not going to make it across the river into the Land of the Dead.

I'm drowning.

Do the ghosts across the river see me? In my soul, I start crying out to my dead ancestors.

"Grandmother? Grandmother, help me! Uncle Badger! Where are you?"

My long hair spreads around me as I sink. It looks like fluttering black tentacles.

"Father?" *I silently scream.* "Father, please!"

In the water above me, a hazy image forms, a man's face. At first I can't see it very well; then the image sharpens . . . and I see Screech Owl. He's watching me with deep sadness in his dark eyes. He must know I have failed.

"Screech Owl! I'm dying. Help me! I don't want to be a Spirit dreamer!"

I hit bottom and lie in the sand staring up. The light is fading. It's growing dark.

At the edge of my vision, I see something.

A green shimmer slithers through the water. Beady golden eyes glint. It's coming straight at me, moving fast, its tail whipping.

Like an arrow, it shoots inside me, and I feel it wriggling around my heart.

I can't even scream.

Another face forms, right above me, and I hear a voice say, "Swim this way, Twig. This way."

I swim after him and make it to shore. I'm dripping wet and icy cold. He stares at me while I cough and cough. Two black braids frame his oval face. He is younger than I am, maybe eight summers, and is dressed in strange hides. The red face of Wolf is painted on his chest.

"Who are you?" *I croak.*

"My name is Runs In Light. I'm the Spirit Helper of lost children. Come with me, Twig."

"Where are we going?"

"On a dream-walk. Just like warriors go on battle-walks, dreamers have to confront their enemies, too. I'll take you. But you must hurry."

I study the curious hides he wears. For all of their beauty, they are thick and covered with a black hair I have never seen before, as if they come from an animal that doesn't live in my world.

"What is your shirt made from?"

"It's giant bison hide," he says, lifting his arms. Then he points to his belt. "And this is cheetah hide."

"What are those animals? I've never heard of them."

"Come with me, and you can see them if you'd like. We're going to take a dream-walk to long ago."

Runs In Light strides out into the moonlight and stands on the narrow lip of rock that overlooks the Land of the Dead. Gingerly, I follow. Above me, a vast, glittering bowl of Star People spreads to the ends of the earth.

"Where do these giant bison and cheetahs live?"

"Far away . . . and a long time ago. When the threads of the One Life pulled apart, the world changed and they died."

"You mean they're all gone?"

He nods wistfully. "Yes. Every time a dreamer fails, a part of Life dies."

Sadness fills me. My soul seems to remember Giant Bison and Cheetah, but dimly, like the recollection of being born that is buried deep inside me. "If they're gone, how can we see them?"

"Spider will help us. You can be a great dreamer, Twig, just like your father, but you must see for yourself what happens when a dreamer gives up."

Runs In Light extends his hand and blows across his palm. Strands of light shoot from his fingertips and lance across the darkness like a spiderweb iced in blue fire.

My mouth gapes when he trots out onto the swaying web. "Please, Twig, we must go now."

"I—I'm coming."

I test the blue web with the toe of my moccasin before biting my lip and racing out after Runs In Light.

CHAPTER 22

HALFMOON DREW HIS buckskin cape more tightly about his shoulders and ducked beneath the flap into Chief Gill's lodge. Fifty hands across, it was the largest lodge in Buffalobeard Village, and the most opulent. Hundreds of prayer feathers hung from the pole frame, twisting gently in the wind, and painted rawhide shields lined the walls. Each bore the colorful image of one of Gill's Spirit Helpers: Bear, Lion, and Condor. In the rear, a stack of buffalo hides the height of a man lay folded.

"Good evening," Halfmoon said, and squinted. Though

he saw better after Father Sun descended into the under-world at night, his vision was still blurry.

The three other elders already sat around the fire. The white-haired old women, Bandtail and Snapper, sat on ei-ther side of Gill. They both looked angry. Gill, on the other hand, looked tired. He had a golden elk hide over his shoulders.

"Good evening," Gill greeted them. "Please sit down and dip yourself a cup of tea."

Halfmoon sat on the buffalo hide near Bandtail. Though his vision was fading, he could still make out her bulbous nose and puckered mouth. She looked like she wanted to spit upon him for calling this late council session.

Gill gestured to Halfmoon. "Since you called us to-gether to talk about your granddaughter's dreams, Half-moon, please begin."

Halfmoon reached for the wooden cup and dipped it into the tea bag hanging on the tripod at the edge of the fire. The scent of tundra wildflowers rose. "Forgive me for being late. I've been speaking with our warriors most of today; then I met with my daughter, our Spirit dreamer, before coming here. She tells me that my granddaughter, Twig, is now studying with Screech Owl."

A sour expression came over Bandtail's face. "Yes, so?"

Halfmoon sipped his tea, stalling to allow them more time to think about what he'd just said. Their village had not sent a dreamer away to study for thirteen summers. It was a rare and important occasion, though the pinched expressions on Bandtail's and Snapper's faces told him they didn't seem to grasp that fact.

He sat up straighter. "I know this council decided that we should not pack up and move our village, but I must tell you that Twig has been having powerful Spirit dreams that should make this council reconsider."

"Bah!" Bandtail said. "She's too young to have Spirit dreams. She is not even a woman yet."

Halfmoon nodded. "I realize it is unusual for a child to have Spirit dreams so young. But do not forget that Cobia—"

Snapper interrupted, "Twig is not Cobia. Twig has always been a normal child. Cobia was terrifying from the instant you brought her here. If we'd been smart, we would have driven her away long before she had a chance to kill Minnow."

"Yes," Bandtail agreed. "Twig is just a girl. Power does not hover around her like it did Cobia."

Gill held up a hand, asking for silence. "Please, before we make any judgments, perhaps we should allow Halfmoon to tell us what his granddaughter has dreamed."

Bandtail and Snapper whispered to each other for a time; then Bandtail flicked a hand at Halfmoon. "Go on. Tell us."

Halfmoon set the wooden cup on a hearthstone before saying, "Twig has been having the same dream for some time. She sees a green flaming ball of light roll through the sky right over her head. Screech Owl told her that it might mean the Star People are going to make war on us."

Bandtail exhaled hard. "And what does young Twig suggest we do to stop this terrible event?"

"Twig thinks we should move west. As soon as possible."

Snapper leaned forward and shook a crooked finger at Halfmoon. "You've been trying to get us to move for over half a moon. The last time you told us we had to move south because the Thornback raiders were going to attack us. But that hasn't happened."

"Yet," Halfmoon said. "It hasn't happened *yet*, Snapper. I still believe they're coming. And if Twig's dreams are true, that is another reason we should—"

"They aren't true," Bandtail insisted. She folded her arms across her chest. "If Twig really is having Spirit dreams, then why hasn't our own village Spirit dreamer brought us this information? Hmm? She's your daughter! We had a village council meeting with her this very afternoon, and she said nothing about Twig having Spirit dreams. As far as I'm concerned, this discussion is over. You will never convince me that little Twig is a Spirit dreamer."

"I agree," Snapper said. "I think you are just trying another tactic to force us to move when we don't want to."

Halfmoon sighed. He had expected this. Bandtail and Snapper generally agreed, and once they'd made up their minds, there was little anyone could do to change them. "When my granddaughter returns from Screech Owl's, may I at least bring her to speak to the council? Perhaps if you hear about her dreams from her own lips, you will be more inclined to heed her words."

Gill looked around the circle, waiting to see if anyone else wished to speak, before he said, "My own opinion is that we should question the girl, as we do all potential Spirit dreamers. Do you agree?"

Bandtail grudgingly answered, "I will be happy to question her."

"So will I," Snapper said, and grunted as she rose to her feet. "Though I think it is a waste of time."

"Then we are agreed." Gill looked around. "When Twig returns we will question her, and then decide whether or not we should reconsider our vote not to move the village."

Snapper made a disgusted sound and ducked under the lodge flap and out into the darkness.

Bandtail propped her walking stick and stood up. She glared at Halfmoon, and then she, too, left.

When they were alone, Halfmoon looked at Chief Gill. "Well, that was unpleasant. I had hoped they would listen carefully, even if they did not believe Twig was a Spirit dreamer."

Gill gave him a tired smile. "They are ten summers older than you or I. They have seen many would-be Spirit dreamers, and most have turned out to be simply children with imaginations. And . . ." Gill lifted both hands. "You've been pushing very hard to get us to move the village. They both naturally suspect you made up the story about Twig's dreams."

Halfmoon rose to his feet. "The fact that my own

daughter, our village Spirit dreamer, has never mentioned Twig's dreams did not help my cause, either."

"No." Gill shook his head. "It didn't."

Halfmoon bowed politely to Gill, then ducked beneath the lodge flap into the night. The cold air smelled of damp earth and wet leather. All fourteen lodges had a golden glow from the fires burning inside, and he heard people talking and laughing.

As he made his way across the plaza, he knew he would not win this battle in the council unless either they were attacked by raiders, or Twig's dream came true.

And by then it would be too late.

CHAPTER 23

FOR AS FAR as I can see, darkness floods outward, rippling to the ends of the sky. My skin gleams blue-white in the eerie light.

Runs In Light stops suddenly and points. "Do you see that, Twig?"

At the end of the blue web, a forbidding wall of ice rises.

Runs In Light trots forward.

"Wait! Where are you going? Don't go out there!"

"Let me show you. Hurry. Come this way." He races up to the top of the cliff and stands looking down into the massive crack.

"Stay back!" I shout. "It's too dangerous!"

"Not if you follow me," he says, and leaps down.

I'm sobbing when I reach the place where he has vanished. But deep in the bottom, I see him. He is standing on a trail that runs between the steep ice walls.

"Come on, Twig. Follow me!"

I'm terrified, but I leap. . . .

And I land as softly as a feather. High above me, a clear patch of night sky shines.

"It's this way," he says.

As we run, the sky vanishes, and we enter a black tunnel.

"Through here." Runs In Light drops to his knees and scrambles forward. "This is the way, Twig."

I crawl through behind him. Darkness weighs down on me, heavy, taking my breath away while it pounds on my eardrums and presses on my eyelids.

But far ahead, I see a tiny spot of light. It grows larger as we near it.

I step out of the tunnel into the sunlight and inhale a deep breath of the chill, bright air. This world smells strange, as though moss and chokecherry had been steeping together for a thousand summers.

"Come, Twig. It's just a little farther."

Runs In Light clambers through the maze of boulders where Father Sun blazes on his black braids. "Up here, Twig. Let me show you what happens when a dreamer fails."

I jump to the next boulder, following him. When I reach the top, I see herds of curious, hump-backed animals with long necks. Their ears and tails switch away flies while they inquisitively study us. Ice-capped mountains thrust up like teeth behind them.

"What are they?" I ask.

"Those are camels. They've only been gone for a short time." He lifts his arm and points to the south. "Do you see the people?"

I look, and there, I see people hunting. They have their prey trapped against a towering cliff. It might be a buffalo calf, but if so, the distance between the tips of its horns is three times as wide as the buffalo in my world, and it is much taller. The animal stamps its hooves and charges, trying to kill its attackers. People dodge and run, using their atlatls to launch long spears into its sides. The animal lets out a roar that sounds like a dying saber-toothed cat. Then, again, it makes a feeble run to scatter the humans. But they just circle and keep throwing their spears.

"Where are we?" I whisper.

Runs In Light crouches down. "This is the land of Giant Bison and Cheetah. That big buffalo down there is an orphaned bison calf. It's the last giant bison alive. Humans killed its mother less than a moon ago. Now they're killing it."

"It's the last of its kind? Why don't you stop them?"

"We tried to. But when the One Life has been turned upside down, only a living dreamer can make it right again. Power finds the best dreamer it can—but sometimes the dreamer fails."

I kneel beside him, watching as the giant bison calf wails and drops to its knees. Even from this distance, I see the blood that froths at the animal's mouth. The calf shoves itself up on trembling legs, but stumbles and falls on its side in the snow field. All of the people shout happily and hug each other as the bison calf's huge head sinks into the drift, and the snow runs red with its blood.

"How could they do that?" Tears make my voice tight. "Didn't they know it was the last giant bison alive?"

"No. But even if they had known, it wouldn't have made any difference. They are hungry. They need its meat." Runs In Light exhales hard. "That's what happens when the One Life is knocked out of balance. Earthmaker created the universe to have equal portions of light and dark, pain and happiness, birth and death, heat and cold. But sometimes the world gets knocked out of balance . . . and the One Life falters."

Tears blur my eyes as I watch the hunters begin the hard work of butchering Bison Calf. With sharp stone tools, they pull back the hide and carve off the rich red meat.

"You see that man on the far right? The one with Owl's face painted on his shirt?"

I wipe my eyes and nod. The man stands with his shoulders slumped forward, a hand braced on the head of a thin little girl who bounces joyfully up and down as she watches the piles of meat growing.

"His name is Tusk Boy. Power placed all of its strength and hope in him. He had Owl as a Spirit Helper from the day of his birth. But in the end, when Power called him to the river that runs before the Land of the Dead, so he could learn how to set the One Life straight again, he couldn't do it. He was afraid to cross."

My mouth has gone dry. "Afraid he would drown?"

"Yes. He knew his starving wife and children needed him, and they meant more to Tusk Boy than Bison Calf did. Only a few dreamers are willing to sacrifice themselves, and their families, so that yellow butterflies may continue to flutter over the *wildflowers in springtime. It is those few that Power seeks out. But not even Power can know for certain who will succeed and who will fail." Runs In Light gives me a sad smile. "No one really wants to be a dreamer, Twig. Not even you."*

The grassy plains before me change, glittering like a swarm of gnat wings before fading into a new vision. . . .

— CHAPTER 24 —

THE LONG, DEEPLY blue twilight of the Moon-When-Thunderbird-Walks settled over the land, bringing with it Wind Woman's fury. The gale had come up early that afternoon, roaring, blasting everything in its path, blowing the snow into deep drifts along the trails.

Greyhawk stood outside Screech Owl's cave, gripping his atlatl while he surveyed the drifts, and beyond them, the smoke that billowed across the western sky in a great purple smear. If he had his directions right, that was about the location of Clearwater Village.

It was burning.

Yipper kept sniffing the air, whimpering, and gazing up at Greyhawk as though to say, *"Why are we still here? We have to go home."*

Greyhawk stroked Yipper's black head, but in the back of his mind, he was going over and over every lesson he had learned in warriors' school. How to hold his atlatl, how to make a good sharp spear point, how to cast, how to track an enemy across bare stone . . . how to survive when you were being chased by killers.

Screech Owl ducked out of the cave and followed Greyhawk's gaze. "Come back inside, Greyhawk. It's too cold to stand out here. Besides, there's nothing you can do."

Greyhawk turned to face him. The old man wasn't nearly as scary today. Instead, he looked frail and worried. Greyhawk pointed to the smoke with his atlatl. "Can you see that smoke?"

Screech Owl nodded. "Yes. I see very well far away."

"Do you think that's Clearwater Village?"

"Probably."

Greyhawk's stomach muscles knotted. "The Thornback raiders must have attacked just before the storm."

Wind Woman whipped long gray hair over Screech Owl's eyes. He squinted through it. "Yes, I pity the poor people who escaped the raid. The snow is so deep. They won't get far."

Greyhawk gripped his atlatl more tightly. He longed to be home near his father. The people in Buffalobeard Village must have seen the smoke early this morning. They would be packing up everything they owned, getting ready to abandon Buffalobeard Village as soon as the trails melted out.

Screech Owl asked, "Did you ever find out what happened to Puffer? At the Buffalo Way ceremony all I heard was that she was dead."

Greyhawk looked westward to where the Ice Giants gleamed in the dawn light. Cobia's cave was there somewhere . . . but Puffer had never even gotten close. "Puffer and her war party were ambushed near the ruins of Starhorse Village. The warrior who escaped, Searobin, said that he never saw men, just black shapes floating through the trees."

"For black shapes, they cast their spears with deadly accuracy."

"Yes, and I—I have to get home, Screech Owl. Someone has to stop the Thornback raiders. Our village is going to need every warrior, even boys just learning to be warriors."

"Well, you can't go anywhere today. Perhaps tomorrow I'll take you and Twig home."

"You mean if Twig wakes up."

"Yes," Screech Owl softly answered.

Greyhawk leaned his shoulder against the ice-crusted boulder. All night long, Twig had moaned and thrashed; then she'd gone absolutely still. She hadn't moved at all today. She just lay lifelessly on the litter. Early that morning, Greyhawk had panicked and demanded that Screech Owl do something, so the old man had checked for a heartbeat, then had placed a mica mirror beneath her nose. Nothing.

Terrified, Greyhawk said, "Is Twig dead? Did you kill her? You killed my best friend!"

Screech Owl ran a hand through his matted gray hair. "Greyhawk, I just wanted her to see the tunnel. I never thought she'd be able to—"

"To dream her way to the skyworld? She's a great dreamer! Didn't you know that?"

His words were torn away by Wind Woman and blown into the white distances.

Screech Owl tiredly folded his arms across his bony chest. The old man hadn't gotten much sleep last night. Every time Greyhawk had awakened, he'd seen Screech Owl sitting in his protective circle, staring at Twig. Throughout the long night, his face had grown more and more frightened.

"I thought she might just be able to peer over the edge into the darkness," Screech Owl explained. "It takes even the greatest dreamers many summers to gain the skill and courage to actually plunge into the spiraling black throat that carries them up to the skyworld."

"But she did it, didn't she?"

"Maybe."

The old man had been half-crazy all day, rushing around the cave, turning first one way then back the other way, as though he were lost in a maze.

"Maybe Twig just decided to stay longer, to talk with her dead grandmother, or maybe her father?" Greyhawk suggested.

Screech Owl hesitated for a long time before he said,

"It's possible. Many dreamers stay in the skyworld for days, talking to Spirits, visiting with old friends. But Twig is so young. . . ." Guilt twisted his face.

A kestrel soared through the sky high above, shrieking before swooping low over the boulders. Screech Owl shielded his eyes to watch its flight. He didn't seem to recognize the bird. For good measure, Yipper growled at it.

"Can't you try to wake her?" Greyhawk asked.

"If she hasn't awakened by tomorrow morning, I'll try brewing a Spirit tea to bring her home. But danger lurks in even the slightest interference. If Twig is struggling against some Spirit creature and I so much as call her name, the distraction could cause her doom. But if she had an accident, if her litter overturned and she's drowning . . . well, she would be running through a country that has no landmarks . . . a country haunted by horrors you cannot even imagine. In that case, my voice might help lead her home."

"Why can't you just go after her and bring her back?"

Screech Owl's hands dropped limply to his sides. "The skyworld is vast. Every dreamer enters at a different place. It spreads out infinitely in all directions. Finding her would take a miracle."

Greyhawk's gaze returned to the streaks of gray that drifted across the heavens. What was happening out there? Elder Halfmoon must already be in war council, planning what to do. The snow would slow the raiders down, but . . .

"The Thornback raiders will be coming for us next, Screech Owl. We have to stop them."

CHAPTER 25

ICE AND SNOW gust by, making it almost impossible for me to see anything. . . . Then a young man appears, standing on the crest of an ice ridge. He wears a white bear hide over his shoulders, and long black hair whips around his face.

Standing alone on the ice, the young man cries, "I'm not the one! I'm no dreamer."

"Who is he?" I ask Runs In Light.

"Wolf Dreamer. He succeeded. He—"

"Wolf Dreamer! Is that who he is? He's one of the Blessed Hero Twins."

"Yes, he dreamed humans into the land where you live, even

though all he wanted was to be a hunter and to raise a family with the woman he loved."

"Power wouldn't let him?"

"He wouldn't let himself. The survival of Life was more important to him than his own wants. Without his dream, humans would never have found the way to your world."

I clench my fists. "So Wolf Dreamer was brave enough?"

"Yes, but not until the very end."

Runs In Light turns to look at me. His young face has taken on a bittersweet expression that melts my heart. Snow blasts by us, whistling, freezing on our eyelashes.

"No one wants to be a dreamer, Twig. But someone must be."

I force a swallow down my throat. "I'm afraid, but . . . I'll try. Can you help me? I've only seen twelve summers."

"So had I," he says softly. "I had seen twelve summers when Power called."

"You were a dreamer?"

"Yes. A very long time ago."

Runs In Light rises to his feet, and the air wavers around him, blurring his body into bizarre, ominous shapes. "It was even harder for me than it is for you, Twig. I was more afraid than you can imagine."

"How did you get over it?"

"I united the worlds of Animal and Human in myself, and became my Spirit Helper."

"Became?"

"Some dreamers are strengthened when they are consumed by fire. Other dreamers need water. Some, like us, have to drown

in blood before they can unite worlds inside themselves. Don't fear it, Twig. That crushing beak will give you wings."

"What do you mean? I don't understand."

I stumble backward when Runs In Light's legs begin to writhe in a hideous dance. As I watch, black fur sprouts from his skin, and he turns into a wolf—a big black wolf. With wistful, human eyes, he peers up at me. "You and Greyhawk must go to Cobia's cave. Eagle-Man waits for you there."

The wolf lopes away at full speed, charging through the icy wilderness as though being chased by an invisible monster.

"Runs In Light, wait! How do I get home? I can't get home!"

In a voice that grows fainter by the instant, he calls, "Go and ask Wolf Dreamer."

I turn to look at the man standing on the crest of ridge. He's smiling at me, but he looks sad.

As I climb toward him, he calls, "Hurry, Twig. The Thornback raiders are approaching your village. Very soon, they will find your family. You must hurry. Hurry."

CHAPTER 26

GREYHAWK AND SCREECH Owl continued to stare out across the white wasteland of snow toward the burning village in the distance. The smoke had started to coil upward like a black tornado.

Screech Owl said, "You are right, Greyhawk. We must stop them, but—" He stopped and cocked an ear.

A sound rose; it barely carried over the wind: soft, mewing.

Then Greyhawk clearly heard a cough and a wheezed, "Screech Owl?"

"*Twig?*"

Screech Owl dashed beneath the leather curtain, and Greyhawk ducked into the cave behind him.

Twig was lying on her side, her body dripping wet. Strange bits of moss clung to her sleeves. She coughed again, desperately, and tried to raise herself on her elbows but weakly fell back against the fox hides.

Greyhawk cried, "Twig! Are you all right?"

Screech Owl ran for her, scooped her up in his arms, and frantically kissed her soaked face. "Thank Earthmaker, I was so afraid."

Yipper trotted over to sniff Twig's head, then licked her arm affectionately. She didn't seem to feel it. She kept coughing.

Greyhawk didn't know what to do. He just stood rigidly, clutching his atlatl, waiting to hear her speak. She looked different somehow, her eyes brighter, and not quite human.

Twig fell into a violent coughing fit. A trickle of water ran from her mouth. She fought to catch her breath and started choking. Screech Owl laid her facedown on the floor and firmly pressed against her back. More water gushed from her lungs, forming a small, crystalline pool on the hides. He pressed again and again, until she seemed to be breathing easily; then he stretched out on the floor beside her to study her face. She smiled weakly. Screech Owl lifted a hand and stroked her sopping hair. "Are you feeling better?"

"Yes," she whispered.

Greyhawk knelt beside her. His throat had closed up, making it hard to breathe. "I thought you were dead," he said. "I missed you badly."

Her pretty face, with its full lips and straight nose, had gone as white as the snow. But her eyes gazed at him steadily. "I fell into the river."

"The river that runs in front of the Land of the Dead? How did you get out?"

"I was . . . was drowning. I saw something in the waves. It came and slithered inside me."

"Snake?" Greyhawk hissed in surprise.

She nodded. "Water Snake. I—I got Water Snake's soul. Then . . . I could swim to shore."

Screech Owl said, "That's good, Twig. You wanted Water Snake's soul. How did—"

"Runs In Light came . . . came to . . ." She started coughing again.

"Wait, Twig," Screech Owl said gently, seeing how hard it was for her to talk. "You need to rest and eat. We'll talk about these things when you're stronger."

Twig nodded, and her hand crept spiderlike across the floor until she could twine her fingers in Screech Owl's buckskin shirt. "I tried very hard . . . to come back to you. I love you, Screech Owl. You, too . . . Greyhawk."

Screech Owl stroked her hair. "We love you, too, Twig. You sleep now. When you wake up, we'll eat and talk."

CHAPTER 27

WIND.

And more wind, howling through the cold moonlight.

Twig watched Screech Owl crouch before the rabbit that was skewered on a long stick and propped near the flames. He turned the stick so the rabbit would cook on the other side, and glanced at Twig. She sat across the fire pit from him. Screech Owl had given her one of his old shirts to wear. It was much too big for her, but it was dry and warm. It was painted green with red spirals and black dancing bears. Screech Owl had explained that it had come from his ritual attire and had been specially blessed by Kestrel Above.

"Twig?" Greyhawk said. "Can you talk now?"

She nodded, but didn't say anything. Her gaze was fixed on the snowflakes that blew past the cave entrance. They were whispering to each other, but she couldn't understand their words.

Screech Owl dipped a horn spoon into the pot of tea, stirring it for the twentieth time.

Greyhawk walked over and knelt beside Screech Owl to whisper, "Why isn't she talking?"

Screech Owl said, "That happens to dreamers when they get new souls. They become disoriented for a time, seeing an old world through strange new eyes. I've known dreamers who went mad from fear. And others who left their homes and families and just ran away into the forest never to be seen again."

"Did that happen to you?"

"Me? No, of course not. I was delighted by the bizarre thoughts that came to me. After I got Pack Rat's soul, I had the urge to poke my nose into dark crevices looking for shiny objects. I didn't realize how dangerous it was. One night I poked my head into a hole in the ground where Weasel lived and Weasel sank his teeth into my nose. See this scar?" Screech Owl pointed to the white scar on his nose.

Greyhawk scowled.

Twig smiled and studied Screech Owl as he duck-walked to the rear of the cave to sift through the basket of dried blossoms. The delicate, flowery scent swirled up when he grasped a handful. He brought them back and stirred the blossoms into the boiling blend of roots.

"I saw Wolf Dreamer," Twig said.

"You *saw* the Blessed Hero Twin?" Greyhawk asked in awe.

"Yes, in the Land of the Long Dark. Have you ever seen him, Screech Owl?"

"No." Screech Owl cocked his head. "But each dreamer meets different Spirit Helpers in the skyworld."

Twig clasped her hands in her lap. "After Runs In Light left me, I didn't know how to get home, so I walked down to Wolf Dreamer. We talked. He told me things. . . ."

She understood why a new dreamer might go mad. The things she'd seen were terrifying and magical. The colors were almost too dazzling to look at, and the faces of the Spirits shone as though coated with liquid moonlight.

Greyhawk said, "What did he tell you, Twig?"

She blinked at the swaying door curtain. She didn't know if she should answer. Besides, a silence lived in her heart now—a deep, bright silence that was perfectly calm. She longed to swim in it forever.

Screech Owl filled three wooden cups with tea, then slid the rabbit into a bowl and tore off the legs. He handed a teacup and a bowl with a leg to Greyhawk, then carried Twig's teacup and bowl over and set them by her knees. She barely saw him.

Screech Owl picked up his own dinner and gently

said, "First, tell us about the journey, Twig. Did Eagle-Man come up through the tunnel in the spruce branch?"

"Yes," she said softly. "He brought the Spirit buffalo. They put their heads through the nooses you made. Then . . . then we started up . . . flying into the dark storm."

Steam rose around Screech Owl's face as he sipped his tea. "Eat while you talk, Twig. You must be starving."

She picked up her rabbit leg and chewed it thoughtfully while her gaze touched each sacred symbol painted on the walls. The spirals and purple starbursts glittered in the firelight.

"The buffalo had a hard time pulling the litter through the river, Screech Owl."

"They always do. It's so deep and wide."

"And fast. It rushed so fast."

"So you fell in and had to turn back?"

She finished chewing and swallowed. At the memory, fear, like a living thing, coiled in her belly. "Yes."

Screech Owl sat forward and gently touched her shoulder. "That's all right, Twig. You did well."

"But I didn't make it across to the Land of the Dead. I'm sorry."

In a hushed voice, Screech Owl said, "Don't be. Very few Spirit dreamers ever reach the Land of the Dead. Especially not on their first try."

Greyhawk looked at Screech Owl. "How long did it take you to make it across the river?"

The old man cocked his head. "I finally made it on my fifteenth try. I'd seen twenty-two summers."

Twig continued, "But I could see things on the other side: old fire pits, stumps with ax marks. And the trees, the trees, Screech Owl! They were so tall their tops disappeared into the clouds. That's when Runs In Light led me to the Long Dark. And . . . and I met Wolf Dreamer."

Twig gobbled a chunk of meat, barely chewing it; then she lowered her eyes, and tears glistened on her lashes. "The Thornback raiders are coming, Screech Owl. Very soon."

"I knew it!" Greyhawk shouted. "We have to go home!"

Screech Owl's eyes narrowed, as though in pain. "Did Wolf Dreamer tell you how to stop them?"

Twig didn't answer. She watched Screech Owl with the bright, unblinking eyes of Water Snake.

It must have scared Greyhawk. He walked across the cave to the entrance and pulled the curtain aside to stare out at the dark night, as though afraid he'd find Thornback raiders camped right outside. The faint scents of mud and soaked rocks blew in on Wind Woman's breath.

"Our families are in danger," Greyhawk said. "We have to get home. I'm leaving tomorrow at dawn. I don't care how deep the snow is."

Twig blinked. Only a few days ago, he'd been afraid of everything—birds, bullies, and fights. But now, he sounded like a warrior.

Screech Owl responded, "I'll take you. I don't want you going alone. If the raiders are out there, I—"

"Screech Owl?" Twig set her cup down and wrapped her arms around her knees. Her heart felt luminous. "Why didn't you ever tell me you were my father?"

Greyhawk's gaze shot to Screech Owl. "You . . . *you* are Twig's father?"

Screech Owl's hand stopped midway in bringing his teacup to his mouth. He seemed to be fighting to swallow past the knot in his throat. Tea sloshed onto the floor when he set his cup down. "Twig . . . I . . . your mother . . . she—she left me. She told me she never wanted to see me again after the dreams I had made her see. She hated me. She thought it would be better if people believed that Shouts-At-Night was your father. She said it would make things easier for you. I wanted to tell you so many times."

"But you're my father. Our people trace descent through the men. You could have made a claim on me."

"Yes," he said gently, "but I loved your mother. I didn't want to hurt her. And I—I thought you would be better off with her than me. I tried to see you every time I went to Buffalobeard Village. I've always loved you."

Twig gave Screech Owl an affectionate smile, and emotion seemed to swell at the back of his throat. He couldn't speak. He just tilted his head awkwardly, and Twig jumped up and hugged him.

"I'm glad you're my father, Screech Owl. There's no-body else I'd want for a father."

Greyhawk leaned against the cave wall, as though he was a little faint. "I feel like someone just kicked me in the belly. Twig, are you sure? Who told you Screech Owl was your father?"

As the flames died down in the fire pit, smoke curled upward in billowing clouds where it crept along the ceiling until it was sucked out through the crack.

Twig sat down again. "When I was drowning, I called out for my father, and I saw Screech Owl's face. Then, Wolf Dreamer told me that's where I get my ability to dream—from Screech Owl." She smiled at him. "I don't know why I didn't think of it myself."

Screech Owl said, "What else did he tell you, my daughter?"

Twig's soul seemed to be floating, moving with the dance of the firelight. She took a deep breath. "Screech Owl, Greyhawk, you have to promise not to tell anyone."

"I promise," Greyhawk said.

"As do I. What did he say?"

Twig exhaled hard. "We have to go find Cobia. Greyhawk and me. We have to do it together."

Greyhawk's knees went weak. "Me? Why do I have to go? I'm no dreamer!"

Twig whispered, "No, you're a warrior."

Screech Owl seemed to stop breathing. He stared hard at Greyhawk. "Yes, and you're about to be tested."

"Tested? What does that mean?" Greyhawk said.

"It means that Twig's Spirit Helper has called you. And having a Spirit Helper call you is a little like meeting Grandfather Grizzly unexpectedly in the dark forest. You never know whether he'll lead you out of the darkness to the trail home—or force you to run for your life."

Greyhawk started shaking his head and backing away, and Twig said, "Greyhawk, our families are in trouble. The Thornback raiders are headed for our village. My Spirit Helpers told me the only way we can really save our people is by finding Cobia."

He nervously licked his lips. "I'm ready to fight raiders, Twig, but Cobia . . ."

"Fighting the raiders won't be enough," Twig said softly. "There's something much worse coming. That's what we have to stop."

"The ball of light in your dream?"

"I think so. I—I don't understand what all of it means, Greyhawk. I just know we have to find Cobia."

Greyhawk gripped his atlatl and squared his shoulders. Yipper leaped to his feet as though he knew that meant they would be going soon. Greyhawk took a deep breath, and when he let it out, he said, "All right, Twig. If it means we can save our people, I'll go."

Twig nodded, and started to say something, but she heard a whisper. Her gaze went to the colorful symbols painted on the walls, and she frowned, listening to them talking to each other. They had sweet, high voices. After ten heartbeats, she said, "We'll leave at dawn."

CHAPTER 28

GET UP!"

The hoarse voice brought Hook straight out of a deep sleep. Dry Cloud screamed as Hook threw off his hides, grabbed his war club, and jumped to his feet ready to club his enemy to death.

"I know where the Stone Wolf is."

Hook blinked. The dark silhouette of a man filled his entryway. Cold wind blew in, fluttering the scalps tied to the frame poles. The man was holding the lodge curtain open, and his body looked utterly black against the bright moonlight.

Breathlessly, Hook said, "My chief? Is that you?"

"The Stone Wolf is in Buffalobeard Village. Find it. And bring me the girl who has it. Leave now."

The curtain fell closed, and darkness filled the lodge.

"Blessed Spirits," Dry Cloud gasped. "What's he talking about?"

"Father?" his oldest son, Blue Dog, called. "Is everything all right?"

"Where are you going, Father?" Slate called, and then his entire family started talking at once, asking questions. Dry Cloud rose and walked across the lodge to check on Slate.

Hook's chest was heaving. He fought to force the blood surging in his veins to slow down.

"Quiet. I have to go assemble a war party. I'll return as soon as I can."

— CHAPTER 29 —

TWIG TUGGED UP the hem of her green dress—actually, Screech Owl's ritual shirt with the dancing bears—to avoid the tangle of old roots that crept across the path. She had pinned her braid on top of her head with a wooden comb, but Wind Woman had torn loose straggles that blew before her eyes. In the pack on her back, she carried all of the sacred things that Screech Owl had used to teach her, a hollow tube to blow away evil Spirits, and her atlatl, plus the clothes she had brought with her. Screech Owl had made a special belt pouch for her to carry the spruce bough from First Woman's tree, and told her *never* to lose it.

Five paces ahead of her, Screech Owl walked beside Greyhawk. Greyhawk carried his spear nocked in his atlatl, ready for a fight. He had been pensive all morning while they followed the winding trail that led to Buffalobeard Village. As the warmth of the day increased, more and more snow melted from the trail, leaving it muddy and slippery.

Greyhawk said, "Screech Owl, I've been wondering about finding Cobia's cave. I don't even know which trail to take. Do you?"

"You follow the lakeshore trail until you see an ice canyon, Hoarfrost Canyon; then you walk into the canyon. It gets more and more narrow as you go. At the end of the canyon, you'll see her cave."

"So, once we enter Hoarfrost Canyon, we can't miss it."

"That's right. Hoarfrost Canyon dead-ends at Cobia's cave. That what makes it a perfect ambush place. The only way out is the way you came in."

"Then if someone blocks the mouth of the canyon, we're trapped."

"Yes, though there are smaller caves that dot the ice cliffs. . . ."

Twig barely heard them. She'd been thinking about her Spirit journey to the skyworld. Memories of her litter overturning in the river had been haunting her. In her nightmares she still gulped mouthfuls of chilling water and felt her lungs go cold before she saw Water Snake slithering toward her.

"Screech Owl?" she asked. He and Greyhawk turned to look back at her.

"Yes, Twig?"

"What happens if I get Rock's soul before I have to go back into the skyworld?"

"What?"

"I said, what happens if I have to cross the river in the skyworld with Rock's soul in my body?"

Greyhawk squinted at her. "Rock's soul?"

"Yes. You know, or something else that would sink. I'm worried that—"

"Oh . . . Oh, I understand. Well"—Screech Owl gestured airily—"I suppose you'll have to roll along the river bottom until you find a firm enough place to roll ashore. You'll want to avoid all the mucky places, of course, because if you get stuck, you won't have any hands or feet to push out with. Not having eyes will be the real problem, since you won't be able to see where you're going. But I suspect that if you feel your way, paying attention to the flow of the current, you'll make it." His bushy gray brows lifted abruptly. "That is, unless one of the grouse with fish fins dives down to gobble you up for its gizzard."

Greyhawk said, "I hope no worm souls try to get Twig before she has to talk to Eagle-Man again. Eagles love worms."

"That's not funny, Greyhawk," she said.

"And, then"—Screech Owl tilted his head—"the other solution is just to cross the river in a different place. A place where it isn't as wide or deep. That will take some searching, of course. You might want to try a place up north, in the heart of the Ice Giants. Cobia once told me the river isn't nearly as wide there."

Twig frowned and walked up the trail. As she shifted the weight of her pack, the hollow tube for blowing away evil Spirits rattled. "Cobia won't kill us, will she?"

He tilted his head uncertainly. "No one can say what Cobia will or will not do. I just wish I knew how much time I have left to teach you. I don't want to push you, but, Twig—"

"We'd better do it, Screech Owl." She bit her lip, recalling the terror she'd felt when her litter had overturned in the sacred river. She could still see the faces of the buffalo as they dragged her litter away . . . and feel the icy water filling her lungs. Could she stand that again? "It might take me longer to learn than we expect."

Screech Owl trudged up a small rise that overlooked Ice Giant Lake. Far in the distance, Twig saw Buffalobeard Village nestled at the base of the rocky ridge. They had almost finished the rock wall. Only one gap remained on the south side of the village. The smoke from the campfires rose into the turquoise sky.

Twig thought she could see fishing boats out on the water, and people moving along the lakeshore, but windblown snow blurred the distances. It might just be boulders. Still, her eyes lingered on those black dots, and her heart ached for her mother.

Greyhawk said, "Come on. Let's hurry. Even if we run all the way, we're not going to get home until after dark!"

Twig trotted down the hill behind Screech Owl and Greyhawk, calling, "When can you teach me more? Tonight?"

"If your mother will let me, yes. In fact, doing this lesson in your own lodge might be best. You'll feel safer there than anywhere else."

Twig broke into a hard run, her legs pumping while the pack slapped her back. Ahead, the trail wound downward. "What will you teach me, Screech Owl?"

His sweat-damp gray hair flopped around his ears with each step. "I'm going to teach you how to cross the river and enter the Land of the Dead, Twig."

"After I cross the river, what do I need to do?"

Screech Owl caught up with her and put a hand on her shoulder to stop her. For a while, they just stood in the trail and looked at each other.

Then Screech Owl said, "After you cross the river, you have to step into the mouth of the Spirit that wants to chew you up."

CHAPTER 30

DUSK WAS DEEPENING into night when Twig made the last turn in the trail and ran headlong for home. As she crested a rise, she saw Buffalobeard Village. The circle of lodges still stood around the central fire pit, but big packs had been piled outside the lodges. From the looks of things, they would be leaving tomorrow.

Mother ducked out of their lodge, and Twig yelled, "Mother? Mother, I'm home!"

Mother turned and ran toward Twig. She had braided her hair and coiled it on top of her head, pinning it with a rabbit-bone pin. The style made her narrow face seem longer and her nose more hooked. Her shell bead neck-lace glittered. "Twig? Oh, Twig! And Greyhawk! We were so worried about you!"

"I'm fine," Greyhawk said.

"Well, you'd better get home and tell your father. Right now. He's been terrified."

Greyhawk lifted a hand, called, "I'll see you in the morning, Twig," and raced across the village for his lodge.

Mother threw her arms around Twig and hugged her tightly. It felt so good to be close again. Mother kissed Twig's hair and face, and Twig's soul ached with happiness. "Oh, Mother, I missed you."

"And I missed you. Let me look at you. Are you all right?"

Twig's pack made her so awkward that she staggered sideways when Mother released her.

"Mother, guess what? I went into the skyworld! Screech Owl made a death litter for me, and Eagle-Man brought Spirit buffalo to pull it."

Mother smiled. "Yes, I made that same journey when I studied with Screech Owl. I think every dreamer in history has tried to make that trip. How far did you go? Did you get out of the cave?"

Excitedly, she said, "Oh, yes, I made it to the river, but my litter overturned, and I fell into the water—"

"You . . ." Mother blinked, and lifted her gaze to Screech Owl, who had come to stand behind Twig. Twig saw Screech Owl nod, and Mother stroked Twig's hair in amazement. "I'm so proud of you, Twig. I tried many times to make it across the river. In fact, I've known only one dreamer in my life who has made it to the river, and crossed it into the Land of the Dead." She looked at Screech Owl.

"Yes, well," Twig blurted happily, "Runs In Light told me that if I try very hard I may be as great a dreamer as my father, Screech Owl—"

"*What?*" Mother's smile faded, then hardened into anger.

A dreadful silence fell. Twig's eyes went back and forth between them.

"I kept my promise, Riddle," Screech Owl said softly. "I didn't tell her. Her Spirit Helpers did."

Mother lowered her eyes disbelievingly before she said, "We'll discuss it later. I'm sure Twig is hungry. I have a fresh pot of grouse stew in our lodge."

Mother marched away, and Screech Owl patted Twig's head as he passed by her to catch up with Mother. "Riddle, please, let's talk now," he said; then his voice went too low for Twig to hear, but she could see Mother's shoulder muscles knot.

They marched straight back to Mother's lodge without saying a word to anyone.

The old people watched Twig as she followed along behind Mother and Screech Owl. She could see the curiosity in their weathered faces, and knew they wanted to ask her what she'd learned. They were probably worried she didn't have a human soul—which, of course, she didn't.

Mother raised her voice to a shout. "I told you I didn't

want her to know about you. We had a bargain! What am I going to do now?"

"Lower your voice, Riddle," Screech Owl pleaded.

Twig felt ill. She had been so afraid of telling Mother about having Water Snake's soul that she had forgotten she wasn't supposed to know about Screech Owl being her father. What would happen because of her slip?

By the time she reached the lodge doorway, the barest sliver of Moon Maiden's face had peeked over the eastern horizon.

CHAPTER 31

TWIG SAT ON her bedding hides with her chin propped atop her knees. The Stone Wolf was whispering to the yellow spider painted on Mother's medicine bundle. She strained to understand the words. Strange that she had never heard them talking before. But Power was loose on the night. She could feel it nipping at her skin with tiny fangs.

She fiddled with the sleeves of Screech Owl's green ritual shirt, tugging at the fringes while she studied Screech Owl and Mother. They sat cross-legged near the fire.

If Twig had to listen to their silence much longer, she wouldn't be able to breathe. What had they said to each other on the way to the lodge? Something bad. Mother's face looked stormy as she filled bowls with grouse stew. Screech Owl wasn't looking at her. Instead, he was drawing magical signs in the hard-packed dirt floor.

Is that what the Stone Wolf and the spider were discussing? Their voices had dropped even lower.

Twig turned to watch the lodge flap sway in the wind. Every now and then, when Wind Woman shoved the flap open, she glimpsed Moon Maiden's face sitting above the rocky ridge. The tumbled boulders stood like dark sentinels against the silver undercoat of moonlight.

"Riddle," Screech Owl said very softly, and Twig took a deep breath. "You don't have to believe us, but—"

"I don't believe you," Mother responded in a low, shaky voice. Anger and hurt flashed in her eyes. "I think you've taught Twig enough. Maybe I won't let her go back to see you ever again!"

The deep wrinkles around Screech Owl's eyes tightened. "Dreamers are not made in a few days, Riddle. If Twig has to learn on her own, the pain will probably drive her away from dreaming. Power has chosen her. This is not something you or I have a say in. She will be a Spirit dreamer. The only choice we have is whether or not to help her. If we leave her to stumble around trying to find her own way—"

"Some people do better stumbling around than being guided by a crazy old fool."

Tears stung Twig's eyes. She just wanted Screech Owl

to teach her for a little while longer—she didn't want to hurt Mother.

Mother tramped across the lodge, tugged the Stone Wolf from her medicine bundle, then walked back and knelt before Twig. The Wolf had a new leather thong on it, turning it into a necklace.

Mother's eyes looked blacker than black when she said, "See this, Twig? I made this so you could wear it when you got home." She draped the thong over Twig's head.

Twig shuddered when the Stone Wolf fell over her heart. Threads of power seeped from the Wolf and soaked into her chest. She barely heard Mother say, "The Wolf will help Twig, Screech Owl. She no longer needs you."

"But Riddle . . ."

A ragged scream shredded the night.

Screech Owl whirled around to look at the door curtain.

Just when he started to rise, war cries rose out of nowhere. The high-pitched shrills slipped up and down like someone playing a bone comb with a chokecherry stick.

Someone cried, *"It's the Thornback raiders! Grab your weapons!"*

Screech Owl dove for the door, jerked the flap aside, and peered out at the night.

Twig could see them, and she knew immediately that she was too late! Too late to tell Grandfather or the elders what she'd learned. Too late to stop them!

As the raiders ran through the village, casting their flaming spears into the lodges, they looked like black scraps of cloth flying on the wind. Lodges burst into flame, and people scrambled out to run.

The ghostly black raiders yipped and fell on the old men, women, and children alike, chasing them down.

A flaming spear landed on the roof of Twig's lodge.

"Fire!" Mother screamed. Smoke rose in a gray haze and started to fill the lodge. "Screech Owl, our lodge is on fire!"

"Riddle, grab Twig! We'll have to break through the poles on the back of the lodge to get out."

"But they'll be watching!" Mother cried in terror. "You know they will. They're probably waiting for us to—"

"It's our only chance!"

Twig shouted, "Look!" and pointed at the roof.

Screech Owl lunged for Twig and knocked her back against the wall as a burning section of roof poles toppled into the lodge.

When Twig sat up, she saw Mother's arm, twisted at an impossible angle in the midst of the flames. "Screech Owl. Save Mother! Help Mother!"

The fire roared, searing Screech Owl's face until he had to close his eyes. Roughly, he grabbed Twig's hand, dragged her to the back of the lodge, and jerked the frame poles apart. "Run and hide, Twig!" he shouted as he shoved her outside. "If I don't come to find you soon, remember what your Spirit Helpers have told you. Their words may save all of us!" He leaped back into the burning lodge.

Twig stood rigid, staring at her lodge. In terror, she cried, "Screech Owl! Mother! Where are you?"

No one answered.

Twig put her hands over her mouth to stifle her sobs and dashed out into the night.

Everywhere dark eerie warriors were chasing after running, screaming people.

Twig climbed up into the rocks, trying to find a good place to hide. Firelight reflected across the boulders, swirling like monstrous creatures with fiery wings.

Twig stumbled over a rock, regained her balance, and ran again until she could crawl into a thick brier of old bushes, where she fell to her knees. She watched in horror as enemy warriors shoved Screech Owl through the village plaza. He was carrying Mother in his arms. Her body, legs dangling, hung limply. She watched until they disappeared into the darkness. Was Mother dead?

A fist tightened around Twig's heart. *Mother? Mother, don't leave me!*

Twig gasped desperate breaths of the cold, smoky air while she tried to spot anyone else she knew. Warriors floated around the charred skeletons of lodges.

"Greyhawk, where are you? Eagle-Man, let him be all right. Oh, Grandfather. Grandfather, where are you?"

Twig crawled to the far end of the brush to see the village from a different angle, and she spied eight raiders creeping through the darkness. They seemed to be checking the base of the rocks for survivors. They flushed a mouse that darted away into the firelight crevices; then Old Man Blood Duck jumped out and tried to run on his maimed leg. One of the raiders pounced on him and clubbed him in the head. The old man crumpled to the ground like a rabbit-fur doll. Twig's heart thundered.

They're going to find me. I have to run. But if I stand up, they'll see me. What . . . ?

Suddenly, she knew. She flopped on her stomach and slithered through the brush, as silent as Water Snake, her movements hidden by the wavering dance of shadows.

—— CHAPTER 32 ——

GREYHAWK HID BEHIND the low rock wall west of
Buffalobeard Village, watching the lodges burn.
All around him, ash fell like black snowflakes.

Raiders stalked around, kicking dead bodies, spearing
the wounded to make sure they would not rise again.
Groans and hideous shrieks rang out.

Greyhawk was shaking so badly he could barely stand.

Yipper, who stood at his side, let out a low growl, and
Greyhawk panicked. He grabbed Yipper's jaws hard and
held them together, hissing, "No! Don't make a sound!"

Yipper stared up at him with wide eyes, but he seemed

to understand. When Greyhawk let go, Yipper sat on his haunches and kept quiet.

Greyhawk moved along the boulders until he could see farther to the east. The raiders had captured several children. He saw Rattler, Buzzard, Little Cougar, and Black Locust huddling together. Two men guarded them. The raiders must be planning on marching them home as slaves. Where were the other children? He saw two dead boys lying on the far side of the village, near the stone wall. Who were they? Which friends?

Ten paces away from the children, Screech Owl sat with seven adults. The old man had his shoulders hunched, staring down at the woman who lay unconscious across his lap. Twig's mother? Greyhawk couldn't see very well, but he thought that's who it was.

"Where's Father?" he whispered to himself. "Where's Elder Halfmoon, Searobin, and our other warriors? Where's Twig?"

He didn't see any of them, alive or dead.

Raiders encircled the villagers, holding their nocked atlatls up, ready to cast. Only one raider stood inside the circle with the villagers . . . and he was big. Tall, and muscular, and dressed all in black, he looked like one of the giants from the Old Stories. All of the raiders had covered their faces with soot. The only thing Greyhawk could make out clearly was their eyes, shining in the firelight.

The big raider walked over and kicked Screech Owl hard in the ribs. "You, what's your name?"

"Screech Owl. What's yours?"

Had the old man's eyes and beaked nose grown bigger? They seemed enormously large in the thin frame of his face. His tan shirt was filthy, covered with dark streaks of charcoal.

"What do you know about a Spirit object called the Stone Wolf? It's supposed to live in Buffalobeard Village. Have you ever heard of it?"

"Oh, yes," Screech Owl said, and mopped his forehead with his torn sleeve. "It did live here, many summers ago. But it vanished."

"What do you mean it vanished?"

"Someone stole it. Quite a long time ago. Isn't that what happened, Riddle?"

The woman lying in his lap turned to glower at the big raider. Her mouth moved, but Greyhawk couldn't hear her answer. Her voice must be very weak. At least she was alive.

The big raider slapped his atlatl against his leg. "I don't believe you. Our chief told us there was a Stone Wolf here and that it possessed great power."

"Well, if it was here," Screech Owl remarked reasonably, "it certainly didn't possess much power. Look what happened to Buffalobeard Village."

The other raiders burst out laughing and gestured to the smoking lodges, but the big man didn't seem amused.

He pointed his atlatl at Screech Owl's gray head. "We've been gathering every Spirit object we can find. We want that Stone Wolf, and the girl who possesses it."

Screech Owl went rigid. "What girl?"

As though annoyed by the question, the raider gripped
Screech Owl's shoulder and shoved him backward. Twig's
mother covered her head, expecting a blow. "We have to
find that Wolf. I know a little girl has it. Where is it? What
have you done with it?"

Screech Owl tucked his hands into the folds of his
shirt, but before he did, Greyhawk saw them shake. After
a few moments, Screech Owl asked, "What do you want
with all these Spirit objects?"

The big raider leaned down and grinned at Screech
Owl with broken, yellow teeth. "Our chief, the Blessed
Nightcrow, has foreseen the destruction of our world. In
his vision, a giant ball of light sets the forests on fire, the
Ice Giants turn black, and war breaks out. He's going to
use the power in the Spirit objects to kill all of you before
you can attack us in the scramble for what is left of the
food."

"Really? Does he know how to extract the power?
That's not as easy as it sounds. Believe me, I know. Is Nightcrow that powerful?"

"He is the Thornback People's most powerful Spirit
dreamer. And once he has stolen all the sacred objects
from his enemies, he will be the most powerful dreamer
in the world."

"And the girl? Why does he need her?" Screech Owl
said.

Hook shrugged. "He does. That is all I know, or need
to know. She must be very power—"

A hoarse shout rent the night, and Greyhawk almost

screamed he was so frightened by it. He desperately peered through the rocks to see what was happening.

Near the eastern ridge on the far side of the village, one of the raiders pulled a child and a man from the darkness and dragged them into the glow of the burning lodges.

"Stop it, let me go!" the boy shouted.

Grizzly! It's Grizzly!

The raider hauled Grizzly by the scruff of his neck while he twisted wildly, kicking, biting, trying to wrench free of the man's iron hands.

Grizzly's father, Black Star, had been wounded. He was dragging his right foot, and blood soaked his pant leg.

"Let me go!" Grizzly screamed, and sank his teeth into the raider's hand.

"You little wildcat!" the raider shouted, and lifted his war club to kill Grizzly.

Before he could land the blow, Black Star leaped upon the raider, and they toppled to the ground in a rolling, fighting blur. Both men roared at the tops of their lungs.

Three other raiders ran forward and began beating Black Star with their war clubs. It took less than ten heartbeats for Black Star to collapse on the ground.

Grizzly stood as though frozen in shock, staring at his father's brain where it was visible through the crack in his skull.

The raider who had threatened Grizzly got to his feet and lunged at Grizzly to finish the job and kill him.

The big raider shouted, "No, Chub! Wait. Bring him here."

"What for?"

"Because I said so!"

Chub lifted his war club, ready to strike Grizzly despite his war chief's orders. "He's a little animal, Hook. The sooner we kill him, the better!"

Another warrior, a very tall man, grabbed Grizzly and dragged him away from Chub, which obviously enraged Chub. He glared pure death at the insolent warrior.

"Here he is," the tall man said, and shoved Grizzly down at Hook's feet.

"Good work, Shrike," Hook praised, and studied Grizzly. "Children are less skilled at lying. Perhaps he knows where the Stone Wolf is."

Grizzly scrambled to his knees, breathing hard, and stared at his dead father, as though expecting him to rise.

"What's your name?" Hook demanded to know.

"Grizzly." His voice broke and tears filled his eyes.

"Grizzly, what happened to the Stone Wolf?"

"Why don't you ask her?" Grizzly responded, pointing at Twig's mother. "Her name is Riddle. She's the keeper of the Wolf Bundle."

Hook didn't deign to glance at Screech Owl or Riddle. He motioned for Chub to step back and knelt before Grizzly, staring hard into his terrified eyes. "Which lodge belonged to Riddle?"

Grizzly thrust out his arm to show where it was.

Hook looked up, and Chub said, "We searched it. We found nothing valuable in the ashes."

Hook turned back to Grizzly. "Where could it be if it wasn't in her lodge?"

Grizzly stared at his dead father, and tears streamed down his face. "M-Maybe Twig has it."

Greyhawk thought he was going to throw up.

"Twig?" Hook almost shouted. He looked excited. "The girl's name is Twig? Where is she?"

"I don't know. I—I saw her run away."

Hook rose to his feet and ordered, "Spotted Skull, take five warriors. Tell our men they are hunting for a little girl. We'll finish the job here; then we'll join you in the search."

"Yes, Hook."

Greyhawk silently eased back into the shadows and, shaking badly, leaned against the cold rocks. Hook was splitting his forces. Greyhawk's father had told him a war chief should never do that unless he had a lot of warriors to spare. Greyhawk counted twenty-one Thornback raiders. With six gone, that left fifteen. If only his father were here. . . .

Yipper stood up and nosed Greyhawk's arm. He didn't seem to be breathing, just waiting for a command.

Greyhawk let out a shaky breath. He had to find Twig before the raiders did. He'd known Twig all his life. He knew her favorite hiding places. He could find her—but how could he get away and start looking without the raiders seeing him?

Greyhawk motioned for Yipper to follow and crawled along in the shadows of the boulders, with Yipper at his heels. Pure black, Yipper blended with the darkness.

When Greyhawk had only ten paces left to reach the eastern ridge, he saw the gap in the defensive wall. He had to cross there, but he would be in full view of the raiders if he did.

"Oh, Yipper," he whispered. "We're in trouble."

Yipper cocked his ears. He knew that tone of voice; it meant he should be afraid, and he understood perfectly. He went stone still.

Greyhawk got down flat on his stomach and motioned for Yipper to do the same. Side by side, they slid across the ground on their bellies until they reached the gap. It was about as long as Greyhawk was tall. If he could just . . .

"Did you think you could escape?" a man roared from behind him.

Greyhawk spun around. The raider had his war club up, ready to swing it at Greyhawk's head.

Greyhawk opened his mouth to scream . . . just as Yipper sprang out of the darkness, knocked the raider to the ground, and leaped for the man's throat. When he clamped his powerful jaws around the man's neck, a horrifying blend of snarls and screams erupted.

Greyhawk lunged into the darkness and ran with all his might.

Hook spun and shouted, "Netsink?"

Two warriors charged out to help their friend, and the sounds of clubs striking flesh rose. Yipper's snarls turned into shrieks of pain, then suddenly stopped.

Hook must have seen Greyhawk. He shouted, *"There's a boy! Catch him!"*

CHAPTER 33

THE MOONLIGHT WAS bright enough that every pebble cast a shadow across the tundra.

Which didn't help Greyhawk where he hid in the crevice in the rocks. Every time he even thought about crawling out and running, he was clearly visible.

Twenty paces away, two raiders searched the rocks for him. Both men carried quivers filled with spears over their shoulders, and atlatls in their hands.

"I saw the brat come this way," the tall warrior said. As he moved, he was little more than a black shape.

"Maybe, but we're never going to find him in the darkness, Copper Falcon," the shorter man replied. "We've been blundering around for three hands of time. We should wait until morning and then track him down. He's a boy. We'll catch him quick once we can see his tracks."

Copper Falcon stopped and stretched his tired back muscles. "Yes, and if I were war chief, that is the order I would have given. But I am only Hook's deputy. I can't disobey his orders, and he ordered us to catch the boy. So we keep hunting."

The short man flapped his arms in irritation. "But we're accomplishing nothing. We're probably just getting farther and farther from the boy's trail. When dawn comes, we'll have to go right back to the village and start over again at the place where his trail begins."

"Well, if we have to go back, at least we'll be able to steal something for our trouble."

Catfish heaved an annoyed sigh. "I wish we'd been assigned to the party hunting for the girl. If we could get our hands on that Stone Wolf first, we'd be heroes."

"I've been thinking about that."

"You have?"

"Of course." Copper Falcon continued in a low voice, as though he feared someone might overhear him, "If we could get our hands on that Wolf, we could run straight home and personally present it to Chief Nightcrow. He would be very grateful."

"Maybe grateful enough to make you war chief?"

Copper Falcon smiled, and his teeth glinted in the moonlight. "Maybe."

Catfish chuckled. "You are an ambitious man, did you

know that? Don't forget that Shrike will object. He's been one of Hook's deputies longer than you have."

"I'm not greedy, just hungry for power that should have been mine two summers ago. I don't know why Nightcrow picked Hook over me, but it was an idiotic choice. As for Shrike, he'll have to fight me for the right."

Catfish lowered a hand to his belly and rubbed it. "Speaking of hunger, I'm hungry, too, but not for power. We haven't eaten since yesterday morning. I'm starving, aren't you?"

Copper Falcon nodded. "My stomach is so empty it feels like a hole goes all the way through me."

Copper Falcon walked to the crest of the ridge and peered down across the starlit tundra. A short distance away, a giant sloth, the size of a buffalo, snuffled the tundra while it used its huge claws to dig for roots. Covered with coarse, shaggy hair, the slow-moving animal made an easy target for supper.

Copper Falcon said, "Let's kill that sloth and fill our bellies before we continue. We'll both be happier."

"Now you're making sense." The short warrior drew a spear from his quiver and nocked it in his atlatl.

They both crept out of the rocks and began circling around, hunting the sloth.

Greyhawk waited until all of their attention was focused on the sloth; then he edged out of the rocks and sneaked away, heading in the opposite direction.

CHAPTER 34

AS NIGHT DEEPENED, the rumbling moans of the Ice Giants grew so loud the ground quaked beneath Twig's feet. She shivered, and tried to stop crying. For most of the night, she'd lain curled on her side in this willow thicket, with her head pillowed on her arm, watching the trails below. Moon Maiden cast a silver glow over the night.

"Oh, Screech Owl. Where are you? Are you coming to find me?"

Maybe he was dead. Maybe they were all dead, and she was alone.

Twig covered her mouth with her hands and sobbed.

All her life, whenever Mother had shouted at her, she'd come to hide in this thicket until the hurt went away. Tonight, she would have given anything to know her mother was alive and angry with her at home in their lodge.

"Mother? Please be alive, please?"

She tucked the edges of Screech Owl's green shirt around her toes. Her teeth had been chattering all night. She was tired . . . so very tired. It took great effort to stay awake, to keep watch on the trails.

"Eagle-Man!" she called desperately to her Spirit Helper. "Help me stay awake. I have to wait for Screech Owl or Mother. They might not see me here. I have to stay awake."

Her voice faded as though the wind had sucked it away and blown it up to the Star People. Twig fought the heaviness of her eyes, but weariness overcame her, and sleep finally numbed her body and began to coil around her thoughts.

She was almost asleep when a sudden spot of warmth grew in the middle of her chest, the place where the Stone Wolf rested.

Faintly, a voice whispered, *"No one wants to be a dreamer, Twig. But someone must be. . . ."*

The hiss of a moccasin against stone brought Twig scrambling up in the darkness, crying, "Who—who's there?"

"Twig? Twig, it's me!"

Greyhawk slowly made his way through the willows and crouched beside her. His black hair was filled with sticks and old leaves, as though he'd been crawling through brush all night.

"Greyhawk," she panted. "Where did you come from? I'm so glad to see you."

"I've been searching for you since the attack. We have to get out of here. There are raiders right behind me, and they're searching for both of us."

She rubbed the back of her neck, trying to wake up. "What do you mean . . . both of us?"

"The raiders are after you and the Stone Wolf. They won't give up until they find you."

Twig rose to her feet. Her knees were knocking. "Why do they think I have it?"

"It's a long story. I'll tell you as we run."

Twig blinked. "Where's Yipper?"

Greyhawk's eyes filled with tears. "I—I don't know. He may be dead. He tried to protect me when a raider found me."

"The raiders found you?"

"Yes, just outside the village. A big man was going to club me, and Yipper jumped on him and knocked him down. I—I ran." A sob caught in his throat. He looked away. "I should have stayed, Twig! I shouldn't have left Yipper to fight the warriors alone!"

Grief made Twig's entire chest ache, but she put a hand on his shoulder. "Greyhawk, look at me." He swallowed hard and turned to face her. "Yipper wanted you to run. He was trying to give you time to get away. And he did. You're alive because of him. That's what he wanted. He loved you."

Tears silently ran down his cheeks. "I know."

"Besides . . . I'm sure he got away. He's probably sniffing out your trail right now."

Hope slackened Greyhawk's face. "Do you think so? Really?"

"Yes. You know how fast he is. He can outrun the wind."

Greyhawk blinked back his tears. "He is fast. Do you remember that time he outran the pack of wolves that were chasing him?"

"I remember. Compared to wolves, outrunning warriors would have been easy. He got away, Greyhawk. He's alive."

That seemed to make him feel better. Greyhawk wiped his eyes on his sleeve and swallowed hard. He looked around at the night before he asked, "Twig, where should we go? We have to find a place to hide!"

"We can't hide. We have to go west."

"West? Why?"

She turned to stare at the shining slope of ice that ran down to meet the land in the distance. "Because that's where Cobia's cave is."

Wild with fear, Greyhawk hissed, "Twig, we can't go after Cobia! Our village was just attacked! We have to find a place to hide, and then we have to find our families to make sure they're all right!"

Twig took a moment to steady her nerves before she

said, "Greyhawk, I—I think my dream is coming true. The attack on our village . . . I saw the flaming spears days ago. If my dream is coming true, we *must* find Cobia. Every Spirit Helper I've ever talked to told me that she's the only one who can truly save our families."

"But the raiders will track us!"

Twig shivered violently before she managed to control it. "Greyhawk? How long will it take us to get to Cobia's cave?"

"I don't know for sure. Puffer said that if she left early in the morning, she would be back to Buffalobeard Village by nightfall—if her scouting party ran the entire way."

"That means it will probably take us around twenty-four hands of time. We can go hungry for that long, and we can eat ice for water. We can do this, Greyhawk. Come on."

One step at a time, she forced her feet to walk toward the lakeshore trail.

Greyhawk glanced around at the darkness before he ran to follow her.

CHAPTER 35

SCREECH OWL SAT beside Riddle, watching the ten raiders that Hook had left to "finish the job." The men were taking turns smacking the wounded in the heads with their war clubs while they searched the smoking lodges, stealing anything of value they could find. Chub trotted back with a polished conch shell necklace that had belonged to Chief Gill's wife. The shell had been traded from the far southern ocean. It was rare and beautiful.

"Look what I found!" he announced, and grinned as he held it up.

The tall warrior, Shrike, reached out and ripped it

from his fist. "Very nice. I appreciate the gift." He slipped the necklace over his head, and chuckled at the surprised expression on Chub's face.

Chub shouted, "That's mine! Give it back, or I'll bash your brains out." He reached for his war club, but not fast enough.

Shrike lashed out with his atlatl, slammed it into Chub's hand, and bone snapped loudly as the raider dropped to his knees, yelling in pain. Chub's left thumb stuck out at an odd angle.

"You broke my hand!" he shouted at Shrike.

Shrike laughed. "Get up. Let's kill these prisoners and go find War Chief Hook. He's probably already captured the girl and is headed home. Besides, we've stolen enough to last us moons."

Screech Owl bent down and whispered in Riddle's ear, "Get ready to run."

Her eyes went wide. "What are you going to do?"

"Try to stall them long enough for you and the others to get away."

As he started to stand, Riddle grabbed his arm and hissed, "No, Screech Owl, don't—"

Shrike said, "What are you doing, old man? Sit down!"

Screech Owl grinned. "Well, I will if you want me to, but I think I know where the Stone Wolf is hidden." He cautiously lifted a hand to point to the rocky ridge east of the village. "There's a little hollow where Chief Gill used to hide precious things."

Shrike turned to look at the ridge, and Screech Owl

readied himself to leap, but hesitated when he glimpsed movement among the rocks. There was something out there. Maybe . . .

Shrill war cries erupted from the rocks, and Elder Halfmoon charged out wildly swinging his war club, as though he couldn't quite see the raiders. Fifteen warriors followed him, including Searobin, who shouted at the captives, "Go on, run! Run!"

The captives went crazy. Women grabbed children by the hands, careened to their feet, and dashed away into the darkness, while Screech Owl and the other men leaped for discarded spears and raced to join the fight.

CHAPTER 36

TWIG AND GREYHAWK watched Father Sun's crimson face rise over the Ice Giants. The ice and snow blazed, turning from pink to a brilliant orange as the ball of the sun slipped above the horizon. They had walked a long way during the night. Here, at this place, hundreds of black caves honeycombed the ice.

Greyhawk breathed, "Elder Halfmoon says that these caves twist back into the ice forever. He once tried to follow out the tunnels to find Cobia, but he got lost over and over again. Many of the tunnels connect far back in the ice, but there are lots of dead ends."

"He never found Cobia?" Twig asked.

Greyhawk shook his head.

Twig said, "No wonder he didn't want to take me. His eyes are even worse today. He was probably afraid of getting lost and never being able to find his way out again."

Greyhawk looked around. "Do you remember Elder Halfmoon telling Puffer that she would have to pass Oakbeam Village to find Hoarfrost Canyon?"

"Yes. But I don't know how to get there. Do you?"

Greyhawk studied the land. "Maybe."

Twig followed his gaze. To the west, the Ice Giants rose like shining white cliffs. They'd been squealing and groaning even more than usual. It was as though they knew something she didn't, and were trying to warn her.

"We should try to find Oakbeam Village first," she said.

Greyhawk frowned; then he pointed with his atlatl. "Oakbeam Village is that way. I think. But I'm telling you, we should *not* go there! We should go back and find our families first. If we just had my father here, and your grandfather, we could find her cave and everything would be all right!"

With a confidence she didn't feel, Twig pulled her shoulders back and said, "I'm older than you, Greyhawk. I know what's best for us. I promise I'm not leading you to your death."

A hard swallow went down Greyhawk's throat. "Why did you say that? Did you dream my death? Or . . . our deaths?"

"Do you think I'd be leading us out here if I thought we were both going to die?"

Greyhawk glowered at her as though he feared she might . . . but when she started walking, he followed her down to the trail that skirted the ice caves.

Silver veils of fog blew in off the lake. They clutched at her with cold, transparent fingers.

Twig filled her lungs with the scents of water and damp earth, and when she exhaled, her breath frosted in the morning air. She saw nothing now, except fog. But the Stone Wolf resting over her heart had grown warm and heavy. Its weight seemed to be pulling her forward.

She stopped and stared down at the Wolf.

Greyhawk said, "What are you staring at?"

"The Wolf. It's getting heavier and heavier. I swear it feels like a lump of granite ten times this size." She pulled the Wolf from her shirt. "Feel this."

Greyhawk reached out and grabbed the Wolf by the thong. The Wolf swung just beneath his fingers. "It *is* heavy! Why?"

"I . . . I think it knows how to find Cobia."

He dropped the Wolf and backed away, but his eyes remained glued to the shining obsidian Wolf. "What makes you think that?"

"The weight of the stone is tugging at my neck, pulling me along."

"Pulling you?"

"Yes, pulling me west."

Greyhawk looked to the west, toward the massive glacier cliffs that glittered as though sprinkled with stardust. "Toward Oakbeam Village?"

"I think so." She rubbed the back of her neck where it hurt. The Wolf had grown so heavy, the thong was cutting into her skin.

Greyhawk said, "Do you want me to carry it for a while?"

"No, I think that right now I need to. But thanks for offering. If it gets too heavy, I'll let you."

Whispering, he asked, "Has it talked to you?"

She put her hand over the Wolf. It warmed her cold fingers. "No, it's been very quiet. I don't think it needs to tell me where we're going. It's showing me the path."

He glanced at the Stone Wolf again. "Then you should lead."

Twig nodded and led the way out into a field of eerie ice pillars ten times the height of a man and half as wide. There were hundreds of them. As they moved between them, following the streams of water that cut twisting trails around the pillars, she felt like she was walking through a forest of tree trunks made of solid ice. Carved by the wind and water, some of the pillars seemed to have sculpted faces. The tallest pillar to her right was speckled with gravel and coated with windblown dirt. When Twig looked at the top, she swore she saw a straggly mop of hair and a man's twisted face, his mouth open in a hideous cry.

She shuddered. "I don't like this place, Greyhawk. Let's hurry and get through it."

Greyhawk was looking around, as though he felt it

too—that strange sensation that they were being watched by something not quite human. "I'm hurrying," he said.

They weaved through the forest of pillars, moving so fast that when they entered the narrow ice canyon, barely two body-lengths wide, they almost stumbled over the first human skeleton.

"Twig!" Greyhawk shouted as he stopped dead in his tracks.

She bumped into him, breathing hard.

The mangled bodies had long since been eaten. Only the bones remained, adorned with shreds of clothing that were scattered among the pillars, along with several discarded weapons.

Twig said, "Who are they?"

Greyhawk's eyes focused instantly on an atlatl, and he ran to pick it up. Red, black, and white designs encircled the shaft. "I think this is War Chief Puffer's atlatl."

"Are you sure?"

"Yes." She was my clan, Smoky Shrew Clan. I used to watch her practice all day long, hoping that one day I could cast my spear as far as she could. I swear this is hers."

Twig said, "Then . . . this is our war party?"

"It must be."

Greyhawk wandered around for a while, collecting spears while he studied the tracks that marked the snow, both human and animal. Finally, he said, "A bear's been at them. That's why the bones are broken and scattered everywhere."

Twig rubbed her icy arms. "This must be where they were ambushed."

"Yes." He stared at Twig, and fear lit his eyes. "If we're smart, we'll get out of here before anyone has a chance to ambush us."

Twig grabbed a spear from the ground and sprinted up the trail. In the distance, she could see the lake again, shining blue, though the shore was still mounded with boulders and dirty ice.

When they rounded the next bend, they left the ice pillars behind, but a low ridge of boulders snaked along the ground to the right. They slowed down, feeling relieved to be out of the strange pillars.

Until they heard a snuffle.

Twig's heart thundered when Grandfather Brown Bear lumbered from behind a boulder and onto the trail in front of them.

"Oh, no," Twig gasped, and stumbled backward.

The bear saw them, and stood on his hind legs to sniff the breeze. The wind was blowing right up their backs, blowing their scents to him. He was three times their height, and when he dropped to all fours again, his massive head seemed too big to be real. A low growl came up the bear's throat.

"He's getting ready to charge," Greyhawk said.

Twig felt faint.

Greyhawk grabbed her by the back of the coat and dragged her behind a boulder.

"Greyhawk," she said in a voice that sounded too high-pitched to be her own voice. "What are we—"

"Quiet!" Greyhawk leaned very close to her ear and whispered, "Follow me. I—I can do this. Father taught me how to do this. Stay close to me!"

CHAPTER 37

GREYHAWK BENT LOW and sneaked around until he found a game trail that led up over the boulder ridge. "Twig, do what I do."

Twig bent low—as he had—and followed him up the trail. When they reached the top, Greyhawk peered over the edge at the bear thirty hands below them. The huge predator had his nose to the ground. He was tracking them. It wouldn't be long until he climbed right up the game trail and found them.

Greyhawk whispered to Twig, "We have to circle around to get upwind from the bear so he can't smell us."

"Do you think we can shake him?"

"I don't know, but if he finds us, don't run. He's much faster than we are. He'll have us down with our heads ripped off in a few heartbeats. Start looking for a place to hide. A place deep enough that he can't reach in with his paw and pull us out."

Twig spun around, searched the rocks, and pointed. "What about that rock shelter? Is it big enough for both of us?"

They ran to look. The shelter, made from three boulders that had toppled together, was deep, but narrow. They'd have to crawl in on their bellies and lie flat.

"You go in, Twig. I'm going to wait, to see if the bear is still following us."

As Twig slid beneath the boulders and into the darkness, she said, "Come on, Greyhawk. It's big enough for both of us."

He answered, "Push as far back as you can, so I'll have space."

Greyhawk knelt and watched Twig slide to the very back of the shelter with her spear clutched in her fist. It was just as he'd suspected. The rock shelter wasn't deep enough for two of them to hide out of the bear's reach. If he crawled in there with her, the bear would just reach in, sink his claws into Greyhawk's flesh, and pull him out.

He rose on shaky legs and wilted against the boulder, trying to force himself to think. He had to remember every lesson he'd ever learned. He glanced down at his atlatl and four spears. His aim was pretty good, but he wasn't very strong. He'd have to get dangerously close to the bear.

He scanned the ridgetop. He could hear his father's voice echoing in his head: *How can you use the landscape to help you with your hunt?* A plan was forming somewhere inside him; he could see how the hunt might play out *if* he did everything right.

Greyhawk trotted to the opposite side of the trail and climbed up to the highest point in the boulders, twenty hands above the trail. The rock shelter where Twig hid was directly across from him.

Greyhawk nocked a spear in his atlatl and hunkered down in the rocks.

"Be Mountain Lion," he whispered to himself. "Watch. Wait."

You choose when to strike. Never let the enemy make the first move. But if he attacks before you're ready, you must—

The bear came up the trail. His massive shoulders rolled as he walked, sniffing out their trail with ease. Though he was a brown bear, his hair was tipped with silver, giving it a shimmer.

The bear suddenly lifted its huge head and scented the wind; then his gaze went directly to the rock shelter where Twig hid.

The bear snuffled as he lumbered toward it.

Greyhawk's throat went tight. He gripped his nocked atlatl hard, but his hand was shaking badly. Would he be able to cast accurately? He checked to make certain his other three spears were within reach.

The bear lowered his head and stared into the shelter. Twig didn't make a sound. The bear growled, and a white cloud of breath drifted away on the cold wind.

Greyhawk could imagine Twig lying inside, staring right into the shining eyes of the bear.

The bear reached into the shelter with his paw to find Twig. When he couldn't reach her, he got down on his belly and extended his arm as far as he could, trying to claw her out.

He must have come close. Twig let out a small cry of shock, which made the bear even more determined. He growled ferociously and scrambled around to stuff both paws and as much of his head as he could into the opening. In the process, he turned sideways.

Greyhawk rose on trembling legs and focused all of his attention on the place right behind the bear's shoulder where the heart rested. He threw his spear with every ounce of strength in his panicked muscles. He cast so hard that the motion of the throw almost carried him over the edge of the boulders and sent him crashing down onto the trail beside the bear . . . but he caught himself just in time.

His spear sliced into the bear's side and went deep inside its chest. The bear roared and scrambled out of the rock shelter; then he spun around and around, ripping at the spear in his side, trying to tear it out.

Terrified and elated, Greyhawk forgot his father's most important lesson: *As soon as you cast, immediately nock another spear in your atlatl. . . .*

He remembered only when the bear saw him, let out a blood-tingling roar, and charged.

Greyhawk reached for another spear, and fumbled to get it nocked as the bear leaped up the boulders as though they were mere stepping stones. He cast again and missed, and quickly nocked another spear. In less than five heartbeats, Grandfather Brown Bear was standing right in front of Greyhawk, with bloody breath blowing from his nostrils and blood dripping from his side.

"Don't run, don't run, *don't run*," Greyhawk hissed to himself as he drew back his atlatl and took aim.

"Grandfather," he prayed, "please, please, let me kill you. Our families are dying. We have to find Cobia."

Grandfather Brown Bear cocked his head, as though listening to Greyhawk's voice. . . . Then he bounded forward with his huge jaws open to crush Greyhawk's skull.

Greyhawk cast his spear and, by instinct, threw himself aside, rolling away as the bear's strong jaws snapped for his leg. When the bear missed, he swiped out with a paw bigger than Greyhawk's head, and gleaming claws ripped into Greyhawk's left arm. The pain was so stunning, it left Greyhawk breathless.

Forgetting every lesson he knew, Greyhawk lunged to his feet and ran.

The bear was right behind him, roaring. The bloody spear in its front shoulder, Greyhawk's last cast, flopped with every bound.

When Greyhawk could feel Bear's hot breath on the

back of his neck, he jumped headfirst over the edge of the ridge and tumbled down the slope like a thrown rock. His head bashed every boulder on the way down.

He landed facedown at the bottom, dazed. For a moment, he didn't know where he was. He crawled to his hands and knees and looked around. He didn't recognize this place. Where was . . . ?

"*Greyhawk!*" Twig screamed.

He scrambled up to look at her.

Halfway down the slope, the bear had collapsed on his side; his strained breathing was like a tearing sound on the wind. Twig stood two paces away with a spear in her hand, ready if the bear stood up again.

"Are you all right?" Twig called.

"Yes," he said, and climbed the slope, taking gulps of the cold air. Blood trickled down his face from his wounded head, and his arm burned as though afire. "At least, I'm alive."

"Thank the Spirits," Twig said when he got close. "When I saw you at the bottom of the slope, I thought . . . You're bleeding! Are you hurt?" She ran to him.

Greyhawk sank down atop a rock five paces from the dying animal. Frozen puffs of breath still escaped the bear's jaws, but the soul was going out of his wide eyes. Greyhawk's first spear had gone true. It must have pierced the bear's heart.

Twig knelt by Greyhawk's side, looked at his head wounds, and pulled back the blood-soaked shreds of his shirt to examine his wound. Her pretty face tensed. "The bear's claws sliced deep, Greyhawk. I'm going to have to bandage this."

The bear's legs trembled in sudden weakness, then pawed the air for a few moments before going still. Finally, his huge mouth lolled open, revealing sharp teeth longer than Greyhawk's hand.

Greyhawk's eyes silently traced the lines of Bear's huge body, noting his two spears. He had killed a bear. By the laws of his clan, he had just become a man.

If his father was alive, he would be proud.

Greyhawk exhaled hard. His arm had started to hurt badly, and his muscles felt like boiled grass stems, but they had to keep going. He shoved to his feet. "Let's cut some strips of bear meat and get out of here, Twig. The raiders are still after us. I know they are."

"First, I need to bandage your arm. Stay here. I'll run back to the ambush site and collect some strips of clothing from our dead warriors. After I'm done, I'll cut the strips of meat; then we'll go."

He gratefully sat down again. His head had begun to throb. Through swimming eyes, he watched Twig trot away down the trail.

CHAPTER 38

BY AFTERNOON, THEY knew they were being hunted. Fresh tracks marked the muddy trail, both in front and behind them. Greyhawk knew because he'd sneaked back down the trail to check. There were two war parties searching for them.

He readjusted his bandaged arm. It hurt badly. If he'd been at home, he would have gone to Twig's mother, and she would have placed a willow-bark poultice on the wound. By now, the intense pain would have eased, and he'd be able to breathe. Instead, every time he filled his lungs, the gashes in his arm lanced him with fiery agony.

He turned and gazed to the south. Just beyond the

tundra, vast forests whiskered the land. He looked at them longingly. In the autumn, his village moved south to harvest the pecans, walnuts, and hazelnuts. He loved the forests best of all. Would he ever live there again?

"More tracks," Twig said.

Greyhawk turned and saw her kneel in the trail ahead. He walked up and crouched to examine the new moccasin prints. The Thornback People made their moccasins differently than the People of the Dawnland. The raiders' moccasins had a seam down the middle of the sole that left a clear imprint in the mud.

Twig nervously licked her lips. Wind Woman fluttered long black hair around her face. "What do you think? Should we go back? Maybe wait until tomorrow, and find another trail?"

"No." Greyhawk rose to his feet, and his bandaged arm screamed in pain. He'd heard the big Thornback warrior's voice. His leader, Nightcrow, wanted the Stone Wolf and Twig. He had ordered his men to find them, no matter the cost. They wouldn't stop hunting Twig until they found her. "No, we keep going."

Fear glittered in Twig's eyes. "Are you sure?"

Softly, he said, "I'm scared, too, Twig. But I believe in your dream. We have to find Cobia. It's the only way to save our people."

"You mean, if any of them are still alive." A sob caught in her throat.

Greyhawk gripped his nocked atlatl in his right fist. She must be seeing in her mind the dead bodies of her mother, and Screech Owl, and her grandfather. Must be imagining them lying in the charred remains of their village.

He knew, because every moment since he'd escaped, he'd been imagining the same thing. One instant he saw his father alive and smiling at him, and the next instant he saw his father sprawled facedown in the ashes of Buffalobeard Village. The worst images were of Yipper. If the raiders had killed him, they would have eaten him, and the only thing Greyhawk would find when he got home was Yipper's bones. The thought was almost too much to bear. Yipper had saved him, not just the night of the attack, but every day. He couldn't even remember a time when Yipper was not there beside him, as loyal as his own shadow, fighting for Greyhawk without ever asking for anything in return. Except maybe an occasional pat on the head, or a scratch behind the ear. His throat tightened with grief.

He swallowed hard to push it away and said, "Some of our relatives lived, Twig."

"How do you know?"

"My father once told me that someone always lives through a battle. He said I should remember that, because when I went on my first battle-walk the survivors would hate me and hunt me forever for killing their loved ones."

"Why did he tell you that?"

"He didn't want me to feel proud of killing. He told me it was always bad, just sometimes necessary to protect our people."

Twig dipped three handfuls of water from a puddle and drank them; then she stood up. "We're both tired. We should eat."

"We can't build a fire to cook, or the smoke will lead the raiders right to us."

"That's all right. Bear meat is good raw."

She reached into her belt pouch and drew out several strips of the rich red meat. She gave some to Greyhawk.

"Let's sit down," he said. "We should rest for as long as we can."

"Even with the raiders so close?"

"Yes, Twig. If we don't rest, we'll be too tired to think, and if we can't think, they *will* catch us."

She sat down, and he sat beside her. They chewed the meat in silence, both studying the trails, looking for their enemies.

The meat was tender and sweet. With each bite, Greyhawk felt strength flowing back into his exhausted body.

"I've been thinking about Cobia," Twig said.

Greyhawk looked at her. "So have I. Every spare moment when I'm not afraid the raiders will kill us, I'm afraid she will."

Twig took another bite of meat and ate it. "I was wondering how I would feel if I'd watched my mother killed, then been kidnapped and hauled far away to be raised by my enemies."

"I know how I'd feel. I'd hate them."

"Even if they'd been good to you? Even if you'd been

kidnapped as a baby and your enemies were the only family you had ever known?"

Greyhawk considered that. "I guess if I didn't remember my real family, and my enemies loved me, I'd probably love them back."

"So would I." Twig started to eat another bite of meat, but stopped. "At least until I found out the truth. Then I think I'd be lost and confused."

"Would you? I'd be scared."

"Why?"

"Because if they'd killed my family, they could kill me, too."

Twig propped her strip of bear meat on her knee and seemed to be watching the ice crystals that blew off the glaciers in the distance. The air sparkled.

"Do you think Cobia was scared? Is that why she left Buffalobeard Village?"

He shrugged. "Maybe."

Wind Woman gusted across the tundra and tugged at Greyhawk's shirt. He reached up to hold his collar closed while he ate his last bite of bear meat.

Twig finished eating and heaved a deep sigh. "Do you think we should try to sleep for a while?"

Greyhawk shoved to his feet and looked up and down the trail. He saw only a herd of buffalo grazing to the southwest, and a few caribou scattered along the lakeshore.

"You try to sleep, Twig. I'll stand guard."

"But you're as tired as I am."

"We'll switch off. Next time I'll sleep while you stand guard."

She thought about it for what seemed like a long time, then said, "Don't let me sleep for more than a quarter hand of time."

Greyhawk nodded, and Twig curled up on her side on the ground. She was so tired, she fell asleep almost immediately. He watched her face go from being taut and anxious to the peaceful relaxation of deep sleep.

Greyhawk walked a short distance away and climbed on top of a boulder. It was as tall as he was. He could see much farther from up here. He wished they could go back in time, to the days before. . . .

The Ice Giants growled and the ground shook. Out in the lake, a huge wall of ice broke away from the glacier and crashed into the water. A splash shot high into the air; then the iceberg dipped and rocked until it settled down. The other icebergs seemed afraid of the new one. They drifted away from it.

The ground shook harder, and the Ice Giants groaned loud enough and long enough to terrify him. He glanced down at Twig. She did not wake up.

Finally, the earthquake stopped, and Greyhawk brought up his knees and propped his injured arm on them, where it hurt a little less; then he concentrated on the trails. There were raiders out there, very close, looking everywhere for them. He had to pay attention.

Barely five hundred heartbeats later, he glimpsed black specks on the eastern trail.

Greyhawk flattened out on his belly and watched them. Were they animals? Or warriors?

Very soon, he knew the answer. The long spears they carried in their quivers swayed as they trotted.

He scrambled down off the boulder and ran for Twig. When he saw her, he whispered, "Twig? Twig, we have to go! There are raiders coming!"

She gasped and staggered to her feet, still half-asleep. "Go on! I'll follow you."

Greyhawk charged for the trail that led south into the forests.

CHAPTER 39

GREYHAWK'S WOUNDED ARM screamed in agony, but he couldn't slow down. If the raiders hadn't already seen them, they probably would the instant Greyhawk and Twig trotted to the high point in the trail, just ahead.

Greyhawk leaped an ice-rimmed puddle and sprinted up and over the high spot, then hurled himself down the other side, getting out of sight as fast as he could.

Twig was right on his heels. He could hear her moccasins pounding the ground.

When they reached the low spot, Greyhawk dared to

turn around and look. Twig's pretty face was flushed, and she was breathing hard.

"Are we safe?" she asked. "Did they see us?"

"Probably. We should act as if they did. Come on. If we run flat-out, we'll be to the trees in less than one-half hand of time."

When they entered the dark shadows of the forest, the temperature dropped, and their breath froze into white puffs. Snow glistened in the hollows.

Every wet scent of the forest smelled incredibly clear to Greyhawk, as if it had soaked into his body and was being carried through his veins. The sweetness of the pines mixed with the bitter tang of rotting oak leaves and the earthiness of melting snow.

"Greyhawk?" Twig called in a low voice. "Let's find a place to hide, and wait to see if we're being followed."

"Let's get deeper into the forest first."

He found a game trail covered with deer tracks and trotted forward.

The deeper into the forest they ran, the taller and thicker the trees grew. He glanced up. High above, the branches of the freshly leafed-out oaks created a dense weave that blocked most of the sunlight, leaving the forest floor in shadow. Towering spruce and pine trees grew between the oaks; their tops seemed to pierce the clouds.

"I can't run anymore, Greyhawk," Twig panted. "Please, let's stop. Just for a little while."

"All right."

Cold wind gusted across his face as he looked around. A big pile of deadfall darkened the forest floor to his right. He veered off the trail and headed for it.

Over many tens of summers, trees had died and toppled over each other to form a tangled fortress of logs. Great crooked branches held the heavy trunks off the ground. Moss covered the smoke-colored bark. As he ducked low to examine the pile, it gave off a delicate fragrance. Animals had burrowed through the interior, creating a warren of tunnels. He saw wolf and bear droppings. A pure white snowshoe hare sat in the back, mostly hidden by the shadows, but his eyes gleamed.

Twig leaned over and said, "Can we hide here?"

"I think so. You go in and rest. I'll cover our tracks."

"No, I'll help you," she said, and started to turn back.

"Please, Twig, it will be easier if I'm only covering my own tracks when I come back."

"Oh." She nodded. "You're right."

As Twig got down on her knees and crawled into the cold darkness, the hare shot away through the tunnels and disappeared.

Greyhawk grabbed a handful of old leaves and began backing up, brushing away their tracks as he went. When he reached the game trail, he stood up and examined it. They had left clear prints in the snow and mud.

If they were being followed, the raiders would be able to track them right to this pile of deadfall.

He adjusted his wounded arm. It ached as though afire.

His father's voice seeped into his thoughts: *When you can't erase your trail, Son, cover it with whatever you can find.*

Greyhawk bent down and began scooping up old leaves and pine needles and dropping them onto their tracks. He tried to make it look natural, as though the debris had blown across the trail, not been dropped intentionally. Would it fool trained warriors?

He didn't know, but he couldn't think of anything else to do.

After a quarter hand of time, he straightened up. He had reached the edge of the trees, where they'd entered the forest. Their tracks continued up the wet trail. He didn't see any raiders, but just in case . . .

Greyhawk carefully stepped beyond the leaves where he'd covered their trail, then placed his feet into the last of his tracks and trotted off to the east, leaving a new trail for any pursuers to follow.

He skirted the edge of the forest, walked on fallen logs when he could, and climbed over rocks. If they were in a hurry, they wouldn't have time to backtrack him, and he hoped they would lose his trail altogether.

One thing he couldn't fake, however, and something they were sure to notice: two sets of tracks, his and Twig's, had made it to the edge of the trees, but only one set continued on. They would know that one of the children was hiding.

"Yes, but they're tired, too. I bet they'll take the easy way and chase after me, rather than go thrashing through the forest looking for Twig."

Greyhawk tiptoed across a narrow line of rocks and stepped into a trickle of water that flowed down another game trail. It would wash away his tracks in no time. But it was very cold!

Twenty paces ahead, a tall pine tree grew alongside the trail. The lower dead branches had been broken off by the animals that used the trail. They made a perfect ladder.

Greyhawk reached the tree and climbed it. He sat on a thick branch thirty hands off the ground and looked out across the land.

It didn't take long. He saw the two search parties run together at the fork in the trail. They stood talking for less than one hundred heartbeats and loped toward the forest.

"They found our trail."

His legs were shaking as he climbed down and jumped onto a fallen log.

For too long, he stood there panting like a hunted animal, trying to decide what to do.

There were two search parties now. He hadn't anticipated they would join up. It meant that the war chief would have the luxury of sending one group of warriors to track him down, and one to search for Twig.

The false trail he'd laid would slow them down . . . but it wouldn't stop them, not when they were this close.

He and Twig were going to have to make a run for it and pray they reached Cobia's cave before the raiders caught them.

With every ounce of strength he had left, he charged back through the forest for Twig.

WAR CHIEF HOOK stopped at the edge of the trees and examined the tracks. The other warriors gathered around him, murmuring as they pondered the situation.

The children's trail had been obvious, until now.

As he thought, Hook rubbed his square jaw. "Two children came in, but only one child—probably the boy from the size of the foot—veered off. So . . ." He looked up and scanned the forest. Dark shadows cloaked the interior. "The other child, the girl, is hiding."

Copper Falcon, his deputy, propped his hands on his hips. Sticky patches of blood splattered his black war shirt. He had his long black hair tied back with a cord. "Shall I pursue the boy or the girl?"

Hook considered. "Take ten warriors and follow the boy. I'll take the rest of our force and find the girl. Meet me back here in one hand of time."

Copper Falcon bowed at the waist. "Yes, War Chief."

As Copper Falcon went about selecting the warriors for his search party, Hook examined the ground. Water dripped from the tree branches and filled every hollow, including the leaf-covered game trail. He knelt. Before her trail disappeared, the toes of the girl's moccasins had been pointed straight onto the game trail. He carefully began removing leaves, one at a time, until he saw the covered tracks.

He smiled to himself. The boy had done a good job. One day, if he lived, he would make a fine warrior.

Unfortunately, it was Hook's job to make sure the boy did not live.

He rose to his feet, held up a fist to indicate silence, and motioned for his warriors to fan out on either side of the hidden game trail.

The boy's skill would cost them time. They would have to go slowly and carefully if they wanted to find the girl.

But, in the end, they would find both children.

CHAPTER 40

ALL DAY LONG they'd been hiding and running. Twig was so exhausted, she felt light-headed. And Greyhawk looked pale, and hurt. The pain in his wounded arm must be unbearable.

But at nightfall, Twig and Greyhawk found Oakbeam Village.

Empty. Burned to the ground.

"When did this happen?" she softly asked. "Can you tell?"

"Not long ago. Maybe yesterday. The fires are still burning."

Fog blew through the smoldering husks of lodges. Everywhere, wooden bowls and baskets tumbled in the wind. Many of the bodies lay just in front of burned lodges, as though the people had been killed the moment they'd ducked outside.

Twig felt suddenly cold. Her clan, the Blue Bear Clan, believed that the souls of the dead stayed in the village for three days before traveling to the Land of the Dead. Twig could feel them. Each time a burned lodge pole creaked in the wind, she thought she heard voices.

Greyhawk kicked at a broken atlatl. Then he picked up two spears that must have missed their targets and been forgotten in the raging battle.

"Where are their families?" Greyhawk asked. "They should have come back to bury the bodies."

"Maybe they're all dead."

They followed the trail through the smoke-blackened chaos and westward around the edges of the ice flow, where the fog was especially thick. It was like walking through a shimmering white blanket. Here, at this place, the glaciers flowed down and spread out across the land to form towering ice cliffs cut by deep cracks and fissures, and honeycombed with tunnels that seemed to go back into the ice forever.

"What's that?" Twig said, and blinked at the canyon that appeared and disappeared as the fog shifted.

Greyhawk stopped. "I—I don't know. Do you think it's Hoarfrost Canyon?"

The sheer walls rose fifty times their height, as though

the frozen waste had been split by a lightning bolt cast by Earthmaker himself.

Twig clenched her fists to keep them from trembling. "Grandfather said that the entry to Cobia's cave was at the end of Hoarfrost Canyon. Sh-should we go look?"

Greyhawk nocked a spear in Puffer's atlatl. "Yes."

Twig exhaled a long, frightened breath and walked out onto the sand and gravel that filled the bottom of the canyon.

The deeper they went, the more the canyon narrowed, as though it were funneling them in to some unknown darkness, and the walls grew steeper and taller. Twig glanced up. In less than two hundred paces, the ice cliffs had soared to one hundred times their height. Caves and tunnels of every size and shape sank into the walls. Twig tried not to look inside them, for fear of what she might see looking back.

The canyon was quiet and still. Twig stopped.

"What's the matter with you?" Greyhawk asked.

"Power is loose. Can't you feel it?"

Greyhawk looked at the birds darting over the high ice walls and said, "No. But I believe you."

"Oh, Greyhawk, I wish Mother was here, or Screech Owl."

"Well, they're not. We have to do this by ourselves."

Twig stopped, and the Stone Wolf radiated warmth against her chest, tugging her deeper into the canyon. "I—I'm going, Wolf," she murmured.

As they kept walking, the ice above them knitted into

a roof, and the canyon became a deep dark tunnel. The huge black maw gaped as though ready to swallow them.

"Don't tell me we have to go deeper into this tunnel," Greyhawk hissed. "We don't have a torch. How will we see?"

"I don't know, I—"

Twig gasped when black flits of cloth darted from the caves to her right and flew straight at them. All she could do was stare at the glowing eyes in their soot-covered faces.

Greyhawk cried, *"Thornback raiders! Run, Twig!"* and he cast his spear. *"I said, RUN!"*

Twig ran. But she'd barely taken four steps when a man tackled her from behind and knocked her to the ground. She smashed her head on a rock. The world started to spin. Above her, she saw the grinning face of the raider, then glimpsed Greyhawk racing toward her with his atlatl up. He cast his spear, and the big raider let out a cry, leaped up, and ran away with Greyhawk's spear sticking from his chest. Greyhawk cast two more spears, but missed.

Pain was swelling behind Twig's eyes like an enormous black bubble. She struggled to get to her feet, but kept falling back to the ground.

The next thing she knew, Greyhawk had grabbed her and was crawling, dragging her by the hand, into a narrow ice tunnel barely wide enough for a child's body to pass through. Inside, the ice had a strange shimmer. Greyhawk stretched out flat on his belly and pulled her deeper into the darkness. Twig tried to crane her neck to see how far back the tunnel ran, but it was black ahead. Utterly black. After dragging Twig about twenty paces, the tunnel grew wide enough for Greyhawk to sit up. He stopped and released her hand. Twig lifted her head to look back down the tunnel into the gray light of dusk.

A big raider tried to squeeze into the opening, but his shoulders were too wide. He cursed and backed out.

"Twig? Your head is bleeding. How badly are you hurt? *Answer me!*"

But she couldn't, because the world was spinning into darkness, spinning . . . and she felt so sick.

CHAPTER 41

SHAKING, GREYHAWK SAT beside Twig and studied her face. Her eyes were sunken in twin black circles, and her breathing was ragged.

"Are you all right, Twig?"

She winced as she turned her head for him, and in the faint light that penetrated the cave, he saw a mat of gore and blood.

"Oh, Twig," he whispered. "You have a bad head wound."

She stammered, "H-how long do we . . . how long before . . ."

"Before they find a way to reach us?"

She nodded. It was obviously hard for her to speak. "I don't know, Twig."

Twenty paces away, outside, the raiders shouted. Several more, smaller men, tried to crawl into the opening, but failed.

Greyhawk leaned back against the ice wall and let out a breath. His wounded arm was bleeding again. The tunnel continued to his right, utterly dark. He had no idea how far back into the ice it went; it might be a dead-end. But for the moment, they were safe.

"Greyhawk?"

"Yes?"

She looked at him with frightened eyes. "We're t-trapped. We're never going to be able to find Cobia's cave from in here."

"I know," he said, feeling utterly defeated. Sweat was freezing on his face, and every nerve in his body screamed at him to run. But there was nowhere to go.

They had come so far, braved so many perils, and all of it for nothing. It made him ache deep down. Maybe they should have given up and gone back when she'd . . .

"So . . ." Twig took a deep breath and squinted her eyes as she said, "I'm going to try to dream my way there."

He jerked around, astonished. "Can you do that?"

Sheer terror strained her face. "I don't know. I—I feel sick, shaky. If I fall into the river at the edge of the Land of the Dead, I may not be strong enough to swim out."

"Then maybe you should wait. Tomorrow, when you're stronger, then you—"

"*Boy!*" one of the raiders shouted into the tunnel.

Greyhawk froze. They had built a fire outside, and he could see the man's shining face. He had a thick bandage around his throat, soaked with blood.

The raider said, "I just wanted you to know that I killed your filthy dog. I clubbed him until his head was mush; then I cut out his heart and ate it for supper."

Greyhawk couldn't speak. Sobs spasmed his chest. He wanted to shout *You're lying!* but he feared it was true. The last time he'd turned to look back, he'd seen two warriors running to help Netsink, and each had carried a war club.

Twig said, "Don't listen to him, Greyhawk. You know how fast Yipper is. He ran. He got away."

"Y-yes, I know he did."

But he didn't.

"*And you, girl!*" the raider called again. "Hook killed your mother, Riddle, and who was that old man with her? Shrike slit his throat clear through to his spine."

A strange numbness seemed to filter through Twig, as though her soul were loose, and preparing to fly away. She kept opening her mouth, then closing it. Was she trying to speak?

Greyhawk slid closer to her. "He's lying. They're both alive, Twig. I know they are."

The raiders' shadows moved across the face of the

cave. Twig whispered, "I have to try now, Greyhawk. I have to try to dream."

"Can I help?"

She shook her head. "No. You're a warrior. I—I'm a dreamer."

With shaking hands, she tugged open the laces on her belt pouch and pulled out the tiny spruce branch from First Woman's tree. It looked black in the dim light. She had tears running down her cheeks.

Greyhawk said, "You can do it, Twig. I know you can."

She closed her eyes.

In an agonized voice, she started calling, "Eagle-Man, Eagle-Man, Eagle-Man . . ."

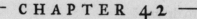

CHAPTER 42

"Eagle-Man, please, please, help me!"

In the middle of the night, Twig was on the verge of giving up. Her throat was raw from calling out to her Spirit Helper, and the pain in her injured head had grown to fill the entire world.

She stopped for a moment and gulped in deep breaths of the icy air.

Greyhawk had positioned himself in front of her, between Twig and the raiders outside, but she could see around him. The raiders had built a fire in the mouth of the cave. They were melting it out, making it larger. The fire's gleam turned the inside of the tunnel a gaudy orange. It wouldn't be long before they'd enlarged the cave enough for a man to crawl in after them.

Twig curled on her side on the floor of the cave and choked out, "Eagle-Man, please, hear me? I need you. I can't do this without—"

The Ice Giants suddenly let out a low, deep-throated growl, and the ground shook.

And from somewhere far, far away, a voice called her name. It kept speaking, but she couldn't really understand what it was saying. She closed her eyes and tried to concentrate. Something about Cobia . . . finding Cobia . . .

Then the Stone Wolf grew warm, almost hot, against her chest, and she clearly heard a boy say, *"It's through here. This way. This is the way, Twig."*

A strange glitter danced behind her closed eyelids. Like a swarm of blue fireflies.

"Twig?" Greyhawk called, but she could barely hear him. "What's happening?"

It was as though Twig's soul had stepped out of her body.

She found herself walking down a dark ice tunnel, alone and scared. She couldn't feel her feet or hands, but her heart was beating. She could hear it.

She walked. And walked.

There were ice mountains, and frozen creeks, and towering blue glaciers that leaned over her like monstrous beings.

After what seemed like days, the tunnel began to grow larger. She must be in the very heart of the Ice Giants, because their voices were deafeningly loud. The deeper she traveled, the larger the tunnel grew, until it became a shining blue cavern. There were ice spires everywhere, and she heard water lapping against a shore, as though a great ocean spread beneath the ice.

And . . . she thought she heard people chanting. The rhythm reminded her of the ghost chants her own people sang to drive away evil Spirits.

"Hello!" Twig shouted.

High-pitched squeals answered. They mixed with the chanting and echoed in a way that struck terror into Twig's heart.

"Hello! Who's there?"

The cavern seemed to close in around her, the ice walls bending down to peer at her more carefully. Twig shivered. This place was not beautiful, though she had the feeling that it was old, very old, and that living humans had never dared to tiptoe beyond the well-worn trails. To her left, tumbled piles of ice choked the floor, and wherever the blue light touched, the ice seemed alive, pulsing.

Twig turned around in a full circle. "Oh, Cobia, where are you? I'm scared. I don't know how to find you. Cobia?"

Sobs clutched at her chest as she started to run again, dashing down a dip in the trail and up the other side.

The chanting grew louder, and life stirred the depths of the cavern. But Twig did not think she knew this kind of life. Feet pounded—heavy, thrashing angrily in a dance that shook the trail.

Twig ran like the wind. Shadows moved at the edges of

the trail, some of them loping along beside her, keeping pace while they hissed their resentment at her presence.

"Cobia? Cobia, please!"

She rounded a bend, and one of the dancers leaped at her. He didn't have any arms or legs, just enormous black eyes and a protruding mouth shaped from pink pipestone. Colorful feathers adorned the dancer's costume.

"What do you want?" Twig asked.

The dancer dodged into a shadow. But Twig saw others moving nearby. Their masks glinted as they floated between the ice spires.

Twig ran on, racing down a winding trail, slowing only when the trail vanished. She couldn't see it anywhere. Which way should she go?

She decided to run straight ahead. Thirty paces later, the tunnel narrowed. If it shrank any more, she would be crawling on her hands and knees.

Suddenly she broke out of the tunnel and stepped into a huge washed-out cavern. High above her, Star People glittered. Trails led off in every direction. Ten or more!

Twig spun around, examining the path that dropped off down a long slope. Then she looked at the trail that climbed into another ice chamber above her.

From out of her memories, she heard a voice whisper, *"To step onto the path, you must leave it. Only the lost come to stand before the entrance to Cobia's cave."*

Tears blurred her eyes. She looked back down the trail. Even from this distance, she could see dark shapes moving. "But the only place without paths is that horrible cavern."

Twig clenched her fists, took a deep breath to fight her fear, and walked down, down through the small tunnel and into the cavern where there were no trails, where dark shadows watched in silence.

The chanting started again.

Twig shouted, "Eagle-Man?"

She waited.

For a while, she thought she might be all right.

Then the masked dancers returned and floated around her like a ring of wolves. She couldn't see them clearly. Just flashes of hideous red mouths, or of long beaks carved from pale wood. When she looked the hardest, the dancers vanished into twists of ice.

"Eagle-Man? Help me! Show me the way to Cobia's cave!"

The shadows went still. Twig jerked around, trying to figure out what they were doing. The strange chant had stopped, the cavern gone silent.

"Eagle-Man?"

Something glimmered to her right. It seemed a trick of starlight when the figure loomed up from the heart of the darkness and stepped toward her.

"I heard you, Dreamer."

Relief made Twig laugh. "Eagle-Man!" She ran to him, weaving between ice spires. "Thank you. I've been so lost, I . . ."

Eagle-Man lowered his head, and his beak opened, revealing sharp teeth. He shrieked like Hawk.

Then he spread his wings and dove at her.

CHAPTER 43

TWIG SCREAMED AS she ran headlong through the piles of tumbled ice.

Eagle-Man's feet thumped the ground behind Twig as he danced his pursuit, spinning and leaping, his wings outspread so that the feathers brushed the ground. The blue gleam coated his body until each feather shimmered like liquid turquoise.

She tripped, stumbled into a rock, and caught her balance. Her knees were trembling.

Shadows flicked through the broken chunks of ice. Every so often she caught sight of a mask, just a glimpse of jasper or shell beads.

Eagle-Man's steps echoed: thump-thump-thumpety-thump. Then they stopped.

Twig looked up and cried out in horror when she saw him perched on an icy ledge over her head. He had tucked in his wings and bent forward to peer down at her, like Vulture waiting for a wounded deer to die. His snakeskin belly glittered.

"Why are you hunting me?" Twig cried. "You are my Spirit Helper!"

"Yes," Eagle-Man hissed, sounding like a snake, "I am." His black eyes gleamed as he shifted on the ledge, stepping back and forth in a strange dance. Gravel cascaded from the ledge with each stamp of his feet.

Movement stirred the shadows, and six ghostly forms shuffled out from the narrow tunnel. Some wore bushy-headed masks of beautifully woven grass; others had animal masks, decorated with the upcurving horns of buffalo. The seashells on their leggings blazed in the light. Through the enormous sockets of their eyes, only blackness showed: empty, ominous, with no glint of life.

They closed in around her and began throwing spruce pollen at her. It netted her hair and stuck to her arms and legs.

"What are you doing?"

Spruce pollen purified and sanctified the way for power. But she did not understand why they were throwing it on her.

Finally, the dancers shuffled backward and opened their hands to Eagle-Man, who was circling near the cavern ceiling. He looked like a black dot.

"Will you give up, Twig? Or will you fly for your people?"

"I want to fly, Eagle-Man! I've always wanted to!"

Eagle-Man let out a cry of triumph and plummeted down, his sharp talons reaching for her.

Twig shrieked when he knocked her to the ground and clamped his talons around her chest, in the manner of Eagle catching Chipmunk.

"Eagle-Man, no! You're my Spirit . . . Helper." She coughed as the air went out of her lungs in a gush. Her arms and legs flailed weakly while his talons tightened, and she could hear her ribs cracking.

The chanting began again.

Eagle-Man lowered his head and stared into Twig's terrified eyes.

"This is the moment Screech Owl told you about. The moment when you must step into the mouth of the Spirit that wants to chew you up. Are you brave enough, Twig?"

A gray haze fluttered at the edge of Twig's vision.

In a bare whisper, she said, "Yes."

With a wrench, Eagle-Man sank his claws deeper into her flesh, and his huge beak dropped out of the gray to tear at her chest and arms. She felt her flesh being torn from her bones as he devoured her.

Twig gave a final gasp as Eagle-Man's beak opened and plunged for her eyes. The last of her body began sliding down his throat, into his stomach.

Then . . . darkness.

CHAPTER 44

A s THOUGH IN a dream, Twig sank into the pool
of blood and it began to sway, rocking her back
and forth. Her soul grew thinner and thinner,
blending with the blood until it melted into the blackness.
And from that nothingness came light.

As though Eagle-Man had opened his beak, a stream of
gold flooded down through an opening above. Twig reached
for the warmth, but her fingers were . . . different . . . like,
yes, like wings. Frail dreamer's wings strengthening, growing. She shook herself, and white bits of down fell away,
revealing brown-speckled feathers.

From deep in her throat, Prairie Falcon's shriek rose: *kree, kree, kree!*

Twig spread her wings and soared upward toward the opening, where she flew out into a vast blue sky. Cloud People twisted and tumbled in the high winds. Twig tested her wings, diving and sailing on the cold air currents, feeling the way that each feather affected her flight when she flapped or tilted her tail. Joy brought tears to her eyes. Such freedom!

As she glided over the Ice Giants, she saw a narrow rushing river below, and a woman sitting on an ice ledge on the other side. Lying in the woman's lap was a small medicine bundle decorated with a black raven.

The woman was looking up, watching Twig.

When Twig soared across the river and flew down to get a better look at her, the woman said, "So. You made it across the river into the Land of the Dead. I knew you would. You are strong."

Twig alighted on the ledge a short distance away. The woman was beautiful. Tall and willowy, long black hair framed her oval face. She had full lips and a turned-up nose with coal-black eyes.

"Are you Cobia?"

"I am, child." She wore a white mammoth-hide cape, and a huge bear claw pendant hung in the middle of her chest.

"Please, help us! We need your help to defeat the Thornback raiders. They're killing us!"

Cobia cocked her head. "You have braved great dangers, and therefore earned the right to talk. But I warn you, I'm not going back with you. *You* are their dreamer now."

"Please, Cobia! You have to. We need you!" Twig cried as she balanced on the ledge, thinking about Screech Owl and her mother . . . and about Greyhawk, who was bravely protecting her even now. They would die if Cobia didn't help them.

Sadness came over Cobia's beautiful face. She patted the ledge beside her. "Come here, child. Let me look at you. You're very young. Too young to have made this difficult journey to the Land of the Dead."

Twig spread her wings, lifted into the air, and softly landed less than four hands from Cobia.

"Yes," Cobia said. "I spend a great deal of time here, talking with my ancestors. Is Screech Owl your teacher?"

"Yes."

Love shone in Cobia's black eyes. She looked away and blinked. "Is he well?"

Tears choked Twig. "He and Mother were captured by the Thornback raiders after they destroyed Buffalobeard Village. Screech Owl may . . . may be dead."

Cobia slowly lifted her head. "When did this happen?"

Twig tried to think. "I'm not sure. I don't know how long I've been hunting for you. Time—"

"Yes, I know, time is different when you're on a Spirit journey. You may have been gone for moments, or moons. This could be the past, or the future. There's no way to know until you return to your world."

"We need you, Cobia. Screech Owl says you're the only person who can defeat the Thornback raiders. You have to help us."

Cobia gently stroked Twig's speckled brown feathers and whispered, "Did your Grandfather ever tell you why I hate him so?"

Twig blinked. "No."

Cobia smiled faintly. "He is the one who kept the truth from me. For many summers I spoke to every trader who came from the far west to Buffalobeard Village. I asked each one about the stories my people, the People of the Duskland, told about me. I was a magical child. Everyone knew my name. When your grandfather killed my mother and pulled me from her dead arms, my people saw it as a terrible sign. They believed they had been cursed by the gods. They tracked your grandfather and almost burned him to death in a cave where he ran to hide. But he escaped." Anger lined her face. "I learned the final details of the story just after I'd seen nineteen summers. That's when I left Buffalobeard Village. I vowed never to return, or to help the people who had killed my mother. Do you now understand why I will not go back with you? I knew you needed to grow wings—that's why I kept calling to you in your dreams. But you must save your people by yourself."

Twig was sobbing when she said, "You shouldn't blame us! You could have gone home after you found out what my people did to your mother. Why didn't you?"

Cobia drew her hand back and closed it to a fist.

"Because too much hope can kill as swiftly as a spear, young dreamer. I knew nothing about the People of the Duskland. They were my people by birth, but they were not the people I loved when I was growing up. They were strangers."

"So you decided it was better to be lonely for the rest of your life than to face your fears?"

Cobia's expression softened. She gave Twig a sad smile and petted her feathers again. "You surprise me."

"Why?"

"For just a moment, you became Truth."

"I don't understand."

Cobia frowned out at the icy wilderness that spread before them. "Truth is not in words, young dreamer, but in a reflection, an iridescence that causes us to suddenly turn and look. That's what you just did to me. You made me turn and look. At myself."

Twig cocked her head. "What did you see?"

"Darkness."

In the cavern far below, masks flashed and ghostly dancers whirled in time to music Twig could not hear. She watched them for a time before she said, "Cobia, please, help us. I know you hate my grandfather, but I didn't do those things to you, nor did my mother. And Screech Owl only tried to help you. He loves you. Won't you at least save him?"

Cobia hesitated. After what seemed an eternity, she stroked Twig's feathered head and said, "The Spirits never give us all the time we need. Your time here is over. You must return now. Greyhawk needs you. *Go back . . . before it's too late."*

Twig bowed her head and wept. She had failed. After all the lessons she had learned, all the terrible trials she had faced, Cobia was not going to help her. Sobs clutched at her chest. It was so cold that her tears froze as they fell, and tinkled like bells when they struck the ice. She whispered, "I'm sorry. I'm going."

She fluttered her wings and rose above the ice, where she hovered, looking down at the vast icy wilderness below. Then she soared south. . . .

— CHAPTER 45 —

A BIZARRE FLASH OF blue light filled the tunnel where Greyhawk sat. He spun around breathlessly, trying to see where it had come from, but the ice cave had turned orange again.

"Once we've eaten," a raider outside said, "we'll pile the last coals from our fires in the tunnel. It won't take long to finish melting out that stubborn patch of ice. Then we'll go in after the brats."

Greyhawk forced a swallow down his throat. The night was very dark, and the raiders' fire cast odd flickering shadows over the tunnel. The wonderful scent of roasted venison kept blowing in, making Greyhawk's empty stomach growl.

A man leaned down and peered into the tunnel. "I want to be the one to go in," he said, and it sounded like Netsink, the man who had attacked him in Buffalobeard Village. "I can't wait to get my hands around the boy's throat."

Greyhawk shivered. No matter what, he wasn't going to leave Twig. When the raider started in, Greyhawk would drag Twig as far as he could. After that, maybe he could fight his way out, then lead the raiders away from the cave long enough for Twig to escape.

The warriors would probably hunt him down, but . . .

Twig let out a breath, and Greyhawk jumped.

Softly, he called, "Twig? Can you hear me? It's Greyhawk."

Cruel laughter rose outside.

Raiders started carrying bowls of coals and dumping them in the tunnel less than ten hands from where Greyhawk sat. The red glow cast a lurid halo over the ice walls.

"Oh, Twig, please wake up."

Water dripped from the ceiling as the cave continued to melt. The raiders cheered and poured more coals on top of the pile.

Greyhawk got on his knees and slipped his hands beneath Twig's shoulders, preparing to drag her deeper into the tunnel.

CHAPTER 46

TWIG WOKE WITH a start when she felt herself being dragged over the icy floor. "Greyhawk?"

"Twig! Oh, thank the Spirits, you're awake!"
Greyhawk gently lowered her to the floor again and
crouched at her side. "I thought you were dying."

Twig sat up. She had a terrible headache that made
her sick to her stomach, but she said, "I did die."

"You did?"

"Yes. I went on a Spirit journey, and my Spirit Helper,
Eagle-Man, tore me apart with his beak and swallowed me."

Greyhawk looked at her with wide eyes. "I definitely
don't want him for my Spirit Helper."

Twig smiled. "He had to do it. When he pecked away my head, I grew bird eyes, and then I could see the hole in the roof that led to Cobia. I flew across the river and into the Land of the Dead."

"Did you find Cobia?" Greyhawk whispered.

Twig heaved a tired sigh. "Yes."

"Is she coming to help us?"

When tears caught at the back of Twig's throat, her head hurt so badly she thought she'd pass out. She took a deep breath and let it out slowly to calm down. "No, I don't think so."

Greyhawk glanced back down the tunnel at the pile of glowing coals that were melting out the ice. Men had started shoving the pile deeper into the tunnel.

He said, "Are you well enough to crawl farther back into the tunnel? They'll be coming soon."

"I—I'll try."

Twig got on her knees and started crawling.

But it didn't take long.

The tunnel ended in less than fifty heartbeats. Just ended. There was no way out.

Twig leaned against the solid ice wall, breathing hard, her head aching, and Greyhawk positioned himself in front of her, holding Puffer's atlatl like a club . . . waiting for the raiders.

CHAPTER 47

IN LESS THAN two hands of time, the raiders had
done it.

Twig shivered when they started raking out the
piles of glowing coals, clearing a path big enough for a
man to slide into the cave.

Greyhawk breathed, "Here they come, Twig," and
gripped his atlatl.

The raider who started in was small across the shoulders. His eyes glinted in the red light cast by the few coals
that still lined the tunnel. When Twig and Greyhawk slid as
far back as they could, pressing hard against the ice wall, the
man laughed, "You brats look like cornered chipmunks!"

The man reached for Greyhawk's leg, and Greyhawk bashed his hand with his atlatl. The raider yipped in pain and instead grabbed hold of Twig's foot.

"Greyhawk! He's got me!" Twig shouted.

Greyhawk battered the man's head with his atlatl.

The raider shouted, "Boy, I am going to roast you like a rabbit when we get outside!"

"Try it!" Greyhawk shouted back, and kept beating the man in the head and arms.

Twig squirmed and kicked as the raider dragged her down the tunnel and out into the starlight, where he shoved her into the arms of another warrior and said, "Here, Hook. She's all yours."

When Hook clamped his big hand around her arm, Twig shrieked, "Let me go!" and as she struggled to wrench free, her eyes landed on the knife tucked into his belt. The long blade was shining black obsidian. Could she—

Hook ordered, "Go back in and get the boy, Catfish."

The first raider slithered into the tunnel again and a little while later dragged Greyhawk out and shoved him hard to the ground.

Greyhawk cried out when Catfish grabbed his atlatl, broke it over his knee, and cast the broken halves out into the darkness, saying, "Now stand up, boy! Just so I can knock you down again!"

Greyhawk, shaking badly, got his feet under him and stood up.

Catfish drew back his hand to knock him down . . .

but Netsink grabbed Greyhawk and dragged him out of the way. "This one is mine."

"No, he's not!" Catfish objected. "Look at my head. He beat me bloody! He should be mine to kill."

"You didn't have to fight off the huge dog he sicked on you! He's mine." Netsink wrenched Greyhawk's arm and flung him to the ground; then he kicked Greyhawk hard in the back, and kept kicking him.

Greyhawk grunted and groaned and rolled into a ball, trying to shield his head from the brutal attack.

When Netsink stopped kicking Greyhawk and pulled a spear from his quiver, hot blood surged through Twig's veins. She dove for Hook's knife.

The war chief had been smiling, watching Netsink. Twig's desperate move took him completely by surprise. He gasped when she ripped the knife from his belt and, before he could stop her, plunged it into his belly.

"*What?*" Hook shouted. He grabbed her wrist and twisted until she cried out and let go of the knife. "The brat stabbed me!"

He slapped Twig hard, and she staggered backward, watching as he jerked the knife from his belly. Dark, foul-smelling blood gushed from the wound.

Twig stared at it and felt sick. What had she done? She'd had no choice, but . . . her stomach heaved. She rolled to her hands and knees and vomited on the ground, over and over, until there was nothing left to come up. Her head was swimming when she looked back at him.

Hook staggered, dazed. He dipped his hand in the blood and laughed.

The other warriors hissed amongst themselves. The tall raider named Shrike sniffed the air and said, "The girl lanced your guts, Hook. You're as good as dead."

Hook blinked and looked around. "Don't even think—"

Shrike called to the other warriors, "I have been Hook's deputy for three summers. He's dying. You all know this kind of wound. He'll be useless before morning. I now claim the title of war chief."

The hissing grew louder. Some of the raiders smiled their support. Others scowled angrily.

Copper Falcon said, "You are not fit to be our war chief! I challenge you for the right." He stepped forward, drew his knife, and spread his legs, prepared to fight.

Shrike chuckled and drew his knife. The two men began circling each other, jabbing and feinting.

Twig quietly backed away, all the while searching for a place to hide. For the briefest of instants, Greyhawk looked up and their gazes locked. *Sealing a bargain . . .*

Neither of them would leave this canyon without the other.

Copper Falcon slashed open Shrike's left arm. At the sight of his blood, the raiders roared.

Hook shouted, "Stop it. We shouldn't be fighting each other! We . . . we have to . . ." As though the gut juices were soaking into his veins, poisoning him, he couldn't seem to remember what he'd wanted to say. Then he shouted, "We have to find the Stone Wolf!"

No one paid him any attention. Every eye was on the fight.

Shrike glared at Copper Falcon. "I'm going to slice your liver out a piece at a time and eat it before your eyes!"

"You arrogant fool!"

Copper Falcon lunged again, but this time Shrike spun out of the way and landed an elbow in the back of Copper Falcon's neck, staggering him. In the half a heartbeat it took Copper Falcon to catch his balance, Shrike plunged his knife into Copper Falcon's kidney and ripped upward.

Copper Falcon shrieked, dropped his knife, and awkwardly pulled his war club from his belt. As he spun around, trying to clip Shrike with a hasty swipe of his club, Shrike kicked the club from Copper Falcon's hand and sent it cartwheeling high into the air.

The raiders cheered and closed in around the two men, waiting for the kill.

Twig looked at Greyhawk, but his eyes were not on her. He was watching the club fall. It landed in the snow three paces from him.

A high-pitched, blood-curdling cry of pain rang out.

Twig jerked around and saw Shrike kick Copper Falcon's feet out from under him. Copper Falcon toppled to the ground and Shrike was instantly on top him, plunging his knife into Copper Falcon's chest. Copper Falcon's hideous cries echoed down the canyon.

When the cries stopped, Shrike stumbled to his feet

and lifted both arms into the air, shouting, "I am the new war chief!"

Most of the men began dancing, clapping, and cheering. But two warriors stood to the side, glowering hatefully at Shrike.

Twig silently took a step toward Greyhawk.

And Shrike saw her.

His eyes blazed. "You. Girl. Come over here."

Twig stood rooted to the spot.

Shrike stalked over and grabbed her by the hair. He wrenched her neck around so he could stare down into her eyes and said, "You are Twig, aren't you?"

She refused to answer.

"A boy in your village said you had the Stone Wolf. Where is it?"

Twig tried to stall, to think of something. . . .

"*Where is it?*" He leaned down and shouted the words right in her face.

Twig was shaking so badly her voice seemed to have left her.

Shrike lowered his face until their noses almost touched and hissed, "Tell me now, or you die."

He lifted his bloody knife and placed it against her throat. The sharp edge burned, already cutting into her skin.

"Stop it!" Greyhawk shouted. He got his feet under him and stood up. He was hiding something in his right hand, tucked up into his sleeve.

Shrike laughed. "You little idiot. Catfish, club the boy."

Twig screamed and threw herself sideways, struggling to break free from Shrike's grip . . . and the Stone Wolf flopped out of her coat and lay shining and black on her chest.

Shrike said, "There it is! I knew you had it."

He grabbed the Wolf and ripped it from Twig's neck. Then he laughed as he looked down at it. "I will be cheered as a hero when I give this to Chief Nightcrow!"

Catfish removed his war club from his belt and stalked toward Greyhawk. When he swung, Greyhawk madly dove out of the way, rolled, and came up with Copper Falcon's war club in his hand. He slammed it into Catfish's lower leg.

Catfish shrieked and dropped to the ground, staring in horror at the broken bone that thrust out of his leg just above his ankle. "The boy broke my leg! *Kill him!*"

Netsink charged after Greyhawk, who was desperately trying to crawl away, kicked the war club from his hand, and grabbed him by the back of the coat. "You're dead, boy."

Twig screamed, *"No!"*

As though she'd triggered it, a fiery gleam swelled on the northern horizon.

Netsink, holding tight to Greyhawk's coat, stammered, "Wh-what's that? Do you see that?" He released Greyhawk to look.

The gleam expanded, growing larger and larger until it filled the entire sky, and they stood in an ocean of orange light. The towering ice walls glittered with it.

"The sky is on fire!" Shrike said, and shoved Twig to the ground to squint upward. "Look!"

Far in the north, a rumble started, growing louder, coming toward them . . . then the gleam exploded! Thousands of Meteor People blasted across the sky, leaving fiery trails, and a rolling wave of flames consumed the heavens.

Greyhawk shouted, "Twig, is this your dream?"

Before she could answer, a thunderous boom split the air and the concussion knocked all of them off their feet. The boom was followed by a deafening ripping sound, like the sky was being torn apart by the hands of the gods.

The raiders screamed and covered their ears.

Netsink shouted, "What's happening?" but Twig barely heard him.

The ripping sound turned into an inhuman shriek and quickly rose to a constant stunning roar, as though a thousand mountain lions were fighting inside the light.

"Blessed Spirits!" Shrike cried. "The girl is a witch! She's called the Star People down upon us!"

While he was staring upward, Twig scrambled over and jerked the Stone Wolf out of his hand. He didn't even try to take it back. He just kept his terrified eyes on the burning sky.

Twig slipped the Stone Wolf over her head and . . .

. . . saw something move in the black maw of the ice cave.

Twig blinked. "What's that? Greyhawk? Do you see that?"

He whirled around, ready for a fight. "What? Where?"

Twig lifted her arm to point.

Against that charcoal background, a slender woman moved, rushing toward them. Tall and willowy, she wore pure white hides and had long shimmering white hair. She was beautiful, with large dark eyes, full lips, and a turned-up nose. A small medicine bundle decorated with a black raven hung from her belt.

In awe, Twig whispered, "Cobia. It—it's her!"

Greyhawk hissed, "Are you sure?"

In her dream, Cobia had had black hair, but the medicine bundle was the same. "Yes!"

The woman moved quickly but with such grace she seemed to be floating through the brilliant orange glare that filled Hoarfrost Canyon. Her black eyes had fixed on Twig. She ran straight for her without saying a word.

The hair at the back of Twig's neck prickled as if stroked by an unseen hand. "Cobia?"

All of the raiders turned to look when they heard her name. A din of shocked cries rose. "It is her! It's really Cobia!"

Thousands of Star People streaked across the sky, leaving brilliant flaming trails as they headed south. And from somewhere in the distance, Twig heard a staccato of thumps as they struck earth.

Shrike cried, "The Star People are hunting us down! Run and hide! We have to get away!"

He dove for the cave they had melted out to get to Greyhawk and Twig, quickly disappearing inside, as though hiding would protect him from the gods. Another warrior scrambled in after him.

Fluid as a ghost, her white cape swaying around her white moccasins, Cobia grabbed Greyhawk's hand as she passed, dragged him to his feet, and hurried for Twig. "Take my hand!"

Twig gazed into those huge haunted eyes and, for the first time in her life, knew true terror. Power like a writhing living thing filled those black depths. She choked out, "Where are you taking us?"

"Come with me! Now."

Twig grabbed her hand, and Cobia dragged both children back into her cave just as the earthquake struck like the enormous fist of the Creator.

The impact tossed Twig high into the air and then slammed her facedown on the rocky floor of the cave. The air went out of her lungs, and stunning pain flashed through her entire body. When she looked up, she saw Cobia and Greyhawk lying a short distance away.

Cobia immediately rolled to her side and got on her hands and knees. *"Follow me! We must get deeper into my cave!"* She started crawling.

Greyhawk was right behind her, but after five heartbeats, he turned back to look for Twig. "Twig? Come on!"

She still couldn't breathe, couldn't seem to make her lungs suck in air. She tried to call to him for help, but no sound came up her throat. Her mouth moved in pitiful cries that no one could hear, not even Twig.

Outside, the Thornback raiders screamed. Twig jerked to look and saw a huge green ball of light tumble across the sky right over their heads, followed by what sounded like millions of lightning bolts crackling through the air at once. For long moments, the raiders just stared up. Time might have stopped.

Then, there was a blinding flash . . . and a searing wave of heat struck.

Without thinking, Twig threw up her arms to cover her face, but her skin seemed to catch fire! It was like being thrown into raging flames!

An instant later, hurricane-force wind blasted the world. It picked her up like a feather and hurled her back into the cave, where it bashed her into solid rock and kept her pinned there. After one hundred heartbeats, the wind stopped. Just stopped.

Twig fell to the floor, gasping for breath, and saw the huge blisters that covered her arms. Her face must look the same way.

She tried to get to her feet, but the Ice Giants let out a magnificent, terrifying roar, and the earthquake smashed her down again. The land itself seemed to be splitting wide open, shattering into splinters of rock and ice that no one could ever piece together again.

Fog rolled into the cave, thick, as though the Ice Giants were vaporizing outside.

Twig tried to shout at Greyhawk, and could tell he was shouting back. His mouth was moving, but his voice was drowned out by the earthquake.

Greyhawk and Twig madly slid forward on their bellies until they could clasp hands.

Ahead, deeper in the cave, Cobia was waving them forward and shouting, though they couldn't hear her.

Together, they scrambled across the heaving floor to get to her . . . and she led them back, deeper and deeper into the darkness.

When Twig dared to glance back through the mouth of the cave, she saw the fog burning red and glowing gravel raining down . . . and water. Water was filling Hoarfrost Canyon.

The Ice Giants were flooding the world.

CHAPTER 48

HOWLING WIND BLEW clouds of dust and smoke up the trail, and the air had a lurid crimson gleam. Screech Owl pulled Riddle's good arm over his shoulders and supported her as they followed the lake trail behind the rest of the Buffalobeard Village survivors, fifteen in all. Each had been badly burned when the sky exploded two days ago. But they were alive. Everywhere he looked, he saw devastation. The Ice Giants, covered with dust and soot, had turned black as night. Vast clouds of steam rose from them and shrouded Ice Giant Lake with fog.

Right after the explosion, the lake had started rising,

and by the next morning, all of the charred remains of Buffalobeard Village were underwater. They'd no choice but to leave, to search for another place to start a new village. Screech Owl feared they would have to travel west for a very long time before they escaped the choking haze that filled the world here.

Riddle winced and moaned.

"How are you doing?" Screech Owl asked her. "Do you need to rest?"

"No. We can't afford to fall behind." She'd broken her arm when the roof collapsed on top of her, and wore it in a hide sling. Clearly in pain, she kept uttering soft sounds of anguish. "The dust is so thick, we may get lost. But thank you for asking." She tipped up her blistered, soot-coated face to smile her thanks at him.

He smiled back, and they kept walking.

From somewhere up ahead, he heard Halfmoon call, "Everyone, stay within sight of the person in front of you! Hold your children's hands. We don't want to lose anyone!"

Screech Owl kept his gaze on Reef's muscular back. The tall warrior had his atlatl in his hand, as always, and a quiver of spears slung over his shoulder. He kept turning around to look back, making sure everyone was still in sight. Many of the old people and children were stumbling, having trouble breathing, and many more were wounded. Now and then Screech Owl caught sight of a bloody bandage encircling an arm or leg. A constant noise of coughing, wheezing, and crying children filled the air.

Oddly, the pack of dogs that trailed in the rear were silent as ghosts.

The orphaned children walked in a single group near the front. Through the blowing dust, he saw Grizzly towering over the others. The boy had his thumb in his mouth, sucking it for comfort. Poor child. He had lost both his mother and father. At least his brother Little Cougar was standing beside him, holding Grizzly's sleeve in a tight grip. Rattler carried a baby girl in her arms. Screech Owl had no idea who the baby belonged to. But it didn't matter now. They had only one goal, to survive. And to do that, they had to take care of each other.

When they reached the crest, Halfmoon stopped and shielded his eyes to look up the trail. Had Searobin returned? At dawn, Halfmoon had dispatched the warrior to scout the trails ahead.

They were under no illusions. If they were fleeing westward to escape the fiery destruction, so were the Thornback People. As well as every short-faced bear and dire wolf that had lived. And all of them would be hungry.

Riddle asked, "What's Father doing?"

"I'm not sure." Screech Owl thought he saw a dark shape moving farther up the trail. "I think he's waiting. There's someone on the trail ahead."

"Searobin? He's back? Is he safe?"

The man came into view, trotting steadily forward.

"I don't see any wounds, but let's go find out."

He carefully led Riddle down the hill and into the group. Halfmoon spoke briefly with Searobin before he turned, looked around with his white-filmed eyes, and said, "Reef? Is everyone here?"

"Yes, Elder. All fifteen of us. We're still together."

People stood with scraps of hide pressed over their noses to block the dust and smoke, and their eyes squinted against the icy wind. Tears had mixed with the debris to form muddy trails down their faces.

Halfmoon held up a hand and called, "I know you are all exhausted and hungry, but we have to keep moving. Searobin just brought news that it's much worse to the south. There are fires everywhere. The forests are all blazing. That's where the smoke is coming from."

Searobin coughed and cleared his throat before calling, "We are lucky to be at the edge of the lake! You can breathe here because of the fog. It keeps most of the smoke away. Farther south, I saw dead animals and people lying everywhere. It looks like they suffocated where they were standing when the star exploded."

People shifted and stared. No one knew what to say. It sounded like the end of the world.

Halfmoon said, "So we must keep moving west. Now! Let's go."

He turned to start up the trail again, and Riddle called, "Father? Father, please wait. What about Twig and Greyhawk? They are out there somewhere. Alone. Shouldn't we wait for them?"

Halfmoon's mouth tightened. He must be as worried about Twig as Riddle was, but as a warrior, he probably assumed his granddaughter was dead. He squared his shoulders and called, "We can't. It's too dangerous. We don't know where the Thornback People are. The safety of everyone is at risk. We must keep moving. But . . ." He coughed and looked around at the scared villagers. "You should all know that my granddaughter dreamed this. She told me about the exploding star a quarter moon ago. I—"

"Yes," old Bandtail agreed. "Halfmoon told us of her dreams, but we didn't believe him. Twig was so young—"

"*Is* so young," Screech Owl corrected. "Twig may be the greatest dreamer our people have ever known. She's alive. I know it. The Spirits of our ancestors would not have let her die."

Bandtail exhaled hard. The old woman's blackened face looked strangely purple. "If only we had listened to her dream, by now we would be far to the west, away from this destruction."

Murmuring broke out, and people began nodding their heads.

Riddle bowed her head and nodded, too—but Screech Owl saw the tears that cut lines through the mud on her cheeks. She whispered, "I should have told the elders about her dreams long ago. We would be even farther to the west. And Twig would be with us."

Screech Owl said, "She will find us, Riddle."

Riddle gave him a brave smile, but she clearly didn't believe him. How could she? Wind blasted the trail, scouring it clean every instant. There would be no tracks to follow.

Halfmoon led them down the trail into a dense choking cloud of red-hued dust.

Screech Owl repositioned Riddle's arm over his shoulders and whispered, "Twig will dream her way to us. You'll see."

"Do you think so? Truly?" Her voice trembled.

"I *know* so."

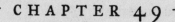

CHAPTER 49

THE FOG BLED pink, then burned orange, and finally became a shimmering scarlet blanket.

As Twig marched through it behind Cobia and Greyhawk, she no longer felt human. She pressed the hide over her nose and fought to breathe. Her senses had sharpened like those of a threatened animal. She could hear, smell, and taste the danger that ghosted by on the howling wind. The ground almost never stopped shaking, and the deep-throated groans and shrieks of the dying Ice Giants were constant.

Over the past three days, she had seen things she never wanted to see again: charred headless corpses blown into a tangled heap by the hurricane, and herds of animals moving with their noses to the ground, trying to sniff out trails because their eyes had been roasted in their heads.

Twig and Greyhawk picked up weapons every chance they got. Both of them carried atlatls in their hands and quivers of spears over their shoulders. They had stone knives tied to their belts.

Only Cobia had no weapons. Perhaps because she didn't need any.

Twig lifted her nose and smelled the air. It was heavy with the scents of burning hickory and spruce, and a strange sulfur-like smell that reminded her of rotten eggs.

All day long, she had thought about Bison Calf, wondering if this was how he had felt on the last day of his life. She remembered the desperate sound of his cries, as though he'd been calling for his mother, or his herd, praying someone would come and save him from the human hunters. Bison Calf could not have known he was the last of his kind in the world. He must have been terrified.

As Twig was.

Twig closed her eyes and prayed that Bison Calf's soul had found its way to the Land of the Dead, and that he would never be frightened again, or hungry, or lonely.

Greyhawk shouted, "Who is that?" and Twig jerked her eyes open.

A human figure appeared to Twig's left, startling her. She grabbed for her knife.

It was an old man. He stepped out of the dense fog, and Cobia stopped to speak with him. Twig could hear their voices, but not the words. The man clutched his elk-hide hood tightly beneath his chin.

Cobia shouted something in his ear, and the old man shook his head and shouted back, *"All dead . . . the end of the world . . . nowhere to hide."*

Had she asked him about his family, or his village?

Cobia said something else, and it seemed as though she was trying to talk him into going with them, but he shook his head again and drifted back into the fog, disappearing as though he'd never been.

Greyhawk turned around and through the hide held over his nose, said, "Did you hear that?"

"No. What did he say?"

"He said that evil Spirits rode in with the bursting star and were roaming the world killing every human still alive. His entire village was slaughtered."

Sensibly, she answered, "His evil Spirits are probably Thornback warriors."

"Yes, probably."

Greyhawk turned back when Cobia continued down the trail, and they walked in single file for another four hands of time without saying a word to each other.

Just before nightfall, when the temperature began to plummet, they came to a river. A black river. Dead fish floated on the surface. So much soot and ash had mixed with the water it ran like liquid coal. If Twig lived long enough to have children, would they ever believe her?

"Are we stopping?" Greyhawk called to Cobia.

She turned around with her long white hair, turned

gray with ash, whipping around her face and shouted, "No! We keep going until we are ready to drop in our tracks. We must get away from this devastation." She waded the river. It came up to her knees, and to Greyhawk's hips.

When Twig stepped in, she gasped at the cold. The water was absolutely freezing, as though it had just poured from the mouths of the Ice Giants. On the other side, she stood shivering. She had totally lost her bearings, with no idea whether they were headed north, south, east, or west.

She said, "Greyhawk, what direction are we headed? South?"

"West," he corrected. "Due west."

"How do you know? There's too much fog and smoke to see the sun."

He shrugged. "I just know. We're headed west."

In another twenty paces, the fog suddenly parted and Twig blinked. Ten paces away, there was a mammoth perched on a boulder. Cobia and Greyhawk saw it, too. They both pointed.

Mammoth's shaggy hair had been burned off, leaving red blistered hide behind. It was seated on its haunches, staring out at the dust storm, as though totally lost and trying to find some familiar landmark to lead it back to its herd. When Mammoth spotted Twig, they studied each other; then the mammoth again looked at the dust and lifted its trunk to trumpet into the storm. It cocked its head, waited to hear an answer, and trumpeted again.

The only sound Twig heard was the shrill howling of the wind.

But Mammoth seemed to hear something else. It stood up, listened, and clambered awkwardly off the boulder. It started walking out across the vast wasteland.

Cobia's eyes narrowed. She watched the mammoth as though their very lives depended upon it.

Then she turned. "Do either of you have Mammoth as a Spirit Helper?"

Greyhawk said, "Not me."

Twig shook her head.

Cobia hesitated a few heartbeats longer before stepping into the tracks of the mammoth and following. In the eerie, gaudy light, the animal seemed magical. Its big body faded in and out of the fog, and often it seemed to be waiting for them to catch up. They would lose sight of the mammoth, then find it standing still in the wavering mist, looking back. When they caught up, it started walking again.

As they wandered through the smoke and fog, they coughed until their lungs ached. Their bellies gnawed at their backbones from hunger, but they kept going.

CHAPTER 50

FOUR DAYS LATER, the smoke cleared a little. They could see farther. Mammoth continued to lead the way, but now she was one hundred paces ahead and still in sight, whereas the day before, if Mammoth was twenty paces ahead, they couldn't see her.

The strange new sounds haunted Twig. There were no birds chirping, or caribou calling. No sounds of life. Night was the worst. The wind became a growling monster, and it was achingly cold. They had no hides and no time to make a fire. When they rested, they curled into shallow pits to sleep for a few heartbeats, or took shelter behind boulders. But never for long. They all knew they might never wake up.

Mammoth suddenly looked back at them.

Cobia stopped. Greyhawk and Twig ran to see what she was looking at.

Greyhawk said, "It . . . it's Tidewater Village. Isn't it?"

Long ago, when Twig had seen eight summers, Mother had brought her here to visit Uncle Banded Bear. Just as she remembered, the caves of Tidewater Village overlooked Ice Giant Lake, but four summers ago, the glistening blue lake had been far in the distance. Today, its filthy black water washed into the caves, swallowing them. Ominously, several caves had been rocked up, as though the villagers had tried to hold back the flood. From the corpses, she knew they'd failed.

"Yes," Cobia softly answered. "It was Tidewater Village."

Her eyes scanned the bodies. Some hung out of the caves; others floated in the distance like tiny islands.

Twig felt as though she'd staggered into the middle of a battlefield. Everywhere, everyone was dead. She sniffed the air and smelled their rot.

"Why didn't they leave their caves and run?" Greyhawk asked Cobia.

She shook her head slightly. "Whatever they saw outside must have been more frightening than the possibility of drowning."

Greyhawk gripped his atlatl and looked around.

They all did, searching for that threat.

But only the bloody mist and scorched land answered.

Mammoth started walking again.

They followed.

CHAPTER 51

Aᶠᵗᵉʳ another day, they found a shore where icebergs had been blown by the ferocious winds and grounded. Ten times the height of a man, they had lined up on the sand and resembled an enormous jaw filled with broken, black teeth.

Cobia said, "Let's sit down and rest out of the wind for a few moments."

Twig and Greyhawk slumped to the ground and heaved heavy sighs.

Cobia used a rock to chip away the filthy surface of an iceberg and handed them each a chunk of ice to suck on.

While Twig and Greyhawk rested, Cobia walked down

the shore picking up dead fish. The entire shoreline was coated with them. Cobia tossed many away—too rotten, probably—and came back with six fish. She handed two to Greyhawk and two to Twig. Twig studied her fish. The slimy skin was falling off the meat. They stank.

"Don't think," Cobia said. "Just eat."

Twig pulled off the rotting skin and closed her eyes. She ate without breathing, so she couldn't smell them. And her empty stomach was grateful. When they started walking again, she felt stronger.

They walked all night, following the mammoth, shivering.

By morning, she knew something had changed. The gaudy red glow that had announced dawn for the past six days was gone. Instead, Father Sun rose somewhere beyond the dense clouds of smoke and ash, and cast a surreal grayish yellow light on the world.

As the light brightened, they saw Mammoth, and beyond her, dark shapes on the trail.

"Cobia?" Twig called. "Are those people?"

Greyhawk reached for a spear and nocked his atlatl in case they were Thornback warriors. "Where, Twig? I don't see them."

"There. In front of Mammoth."

Shouts rose from up ahead. The people had seen them . . . or perhaps they were hungry and had seen Mammoth.

Twig's belly muscles went tight with fear.

Mammoth lifted her trunk and trumpeted as though

signaling victory . . . and then she charged off at full speed, heading south into the denser smoke.

Ahead, people gathered on the trail, staring back at Twig, and she thought . . . but she was afraid to hope . . .

"Who are they?" Greyhawk asked. He had his spear up, ready to cast.

Cobia said, "I think they are People of the Dawnland. See the way they dress?"

Greyhawk's eyes widened. He lowered his spear. "Are you sure?"

Twig's heart suddenly ached so desperately for her mother that she couldn't stand it any longer. She broke into a trot, swerved around Cobia, and dashed headlong up the rocky ridge that curved around the lake.

She could hear Greyhawk's steps right behind her. As she raced forward, he called, "Twig! Wait! They could be enemy warriors!"

Breathing hard, her heart about to burst, she ran harder.

The people watched her, and . . .

"*Twig!*" Mother cried, and shoved through the crowd. She had her arm in a sling, and her face was coated with soot and grime. "Twig? Look! Screech Owl, *it's Twig and Greyhawk!*"

Mother started running back for them, and everyone else in the village followed her. Screech Owl lifted a hand to Twig, and she waved back.

Greyhawk's father, Reef, shouted, "Greyhawk!"

Yipper, who had been standing at Reef's side, wildly

spun around to look. The dog's head had a bandage wrapped tightly all the way around it.

When Yipper saw Greyhawk, he took off running like a spear cast from an atlatl, bounding up the trail as though desperate to make certain Greyhawk was safe.

Greyhawk knelt in the trail and opened his arms. "Yipper! Yipper, come here, boy!"

The dog launched himself into Greyhawk's arms, knocked him flat, and started ferociously licking his face while Greyhawk squirmed and laughed.

Mother hurried up the trail and fell to her knees to hug Twig. Crying, she said, "Oh, Twig, I was so afraid! I love you. I love you."

When Cobia crested the ridge, Mother suddenly released Twig, staggered to her feet, and whispered, *"Cobia."*

Cobia stared at Mother through bottomless, pitch-black eyes and said, "Yes, I'm back."

Cobia walked over the crest and down the trail . . . and as people began to recognize her, the world seemed to stop. No one moved. No one spoke. Not even the dogs barked at her. No one had seen her in twenty summers—not since she'd killed Chief Minnow with a breath across her palm.

Then her whispered name began to pass through the villagers like the hiss of a serpent: *"Cobia. It's Cobia."*

Screech Owl suddenly broke away from the crowd.

He ran up the trail and embraced Cobia in a powerful hug. "I'm so glad you're safe. Thank you for bringing Twig and Greyhawk home."

Cobia said, "I didn't. Mammoth led us here."

"Did she?"

"Yes. I think Twig may have a Spirit Helper she does not yet know."

CHAPTER 52

NIGHTCROW FELT OLD. He shivered in the freezing wind as it gusted across the top of the hill. He had led his people away from the worst of the destruction, but the fires were coming. He could see a wall of flames in the distance, racing across the hills as though pushed by hurricane winds. He could also see the two men running toward the makeshift village they had thrown up last night. Both wore black shirts. So, two of his warriors had survived. Others must also see them, for yelling and shouts filtered through the smoky air. People began to run out, to meet them.

He waited.

In a few hundred heartbeats, Shrike and Blackfoot came trotting up the trail to the hilltop. Both smelled of sour sweat and old blood.

Nightcrow blurted, "Tell me quickly. Are you the only survivors?"

Shrike nodded. His face was soot-blackened and streaked with tears from squinting against the smoke. "Yes, my chief. Everyone else is dead."

Blackfoot wiped his grimy forehead on his sleeve. "The girl is a powerful witch. When Shrike tore the Stone Wolf from her neck, she called down the Star People to kill us."

Nightcrow peered out at the blazing forests, wondering where she was. "The *girl* did this? A little girl?"

"Yes, and she killed Hook, knifed him in the belly."

Shrike nodded. "Even worse, Cobia is her ally." He dropped his voice to a whisper when he said her name, and fear lit his eyes. "Just before the searing heat struck, Cobia ran from her cave and dragged the children inside to protect them."

Nightcrow studied his frightened expression. He held out a hand. "Give me the Stone Wolf."

Shrike shifted his weight to his other foot. "When the Star People started shooting down at us, I—I lost it. I—"

Blackfoot's gaze flicked at Shrike; then quickly he looked away. Nightcrow clenched his fists in understanding and asked, "Now, tell me the truth. What happened to the Stone Wolf?"

Shrike seemed surprised. He just stared at Nightcrow.

"Go on. Tell him," Blackfoot said.

When Shrike kept his mouth closed, Blackfoot said, "The girl grabbed it from his hand and ran away with it."

In an unsettlingly soft voice, Nightcrow asked, "And how did you two survive, while the others did not?"

"We dove into an ice cave and hid until the rising water drove us out; then we swam away."

As silent as Eagle's shadow, Nightcrow rose to his feet to face Shrike. "You were Hook's deputy. You abandoned your men?"

"It's not my fault! The others"—Shrike gestured as though it was of little concern—"could have scrambled into a cave. They did not."

Nightcrow smiled, and Shrike smiled back, not realizing the source of his chief's amusement. "I see." He pulled out the sacred stiletto, the one Hook had stolen from Starhorse Village, from his belt.

"No, you do not see! There were dark Spirits all around us. The only thing that saved us was that we kept repeating your name. Over and over! We screamed your name! It must have scared Cobia, because neither she nor the girl came after us. You are the only reason we made it back alive. Your power shielded us!"

Nightcrow hesitated, his stiletto perfectly still, the carved bone shining red in the strange light. There was something in the way Shrike's devious eyes burned. It was like gazing at a trapped wolf. Nightcrow studied him. He was clearly waiting for the stroke that would end his life.

"Is that true, Blackfoot? Is that how it happened? My name shielded you?"

"Yes, my chief," Blackfoot answered, but his face showed no emotion at all.

Nightcrow smiled again. They might still be useful. He put a hand on Shrike's shoulder, and could feel the man trembling. "Well, then, you are brave indeed, Shrike. I name you my new war chief."

Shrike, who had clearly been expecting a blow to the heart, straightened as though he had not heard right. "My chief?"

"Yes, I want you to lead our warriors. You can start by running down this hill and telling everyone your story. Tell them how my name saved you from Cobia's wrath."

"Of course." He glanced at Blackfoot. "We will tell them Cobia *ran* at the sound of your name. We will shout the truth to the—"

"After that," Nightcrow interrupted, "I want you to find the People of the Dawnland and capture the girl."

"Yes, my chief."

As Nightcrow tramped down the hill toward the villagers who were waiting below, he heard Shrike let out a happy whoop.

The fool. He understood nothing.

CHAPTER 53

BY NOON, THE survivors of the People of the Dawnland marched through an eerily quiet black blizzard.

Twig cast a glance over her shoulder. The fires in the south were spreading through the forests, and ash fell like charcoal snowflakes. All of the animals had fled in front of the fires. Not a single deer or buffalo could be seen anywhere. Even the slow-moving sloths had vanished.

Screech Owl and Cobia walked out front. Twig, Greyhawk, and Yipper came next in line, and several more paces back, Mother whispered with Grandfather.

Though many people seemed frightened of Cobia, no one complained about her presence. In fact, they seemed strangely comforted to have the most powerful dreamer in the world leading them.

Twig coughed and tried to breathe. It wasn't easy. The smoke and dust were so thick they were all having trouble breathing. Many people walked with their hide collars held over their noses. But coughs and wheezes filtered down the line.

And in the strange black blizzard, Twig kept seeing things. Huge things, moving around Cobia.

Greyhawk, who was walking beside her, said, "What's wrong, Twig? You keep staring at Cobia."

She turned to him. He had the front of his face tucked down inside his coat so that only his eyes showed. "Do you see them?"

Greyhawk frowned. "See what?"

"I think . . . nothing. I'm probably just tired. My eyes are playing tricks, but—"

Yipper let out a sudden sharp bark, charged forward, and leaped into the air beside Cobia, snapping at something. Screech Owl and Cobia had their heads together, talking. They didn't even seem to notice him. But Twig and Greyhawk did. When Yipper landed, he stalked around stiff-legged with his hair standing straight up, whining and growling.

Greyhawk's eyes widened. He carefully searched the torrent of black snowflakes before saying to Twig, "Should I be afraid?"

Yipper trotted back toward them, but he kept looking over his shoulder, growling, as though in warning.

Twig whispered, "Do you remember the story Elder Bandtail told about Cobia? About the—"

"About the armless things that danced around her bed when she was a child?" Greyhawk hissed. "Is that what you and Yipper see?"

"I think so, but I don't think they're evil. I—"

Two paces ahead, she heard Screech Owl ask Cobia, "The Thornback raiders are behind us, aren't they?"

Cobia's head dipped in a single nod. It had been so subtle people farther back in line would have never seen it, so it could not terrify them the way it did Twig and Greyhawk.

Screech Owl nodded and exhaled hard. "I thank the Spirits that you are here. Have you dreamed where we should go? Where we will be safe?"

Cobia stopped in the trail and waited for Twig and Greyhawk to catch up. When she looked at Twig, her eyes shimmered. "Where will we be safe, Twig? Have you dreamed of it?"

Twig hesitated.

Greyhawk said, "What's she talking about, Twig?"

Twig took a deep breath, then softly answered, "I—I keep seeing things, and the Stone Wolf is pulling me due west. I think we have to go all the way to the Duskland."

"The Duskland?" Greyhawk half shouted. "Why?"

The other villagers heard him, and stopped.

Twig wet her lips, afraid to answer. Cobia had told her that too much hope could kill. Finally, she said, "There is still sunlight there, Greyhawk. Towering trees grow along the coast, and there's plenty of fish and animals. If we can just get there . . ."

People came forward, surrounding her. The faces of the elders were especially serious. They all listened intently for her next words.

Twig blinked, astonished.

Elder Bandtail hobbled forward. "Are we on the right path to get there, Dreamer?"

"Yes."

Elder Snapper shouldered through the crowd next. "How long will it take us?"

"I don't know, Elder. Many moons, I think." Twig picked up the Stone Wolf, and it tugged her onward, due west.

Everyone seemed to be waiting for her.

Slowly, hesitantly, Twig walked out in front of them, taking the lead.

Cobia, Greyhawk, and Screech Owl fell into line behind her, and the others followed. They followed her—Twig, daughter of Riddle and Screech Owl, a child of the Blue Bear Clan of the People of the Dawnland.

When she looked back over her shoulder, Screech Owl gave her a proud smile.

Twig smiled back, and as she led them down the winding trail toward the far, far Duskland, hope swelled her heart.

She started to walk faster, and Greyhawk called, "Twig, wait for me!"

He ran up to walk beside her, and Yipper shot out in front of them, running down the trail with his tail wagging.

Greyhawk whispered, "I always knew you were a dreamer."

She turned to look at his soot-coated face. "I only made it to Cobia's cave because of you. You are the bravest warrior I will ever know."

Greyhawk smiled, and they both focused on the ash-coated trail ahead.

As she walked, ghostly images formed in the smoke, twisting and shimmering. Somewhere out there, a mammoth trumpeted, loud, tying itself to the forming vision.

Twig stopped suddenly—as the vision became her world.

. . . *I see the smoke break, and ahead of me is Mammoth, looking back over her shoulder, waiting for me to catch up. Her long silky brown hair has grown back. Her ivory tusks shine, and her eyes are bright and happy. My fear slips away like Buffalo's winter coat in spring. I trot to the crest, my lungs heaving, and suck in an awed breath.*

Below, thick grasses waver beneath the caress of Wind Woman. Green meadows roll all the way down to touch a vast blue ocean, where wolf pups roll on their backs in the sand, biting their toes before tumbling sideways, then rising and chasing each other along the shore. Their playful yips are like music on the sea-scented breeze. And far out in the grass, Mammoth runs, greeting Caribou, Fox, and Raven as she heads for the herd of mammoths that stand belly-deep in wildflowers. When the other mammoths see her, they trumpet wildly. The entire herd rushes to meet her. They surround her, trumpeting, tossing their heads and gently smoothing their trunks along her sides and over her back in greeting—as though their lost sister has returned home, and they are joyous.

I smile. The air is filled with birdsong and brilliant sunlight.

I can barely hear myself whisper, "The Duskland. This is the Duskland. . . ."

Why did the Laurentide Ice Sheet collapse and cause the draining of Lake Agassiz? Scientists have recently discovered that around this same time a comet may have exploded over the Great Lakes and eastern Canada. Archaeologists have always been fascinated by the strange "black mat" that covers most Clovis culture sites. Clovis archaeological sites date to between 13,500 years ago and 12,900 years ago, and are never found above this carbon-rich mat. Clovis culture is best known for the beautiful "fluted" spear points its people made to harvest mammoths, mastodons, and buffalo.

Thanks to the efforts of two physicists, the black mat was recently analyzed and found to contain high amounts of iridium, plus carbon spherules and tiny lumps of glasslike carbon that can best be explained by the explosion of a comet in the earth's atmosphere. When the comet exploded, fragments shot out and slammed into the land, leaving over one million depressions that today we call the Carolina Bays. The impacts set off forest fires and undoubtedly caused the collapse of the Laurentide Ice Sheet that still covered most of Canada east of the Rockies.

If a comet did explode around 12,900 years ago, it must have happened when the comet entered the atmosphere, because we have no gaping hole, no crater to mark its point of impact. Scientists speculate that it was an extinction-level event. When the comet struck, it super-heated the atmosphere and sent a shock wave across North America, causing the largest firestorm in the history of the world. A few seconds after the explosion, a blast of high-pressure wind, over 300 miles per hour, swept the continent; then red-hot debris started falling. About thirty minutes later, a tsunami 600 feet high, consisting of dozens of massive waves, rolled across the oceans, devastating coastlines around the world.

It took years for the clouds of debris, dust, and smoke to finally settle. By then, the world had been thrown back into another Ice Age that we call the Younger Dryas.

But human beings survived, as did buffalo, deer, elk, and most other life-forms.

The journey ahead was difficult, but the adventures of Twig and Greyhawk had only just begun. . . .

── READER'S GUIDE ──

ABOUT THIS GUIDE

The information, activities, and discussion questions that follow are intended to enhance your reading of *Children of the Dawnland*. Please feel free to adapt these materials to suit your needs and interests.

WRITING AND RESEARCH ACTIVITIES

I. CLOVIS CULTURE

A. Go to the library or online to learn more about Clovis and pre-Clovis archaeological sites across North America. Divide into small groups to create informative posters about individual sites and how discoveries made there have contributed to our understanding of ancient human history.

B. Go to the library or online to learn more about mammoths and other megafauna (great beasts) that became extinct around the end of the Ice Age. On a large (at least 4' X 6') paper surface, create a mural depicting great beasts in their late Ice Age habitat, using information from your research. On index cards, list 4-5 facts about each beast depicted in your mural.

C. Divide into four groups to debate the question: How did the great beasts become extinct? Each group should argue in favor of two of the following theories: (1) overhunting by humans, (2) climate change, (3) disease, (4) an extraterrestrial impact. When the discussion is over, have each group reassess their conclusions to include, if they think it's appropriate, information presented by the other groups. Go to the library or online to research these positions.

II. DREAMS AND DREAMERS

A. Research and write a short report about the role of dreams in African American, Native American, Chinese, or another culture.

Learn to make a Native American dream catcher or study the importance of the mandala in Hinduism and Buddhism. Think of a favorite novelist, musician, or visual artist who explores the theme of dreams and study one of his or her dream-related works.

B. Twig's dreams suggest a troubling fate for her people. Use chalk, watercolor paints, or other visual arts media to depict a scene from one of Twig's dreams. Share your completed artwork with friends or classmates and invite them to share their drawings or paintings. Are colors, images, or other elements common to several pictures? What was most challenging or exciting about trying to depict a dream through art?

C. Review passages in the novel, written in italics, in which Twig experiences powerful dreams. Examine the word choice, point-of-view, tense, sentence structure, and other elements of these passages. Then, in a style inspired by the novel, write your own 2-3 paragraph dream story. It can be based on a real, recalled dream, or a fictional dream idea.

III. CHANGE

A. With friends or classmates, take turns role-playing a conversation between Twig and Greyhawk in which you discuss the animals you encounter, such as terns and short-faced bears, and those which have disappeared, such as mammoths. How do you feel when elders tell stories of lost beasts? Do you worry about the melting Ice Giants or other natural occurrences? Can you imagine what your world will look like when you are Twig's grandfather's age?

B. Twig and her people live in a time of great climatic change. In addition to a threatened environment, our world is undergoing dramatic economic and environmental changes. Divide a sheet of paper into two columns headed, "Prehistoric Changes" and "Modern Day Changes," listing at least ten changes for each below. Compare and contrast the lists. Does this exercise help you better understand Twig's world? How might Twig's story help you gain perspective on what is happening in the world today? Write a 2-3 paragraph essay discussing one or two comparisons which you find particularly interesting.

DISCUSSION QUESTIONS

1. From whose viewpoint is Chapter One told? What does this perspective help readers learn about the world in which the story takes place? What elements of the landscape seem frightening or worrisome to you?

2. What are the Ice Giants? How are their actions explained and understood by Twig, her mother and their people? What are Thunderbirds and Cloud People? What do such names reveal about the prehistoric peoples' understanding of natural occurrences, such as rain?

3. Who is Cobia? Why was Twig's grandfather sent to kidnap Cobia as a child? Why are warriors from Buffalobeard Village sent to find Cobia? What happens to the warriors?

4. How does Chapter Eight change your understanding of Twig's character and your sense of the story? How does this chapter, and other dream chapters, make the novel unique? Do you believe in Twig's dreams? Explain your answer.

5. What frightens Twig about her Spirit dreaming powers? What makes her nonetheless want to understand her dreams? If you were Twig, would you keep your dreams a secret? Why or why not?

6. On page 98, Twig asks Greyhawk and Grizzly "Do you want the buffalo to go away forever, like the mammoths have?" What is important about her question? How does it help readers to better understand the time in which Twig lives? What resources do we fear losing in our own time? What other modern-day comparisons might you make to Twig's concern for the buffalo?

7. Why does Riddle finally allow Twig to study with Screech Owl? What does Screech Owl mean whenhe tells Twig that ". . . every great Dreamer, at some point, must step into the mouth of the Spirit that wants to chew her up" (Chapter Sixteen)? How might this also be an important piece of wisdom for Twig's entire community? Does it have meaning for modern leaders?

8. How does Water Snake's spirit help Twig elude the Thornback raiders? What terrors does Greyhawk witness? How does Twig persuade Greyhawk to continue their search for Cobia, despite their village being raided?

9. What happens when Twig calls for her spirit helper, Eagle-Man? How does this terrifying moment lead her to Cobia? Is Cobia a real person, a spirit, or another type of being in her early conversation with Twig? Explain your answer.

10. How does Cobia protect Twig and Greyhawk? How do Twig's dreams help lead her back to her people? Where does Twig tell the Sunpath People they must go? How do you understand the relationship between Twig and Cobia at the end of the story?

11. Do you think it is important that the final paragraphs of the novel are told from Twig's dream viewpoint? How does the Afterword affect your understanding of the novel's end? Had you been Twig, would you have had the courage to dream and to embark on a journey to the Duskland? Why or why not? Do you ever feel you need a similar type of courage in your own life? Explain your answer.